PRAISE FOR LINDSEY RO

"Evoking the South in language as rich as tl Lindsey Cook has confirmed her place in th fiction. We meet Lex as she is at the edge of losing everything but her beloved love of words, language, and how they shape our lives. You will dwell deeply in the lyrical narrative of *Learning to Speak Southern*, and you will not want to leave. Imaginative, immersive, and beautifully intense, this is your new favorite read!"

—Patti Callahan Henry, *New York Times* bestselling author of *Surviving Savannah*

"In pitch-perfect tones, Lex and her late mother, Margaret, spring to life on the pages of *Learning to Speak Southern* in a story that reminds us that sometimes, in order to move into our future, we must come to terms with the past. Women's fiction lovers won't be able to put down this story of transformation, coming-of-age, and the true meaning of family. Lindsey Rogers Cook has hit her stride!"

—Kristy Woodson Harvey, *USA Today* bestselling author of *Feels Like Falling*

"Lindsey Rogers Cook has blessed us with this penetrating, page-turning mystery about that greatest mystery of all: family. *How to Bury Your Brother* is a deeply wise book about the secrets that families keep, about the dysfunctions that grumble just beneath the surface. A profoundly honest and insightful and beautiful novel."

—Nathan Hill, *New York Times* bestselling author of *The Nix*, for *How to Bury Your Brother*

"With *How to Bury Your Brother*, Lindsey Rogers Cook has penned a deeply felt novel that unspools the threads of secrets long buried beneath the seemingly sunny surface of one Southern family."

—Mary Kay Andrews, *New York Times* bestselling author, for *How to Bury Your Brother*

LEARNING

to

SPEAK
SOUTHERN

Lindsey Rogers Cook

Published by Sourcebooks Landmark, an imprint of Sourcebooks
P.O. Box 4410, Naperville, Illinois 60567-4410
(630) 961-3900
sourcebooks.com

Library of Congress Cataloging-in-Publication Data

Names: Cook, Lindsey Rogers, author.
Title: Learning to speak southern : a novel / Lindsey Rogers Cook.
Description: Naperville : Sourcebooks Landmark, 2021.
Identifiers: LCCN 2020053745 (print) | LCCN 2020053746
    (ebook) | (trade paperback) | (epub)
Subjects: LCSH: Single women--Fiction. | Mothers--Fiction. | Families--Fiction.
Classification: LCC PS3603.O5725 L43 2021 (print) | LCC
    PS3603.O5725 (ebook) | DDC 813/.6--dc23
LC record available at https://lccn.loc.gov/2020053745
LC ebook record available at https://lccn.loc.gov/2020053746

Printed and bound in the United States of America.
VP 10 9 8 7 6 5 4 3 2 1

To the friends who are also family and
the family who are also friends.

PART I

"The only difference between Memphis and Hell is that
Memphis has a river running along one side of it."
—*ST. LOUIS POST-DISPATCH* (1905)

MEMPHIS CENTRAL BAPTIST CHURCH

—Church Bulletin—
Week of June 22, 1991

"Let the word of Christ dwell in you richly, teaching and admonishing one another in all wisdom, singing psalms and hymns and spiritual songs, with thankfulness in your hearts to God."
Colossians 3:16

9:30 a.m. sermon, "Learning How to Build," I Corinthians 3:9–17
11:00 a.m. sermon, "Of One Mind," Philippians 2:1–18

PASTOR VISITS
Call for preferred times.

The flowers on the altar today were donated by local Boy Scout Troop 2131 in honor of their departed teacher and coach, Mr. Kings.

CHURCH, FAMILY, AND FRIENDS
We care and want to share— please call with news and concerns.

Dear Church Friends,
Thank you so much for the lovely reception in honor of our son's christening. As many know, we've struggled in this realm for years and have prayed to God to bless our marriage. It was so joyful to celebrate Grant's christening, and we look forward to seeing him grow up surrounded by our

church family and with the love of God, as God holds him in His heart, as He does all children.

—*Gerald and Rebecca Taylor*

Dear all,

I thank you for your prayers these last few weeks during my illness. This works! I am feeling much better and will return next month to the nursery.

—*Rose Adler*

In the Hospital

Elk Johnson, Rm. 304

Jolene Swanson, Rm. 212

In Christian Sympathy

The brother of Pat Stevens has died at his home in Nashville, where services were held on Tuesday. Please send your remembrances and kind regards to the Stevens family.

LET'S CELEBRATE

Congratulations to Mr. and Mrs. Dennis Henry on the birth of their daughter, Alexandra Henry, on June 15. The happy father reports that mother and daughter are healthy and happy and looks forward to introducing the new addition to the church family.

INQUIRERS CLASS

Sundays at 2:00 p.m. during the month of July in the pastor's study. All are welcome.

MEET OUR NEWEST MEMBERS

Though they were raised outside the church, when James and Jennie Powell first walked through the doors of Memphis Central Baptist, they knew they had found their spiritual home. They participated in weekly services for some time, saying they were inspired by the

Continued on next page

CHAPTER ONE

"So you've got this, then?" Otto says, standing with his hands in the pockets of the torn pants he found in the dumpster of the tea shop last week.

I stare at him with gritted teeth, but he only looks at me blankly. "What?"

"This"—he gestures to the beeping machines, my swollen body strapped to the monitors buzzing with their secret tasks, the blood that's stained the nurse's glove in a shape that looks like the Arabic letter *seen*, س—"it seems like you've got it handled, so I'm going to…" He makes thumbs-up signs with his hands and tilts them toward the door.

He's talking in English, but even the nurses have to know he's leaving me. They've probably seen it before, or maybe my life really has reached unprecedented levels of fucked up.

"You're leaving?" I yell in Bahasa, and the young nurse's head snaps up; she'll learn in time to hide her surprise. "How can you possibly leave right now?"

Otto comes over to me, his back to the destruction ravaging my lower region.

"It's dead."

"*He's* dead," I correct, just to see him wince. But another round of nausea slams my eyes shut, and I miss his reaction.

"This is good. Now I can go back to school, and you can go back to…whatever."

As he continues his explanation, his voice gallops ahead like it did when he was high two weeks ago, talking about all the things he'd teach this child of ours: the most artistic method of applying finger paint or the sky map from May 15, its due date, three months from now. "Can't you see, you—we're—one big cliché, and this is our chance to break it? A sign from God…or you know, whoever."

Whomever. The word dances maniacally in front of my eyelids, gaining speed with each second I hold my breath. The machines beep, loud and angry, sounding vaguely like the bass line in "Another One Bites the Dust." The older nurse shushes us.

"Let me call someone for you," Otto says, though he knows I have no one here to call.

He strokes one finger down the curve of my shoulder, past the scar he told me was beautiful. I've heard so many stories from my parents about how I got it. All lies, probably. "How about your dad?"

"No!" I yell, in tears now.

B e a t i n g.

B e a t i n g.

A l l i n m y b o d y.

The "good news," according to the cute doctor, is that since the baby is dead, I can have all the pain medication I want. Instead of telling him I always hated the wooziness anyway, that the pills would only make me sick, I was stuck on translating the words he exchanged with Otto about the reason for the silence on the fetal heart rate monitor.

"Lex, how do you think you're going to pay for this? There's going to be a bill here, and without me, rent. You can't bike to work tomorrow like normal."

Across the hall, a newborn baby cries. Not mine; even when it was ours, it was always mine.

"Not…my father… Call…Cami." I cough out the number of my mother's best friend, my godmother, Camila. In Arabic, *kāmil* means perfection. In Roman mythology, she was a warrior. That spirit hurled me over many rough waters during my mother's life and stayed with me after her death. It's a spirit I need now, I think, even as my mind tells me I shouldn't open this door.

I let out the last digit. A mouth-breather in scrubs squirts more liquid into my IV. Soon,

I'm sinking,

sinking,

sinking.

It feels nice—

this nothingness.

The coven (Latin, *conventus*) of nurses starts bustling again, scurrying about purposefully, running to get the doctor with the Australian-accented English. I hear them tell me to push but I don't know what that means, the feeling I'm meant to seek. Birthing class is next month.

I concentrate on Otto instead. I want to tell him: I am not a cliché.

You're not like my father. All girls marry their fathers. See?

Not that we're married. So maybe, instead, I'm the high-school rebel with that guy from *The Breakfast Club*. What was his name?

I try to push again, until the absence of cries hushes the room.

My eyelids are heavy, but I raise the right one as if it's on a crane, millimeter by millimeter, to see if Otto is gone.

That's when I see it. That little scrunched-up, pruny face that's all wrong somehow, even wrapped in a blanket like the baby is only sleeping. A nurse offers him to me wordlessly.

I shake my head no and try to unsee what I've seen, but the face remains inside my right eyelid, dancing in circles where "whomever," my correction for Otto's grammar, used to be.

A face only a mother could love.

But is that a cliché? An idiom, maybe. Just now, I can't remember the difference.

I used to know such things.

Is this death? Dying in childbirth? Like a cliché in Victorian England and now, for some Americans?

If I am dying, I might as well be happy. I cycle through my favorite idioms. At least I think they're idioms.

In Spanish, *Buscar la quinta pata al gato.* "To look for the fifth leg of the cat," or to make something more complicated than it has to be.

In Swedish, *Att glida in på en räkmacka.* "To slide into a shrimp sandwich," or someone who doesn't need to work hard, like Otto, maybe.

In English, "Under the weather." No, you don't have an umbrella over your head to protect you from rain.

Dr. Australia pats my hand twice. My father used to do the same thing—a gesture of comfort from those who don't want to touch you. "You're going to be fine," he says.

I want to tell him I don't care what happens, and because of that, I'll be fine no matter what. I want to tell him that's the beauty of not caring, but instead, I remember one of my mother's threats.

"If you have kids," she said, smirking, pausing for emphasis, "I hope they are just like you."

"Thanks, me too," teenage Lex said, returning her smirk.

"You'd probably screw them up anyway."

"Probably." The younger Lex slammed a door in her face and ran to her room, where an Italian travel CD still played on the boom box.

Salve! Mi chiamo [LEX]. *Sono americano. Un tavolo per uno, per favore.*

That door slammed too.

Now, in my drug-infused memories, on the back of the door is a snake I killed at the Crystal Grotto. I offered my mother's spirit a half-hearted apology there, an apology for being me as much as anything else. Her spirit slips under the bedroom door to join the snake, who seeks revenge by mashing us together in an embrace neither of us enjoys. It's the longest I've been this close to her.

She smells of lavender soap and graphite from the pencil she keeps behind her ear. In life, me ending a fight always annoyed her more than the actual meat of the thing. The same is true in her—our?—death.

While my mother struggles against the snake, I relax into its grip.

Cool as a cucumber.

An idiom.

CHAPTER TWO

You know that period right between waking and sleep? You're not in a deep sleep, dead to the world, but skipping along the earth's surface, floating on your back, like in the green-blue waters of Bali. That's when I always seem to think about the origin of time.

Before "time" existed, before we could say to each other, "I don't have time for that," or "There's still plenty of time," is this what living felt like?

Many centuries ago, before "time," there was only "tide." The passage of time marked by the ocean's unstoppable tides, coming and going, paying no mind to the fragile humans and their short-lived problems. The earth cared only for seasons and eras, not for hours and minutes and seconds. "Noontide," "Christmastide"— these are words I'd like to bring back, because "tide" (limitless) is much more generous than "time" (always limited).

I've always liked that about linguistics, how one word can send you on a trail through dictionaries, origins, languages, and all the connections between them, overlapping in strange ways. I've always loved languages more than the people who speak them.

Eventually, I create a barrier between myself and the nothingness. I divide, like the *da-* root that eventually led to the English word "tide." I open my eyes, if only to prove to myself that I'm still alive.

I'm in a hospital bed in a different, larger, and quieter room. The sun rises over a graveyard out my window where stones jumble and grow together, fight for space, overtake one another, as the bodies below them did on earth. Is this where they've taken him? I shake my head, and the image of the scrunched-up half face disappears.

On the table next to the bed sits a stack of books from the beachfront shack that Otto said had good light for an artist's studio. The tomes I've carted from Tennessee to Mexico City to Quito to Bali and everywhere in between. On top are my passport and my rubber band "wallet," containing one credit card (mostly for decoration because of my shit credit) and the money I usually don't dare carry with me. Otto missed most of the places I hid money around the house, I notice without feeling. Or maybe he spent some bribing the nurses when we checked in, hoping for better care for the baby that wouldn't wait.

From a counter across the room, a crystal vase reflects the window's light, bouncing it around the ceiling in a dash of blue. An assortment of roses sits in the vase, ordered by Cami, certainly, but in an arrangement of which she would never approve. The white and yellow and pink ones pinch together without artistic direction, as if they're still held by twine.

I try to get a better look at them, but moving even an inch up feels like a punch in the stomach. The flowers tell me everything I need to know, though. She's not here; she's watching me. The hospital bed creaks in alarm as I slither back down under the covers and a nurse comes in.

"Good morning," I cough to her, to show my new overlord that I speak Bahasa (enough, anyway), but she doesn't respond. She sets down a tray with food, jabs her finger at an envelope on it, and then squeaks out in her clogs.

Alone again—perfect. How I like it, I remind myself as I reach for my tabbed, creased, and highlighted *Word Origins* dictionary and flip to the entry on **clogs**.

First, "a block of wood to impede an animal's movement," from which the verb meaning "to block" arose. Reference to wooden shoes in late Middle English.

I could be quite comfortable here. My little room overlooking the graveyard, my books, tea, and free breakfast. As Oscar Wilde wrote, "I can be perfectly happy by myself. With freedom, books, flowers, and the moon, who could not be happy?" A quote I remember from my mother's office. Ironic, since she was very rarely happy.

After stirring my oats and fruit, I dip my spoon ever so slightly into the bowl. Like I imagined Italian women did with their gelato, oh so elegantly, while I listened to those travel tapes.

I reach for the note, thinking it will be from Otto. An apology, maybe, even though I'm sure he's already gone. He's probably on his knees in Germany, begging his parents to let him come back and finish school. I hold on to that image, because I know it won't take long for me to put him out of my mind entirely. I'm good at that, not thinking about people.

But the note is a printed email from Cami, sent to some random hospital email address. Always the pragmatist, she has written one word to me, a command—"Rest." Below that is a one-way ticket from Denpasar, Indonesia, to Memphis, Tennessee, departing on February 25.

My heart begins to race.

Memphis?

Snatches of our conversation during the labor come back to me.

The sound of Otto bargaining with Cami on my behalf as if he were speaking underwater. Everyone agreeing—maybe even me—that I should return to Memphis, and as if in a hostage swap, the larger-than-expected bill for the hospital would be paid in exchange, the shack vacated and my books retrieved, my boss informed.

Every ache in my body suddenly demands attention: the burn in my abs from pushing, the soreness in my back. I'm aware for the first time that under the hospital gown, my stomach is still swollen, flabby, lined with stretch marks that seemed beautiful because of their purpose but now mock me with pointlessness.

My spoon is frozen in midair with overcooked oats on it, and I set it down on the tray. How much has Cami thought this through?

I go through the possibilities in my head: grabbing my clothes and my books, running out, screwing the hospital out of the money, using the last of my cash to hop to some other city— somewhere I could forget Bali, forget Otto, forget Bahasa, and learn something new. I've always wanted to learn Yoruba, master how the tones turn each word into its own little song. There's always another English school, always another group of expats.

I don't want to go to Memphis.

I think about the shack where Otto and I moved three months ago, after his parents cut him off. The box with the blanket where we were going to put the baby. The drawer of maternity clothes and a few German pregnancy books Otto never read.

I picture him leaving the hospital. He would go straight to our house, turn up his terrible German rap, and splatter paint on canvas until he decided what to do next, then slink out of the house, glancing behind him with each step, as if my ghost could follow him. I don't blame Otto enough to haunt him; I would have done the same thing if I could. If I hadn't been the one hooked up to the machines, I would be two planes deep by now.

I pick up the spoon and eat the oats, then take another bite, until I'm scraping the sides of the bowl. I drink the water and tea and eat a piece of toast with jelly. The sun finishes its ascent over the graveyard.

What day is it anyway?

It doesn't matter, I realize. Cami will no doubt have thought of everything, arranged for me to stay, then arranged for me to leave in the quick, effortless way she always does, the exact opposite of my mother and of me. This will be the most civilized getaway I've ever made. By far.

That's when I decide to go. Because if I don't, it will prompt a hundred more decisions that I don't want to make, like what to do with the baby's box and how to tell people what happened, what to do about my job, where to go next. How would I explain this blip? An explanation for myself seems harder to conjure than whatever I would tell the strangers that surround my life.

After making this big decision—to have the baby with Otto, to create for it the type of family I never knew, to will myself to be the type of parent I never had—and seeing how that choice blew up, I don't trust my decision-making abilities. Maybe I never did.

It seems much easier to lie here, read my books, eat my oats, allow the nurses to continue administering the liquid with which they are filling my body's newly empty spaces, and wait for Cami to set her plan in motion.

I press a button to summon the nurse (multiple times, now that Otto is gone) and ask for another bowl of oats, this time in English.

CHAPTER THREE

When Cami's plan progresses, it does so quickly.

A nurse walks in with what can only be described as a fresh diaper and a plastic grocery bag holding my athletic shorts and the XXL men's T-shirt I wore here as maternity clothes, a send-off akin to that of newly released prisoners.

I struggle into the clothes, cursing myself and Otto for not thinking to pack something else. It wasn't time for a hospital bag though. Not yet.

The nurse pushes a wheelchair up to the side of the bed and points to it insistently.

"I'm going to have to walk at the airport," I say.

She answers with another determined point, so I climb aboard. I decide not to be difficult, my mother's favorite description of me. Surely, like with Cami, arguments are futile anyway.

Another nurse dumps my books into a triple-lined plastic bag, sending answer keys for English worksheets and random notes from linguistics classes at Vassar and musings about Bahasa cascading down, and plops the makeshift luggage in my lap.

A male of unknown medical training comes to wheel me to the car. He shakes hands with the driver, which I take as a ritual transferring of ownership; I am this other man's problem now. The type of male arrogance I had planned to raise the baby to avoid. He would have been a mama's boy, southern despite my resolve never to let him set foot there. He'd look at me like Grant looked at his mother, a habit I hated in our childhood but yearned for with my own child.

I nod once to the wheelchair-pusher, who is sweating from the effort of wheeling me and my books to the car because of the humid, sticky heat. I linger outside the door before climbing in. This is one of the last times I will feel Bali's heavy air settling on my skin, like being buried in warm sand, like tumbling through the waves when the baby was a secret inside me. But I hadn't yet decided to let the unknown keep growing there, from an olive into a rutabaga and eventually a watermelon. I wasn't sure that I could be nothing like my mother.

Was that what I did wrong, that brief period of doubt? The questions I turned over before I decided I wanted—maybe needed—the baby, even if it meant I needed Otto too? Or was it all that happened before?

I scan the scene one last time: Mr. Sweaty Wheelchair-Pusher, my buddies (the nurses with their varying levels of meanness), a man riding up on a bicycle who is bleeding from his wrist. I try to remember it all. This is what I saw before I went back... But where? Home? That's a place I thought I would finally make here, with the baby.

Once I slide into the back seat and shut the car door, all the air conditioning has seeped into the sand air. The driver's reflection glares at me in the rearview mirror as he pulls out of the parking lot.

CHAPTER FOUR

We leave Canggu for the half-hour journey to the airport, and I watch my so-called life here pass through the car window. The road toward the house Otto has already fled, my bike route to the night school where I've been teaching English to a group of older Balinese businessmen who also speak Chinese. I hope they learn to conjugate their verbs properly, and to understand the difference between "him" and "he" and when to add "the" before a noun, and English's other oddities, but it won't be from me.

It's ironic that I always seem to end up teaching English, because it's my least favorite language. In conversations, I turn to English only when no other common language can be found, which is rare in Bali. The grammar, the vocabulary, and the tilt of English sentences read like a Dutchman, a Spaniard, and a Frenchman got drunk one night and made up some nonsense language for writing in code. English steals and borrows without giving anything back, other than "LOL" and "dude" and "gerrymander." Also, "hipster" and "hot dog." American English—a linguistic slush pile of "abbrevs," bastardized food, and legitimatized racism. That's what it means to be an American, #USA.

Nothing like Spanish, the first new language I learned, back in first grade, on a summer trip to Cami's when she still lived close to where she attended business school at the University of Florida. I learned it before I even knew it was called Spanish, only that it was Cami's secret language, and mine when I was with her. The language I later screamed at dinners overflowing with kids and families and food during most childhood summers after, cheering for Puerto Rican boxers, Cami encouraging me to make friends, before I met Grant.

"I have you!" I'd say to her.

"Someone your own age," she'd respond, as if age mattered.

Even then, I liked how the Spanish words blended together, unlike English's harsh stops between each word. Spanish's romance—all those vowels—later beckoned me from the Vassar College campus, where I'd never bothered to belong, to Mexico City, the start of the four-year-long trip that's about to come to an unexpected denouement.

In Bali, my plan was much the same as it had been in India and Ecuador and all the other places I've been since Mexico City: Find the expats—the smelly kids living out of backpacks and off the remainders of their trust funds, the "digital nomads"—these are the types of words English provides—who were paid to Instagram—again, thanks, USA for that noun-verb interchange—and like a Windexed mirror, reflect back someone exactly like them.

"You were one of five? Me too!" I would say.

"How crazy is that?" a girl with blond hair and brown roots would answer.

"Cray-zee," I'd say, like the word had a period in the middle.

"I feel like we've known each other much longer than two days," she'd respond. The fact that I spoke their language,

knew their hometowns, said "warsh" like their grandmothers—
"Arkansas, right?"—made up for months of friendship, and
they'd let me crash on their couch or introduce me to someone
who could get me a job.

I always gave my new employer references, telling him (always
him) that they only spoke a language he didn't. If he had called,
my previous employers would have told my soon-to-be employer
that I had a habit of leaving, abruptly and without notice. But
they never called.

People who get too close too fast are my favorite; they make it
all look natural, being vulnerable. And each time I leave another
city, burning the bridges built behind me on a mound of com-
monality, a part of me thinks those stranger-friends should thank
me for teaching them this lesson about trust. It was one I had to
learn at a young age, from my father, no less, and one that I was
later glad to have learned.

Otto and I met when I had been in Bali for a few months,
at a "bar" on Echo Beach—more accurately described as a tin
roof supported by two wooden beams with a dirty counter in
the middle that served one type of local beer. I went with an
American who taught English to Dutch expats, but she quickly
joined another group of girls. After standing awkwardly behind
them for a few minutes, I headed off on my own. I've always been
better at sussing out where I don't belong than where I do.

I leaned against the wall to watch the tide come in, listening to
the yelling down the beach and the thump of bass from a famous
bar with a skateboard bowl in the center. The front always seemed
to be decorated with young couples making out, as if the owners
paid them to advertise there.

In a crowd, my mind never rests, which is how I like it. I drown out my thoughts by listening to everyone else talk; each person's language, as unique as a fingerprint, betrays decades of history.

I listened for a while to a pair of honeymooners who apparently thought that because they had ventured beyond a Caribbean Sandals, no one nearby knew the names of English sex positions. I was thinking I'd make a good fortune-teller when Otto found me outside.

"Waiting for someone?" he said in English, with a German accent.

I glanced back to where my ride stood with her friends.

"No," I answered.

He leaned against the wall next to me, holding his beer bottle between his fingertips. He looked lost, like an affection-starved puppy I saw in Mexico and desperately wanted to take with me to Ecuador. If I reached out my hand, I felt sure this boy's head would duck under it, running his long, blond curls against my palm.

"Where are you from?"

"California," I decided. I was in a California kind of mood. Sunny and happy despite the rain earlier that had soaked my still-damp jean shorts.

"What's it like there?"

"Sunny, like here, but with better bars," I said in German.

He immediately brightened, dropping his cool bravado and spinning to face me. "You speak German?"

"Only when I can't help it."

He was so easy to play with, asking me questions about how I learned German, my parents, my childhood—the type of questions I never answered honestly. In the years since I left Tennessee, I've tried on hundreds of personalities, pasts, and backgrounds in the hope that one day I'd find answers to these questions that fit. The real ones never did.

Otto was so nonthreatening that when he asked me what my parents did for a living, I answered honestly.

"They own a hardware store. My dad does the...hardware, and my mother did the accounting."

"What does she do now?"

"Oh," I said, remembering why I avoided honesty—because simple questions often lead to ones with more complex answers. "She still does the accounting. Does the accounting," I laughed, as if the slipup were nothing more than drunken confusion, and asked about his family.

He told me he'd left Germany because his parents didn't approve of his art, to which I asked how old he was.

"How do you say? 'If I tell you, I have to kill you.'" He laughed at his joke and said he would get more beers. He was twenty-one, six years my junior, I'd later find out.

Eventually, I sat on the sand and began answering all his questions with "no" to see how long that could go on.

"Do you have any siblings?"

"No." True.

"Did you like California?"

"No." I'd only driven through, but I did like it.

"Do you like dogs?"

"No." I didn't have much of an opinion on dogs. My father was so allergic that he was sure he could detect even one stray hair.

On the fifth "no," he veered, unfazed, into talk of his sister, who played piano, the relative I'd later imagine would buy our baby gifts too expensive for my unguarded approval and sing to it through the speakerphone. Otto had only been gone a month then, but he talked about all the things he missed in Germany like it had been years. Once I had buried half my calves in the sand, he set his beer aside and asked shyly if he could kiss me.

I'd had just enough to drink to say yes. One fewer drink, and I'd have pointed to my cheek and smiled. One more drink, and I'd have been lying down in the sand, slurring philosophically about the words for "ocean" in different languages and their origins, and what that means about all the societies with whom we share this earth.

He kissed me hard, like he had something to prove. I sank into the familiar feeling of unfamiliar lips on mine. This was simple; this made sense.

I like language because when I learn a new one, I can't think about anything else, a short respite from my thoughts. Sex is like that. The more sex I need to block out thoughts of everything I want to forget, the closer I get to trying a new country or continent, disappointing another employer, another person who thought the Texas-born daughter of an engineer was their friend (or existed at all).

Otto was my first in Bali. He led me back to his apartment, in a nicer area I'd yet to explore. The apartment smelled of lemony furniture polish I doubted he applied himself. A picture of his family sat on his bedside table. I examined it; all the blond German curls everywhere made me think unavoidably of Hitler while Otto fumbled over my breasts with his mouth.

I wondered if his teachers in Germany had taught the students about the casual language the Nazis used—*Sonderbehandlung* translates into English as "special treatment" but meant execution. I wondered if they taught schoolchildren that in war, words come before weapons, a fact the country of my birth has yet to admit.

Otto yanked me to the end of the bed and went down on me, drawing tight spirals with his tongue an inch below the prime location. I scooted closer in an attempt to reposition him. German words used by the Nazis left my mind.

Eventually, he came up for air with a self-satisfied grin. He tried to enter me, and I shot my hand down to guide him before he rammed into the wrong orifice. After I waved him into home base—I love a good baseball idiom, either because of or in spite of my parents' love of the sport—he grunted and finished. He flopped over onto the bed facedown, spent.

"Now me," I said, and he sprang up from push-up position, unaware that he'd left a task unfinished. I instructed him on exactly what to do, after which he immediately fell asleep. I let myself out and walked along the road back to my apartment, running through my favorite German phrases, thinking about how he'd egged himself on before he came. "*Härter, härter, härter!*" I'd never had sex with a German before. He was cute, but I knew I was done with him. I'd already put the wrong number into his phone hours earlier.

When the driver finally pulls into the airport, he finally hands me the plane tickets as if the men couldn't trust me, like when I was a child, traveling to Cami's, and the flight attendant would pick me up at the gate, insist on holding my hand and escorting me off the plane. The driver also gives me two hundred dollars, which Cami added to the paid bill, I suppose. Unfortunately, the gesture reminds me of the cryptic way my father would offer me a stack of twenties in college when I submitted to a visit from him (my mother never bothered), trying to buy my affection. All with stolen money, but I didn't find that out until later.

I give the money to a homeless man standing outside the airport.

PART II

"It occurred to me almost constantly in the South that had I lived there I would have been an eccentric and full of anger, and I wondered what form the anger would have taken. Would I have taken up causes, or would I have simply knifed somebody?"
—JOAN DIDION, *SOUTH AND WEST*

CHAPTER FIVE

On the first plane, I take a pill from the nurses' parting goodie bag and fall into such a deep sleep that I miss the stop in Seoul. Other than stumbling back and forth to the bathroom, I don't really wake up until Detroit, to a flight attendant yelling, "Ma'am. Ma'am. Ma'am!" in my ear, expecting me to rise from the dead and respond.

Currency exchange. Four hundred and fifty-seven dollars to my name. Less once I buy an "I ❤ DETROIT" sweatshirt at an airport gift shop to better withstand the February temperatures in the United States. Another plane.

More thoughts of the baby and my mother, their deaths and my place in them, guilt over leaving and guilt over staying. Thoughts of whispered childhood dreams with Grant, always unavoidable on planes. Thoughts I don't want to have, especially with hormones leaving my tear ducts unguarded. Another pill, and in an instant, it seems, the pilot announces we're approaching the Memphis airport. I take in the Mississippi River through the window.

I pick out the airport, filled with FedEx planes. In the 1960s, it was modeled proudly to look like a bunch of martini glasses, continuing a uniquely southern tradition of cities stubbornly drenched in Jesus and booze, littered with purity rings and strip clubs, hands clasped in prayer and open palms across mascara-streaked faces; endless contradictions.

The plastic handles on my pathetic luggage dig into my hands as I amble down the Jetway toward the airport. I make it five feet before the first Elvis reference—BLUE SUEDE SERVICE, a sign proclaims, followed only a few feet later by a row of colorful portraits of Elvis painted by local high-school students. Yes, we get it. Elvis is from here.

The first time someone smiles at me, I jump, thinking I know them from somewhere. *Puñeta*, don't let it be someone from high school. Or worse, one of the two men I am most hoping to avoid. Coincidentally, I don't know for certain if either is still living. Has my father died at home and Grant been blown up in a cockpit hovering 1,200 feet above some Middle Eastern desert? I suppose I'll find out soon.

But the person is only a stranger. I forgot how in Memphis, everyone smiles at you and talks to you like they know you. "Stop looking at me!" I want to scream.

That's the southern way, though—smile and say, "So nice to see you, Mrs. Henry," to your mother, then circle a finger around the ear, *crazy*, to you. My mother saying, "That girl is always so nice, why can't you be more like her?"

Southerners hear you've been fighting with your mother again and come up to you both in church, telling you that they'll "pray for you," which in some contexts is the most condescending phrase one person can say to another. "Bless your heart" is the same, as in, "Lex is so odd, bless her heart," met with counterarguments from Grant, which I'd scurry to another room to avoid.

These are the types of linguistical nuances students can't learn in English studies. Sarcasm and passive-aggression, two tenets of Southern speech, are difficult for non-native speakers.

Bless their hearts.

I left my flip phone in the hospital room since it wouldn't work outside of Bali anyway, so I have no way to contact Cami. I scan the airport lobby, listening to blues music playing on the stereo and looking for a pay phone that exists only in a nineties time machine.

One wall displays photos showing the body of Martin Luther King Jr. leaving Memphis, something I've never understood why they would spotlight. *Welcome to Memphis: the home of FedEx and Holiday Inn and self-serve grocery shopping, and yes, the most important figure of the civil rights movement died on our watch!*

Outside, there's a man in a black suit and tie holding a piece of paper with Ms. ALEXANDRA HENRY written on it.

I walk as quickly as possible to meet him, forcing myself to concentrate on the pang in my abdomen rather than on my thoughts. Thankfully, it was so small, there wasn't a tear—that's what the nurse said. Thankfully. Thankfully, he was so small and dead that my vagina is intact for future male pleasure. #Blessed.

The car's back seat is surprisingly empty. Maybe Cami is finishing a flower arrangement at her store, or maybe she wants me to live through these last minutes of loneliness to draw a sharper contrast with what I'll find upon my return to her house, to my hometown, to my past.

The journey from the airport to where I grew up is only about fifteen miles, and the signs along the roadside quickly begin to taunt me—the Children's Museum, St. Jude Children's Research Hospital, signs for Memphis's bicentennial. I can no longer hold back my penchant for self-flagellation: I ask the driver to pass by 345 Madison before going to Cami's.

When we get off the highway, I recognize the now-boarded-up buildings as the shops of my childhood, filling spaces in between the shiny new stores and restaurants. There's the parking lot where I lost my virginity. There's the park where my mother used to drop me off, expecting me to walk or run home. Only now, it's called Health Sciences Park and has an empty pedestal that used to house the statue of the first grand wizard of the KKK. As we continue toward Sun Studios, I turn around in my seat to get a better look at the park, surrounded by a fence and orange traffic cones, proof that the city continued to grow in my absence.

In the distance rises the gaudy Pyramid, where I saw my first concert (NSYNC, with Memphis star Justin Timberlake). I see a building I don't recognize with an Elvis cutout in the window—are we ever going to acknowledge that he married a woman he started dating when she was fourteen and he was twenty-four? The dress shop where my mother and I were asked to leave still stands a block up and over.

"What I wouldn't give to go to prom in a dress like that!"

[The reflection of one Lex Henry enters dressing-room mirror, stage right, in a puffy pink ball gown that might as well be from a Disney movie.]

Delicately, carefully, don't look her in the eye, that will set her off. "Pink isn't my color."

"Sure, I get it."

"Really?"

She turns, but the temperature in the room has already gone up ten degrees.

"Why am I even here? I'm nothing to you. My opinion is nothing to you. You do what you want."

"No, I—"

"I'll just go."

"Mom, don't. It's...fine. It's..."

"Just take it off."

"Maybe if it was—"

"Take it off!"

[Mother Henry, center stage, pulls the dress's sleeve, inadvertently grabbing her daughter's necklace, choking her. She's been wearing the gifted chain with the single pearl since her grandfather died.]

"STOP, MOM, STOP!"

"You stop!"

[More grabbing, and then the sound of ripping fabric. Sequins explode, over the small space, the tear exposing a rose tattoo on the daughter's breast.]

"What the HELL IS THAT?"

[Offstage: "Ladies!" The sound of clicking heels on the hardwood floor.]

My mother and I spent our entire time overlapping on this earth arguing over who was at fault for my existence.

Was it my fault for being born or her fault for having me? Discuss.

The car passes the road where my grandfather, my mother's father, told me he had seen the police the evening the FBI murdered MLK. He always made Memphis come alive for me; the city I admired lived only in his stories.

They featured the Peabody ducks and the trolley cars and the old buildings he helped restore. They took place at the demolitions of Memphis's historic buildings, which he attended as if they were funerals. He never stopped mourning the loss of the original Cossitt Library—a spiraling sandstone turret that was once the pride of Memphis's skyline—along with the Napoleon Hill House and Union Station and the Masonic Temple at Madison and Second.

No matter the year or reason ("More parking lots!" he roared) or if his only experience with the building was through an old photo, my grandfather claimed leaders had "no damn excuse," since unlike the rest of the South, Memphis's historic buildings were left untouched during the Civil War. He liked to say "the only just" building loss was that of the Grand Opera House, which burned to the ground in the 1920s during a striptease. That always made me laugh.

Even though I wanted to see my father's store (his father's before him), I sink down in my seat when we approach. I told myself I would never see this store again.

I sit up suddenly.

"What the hell?" I say to myself, paralyzed by the half-constructed set of condos where the Henry Hardware building used to be. The car lingers in front of a sign urging me to call now about leasing "opportunities."

A train whistle in the distance startles me out of my confusion. During my childhood, I didn't even hear them. So many train tracks carve through Memphis, everything seems to be on the wrong side of one.

"Okay, go to Cami's. Thanks."

Even as I tell myself I don't care, I can't help but wonder—Where is my father?

CHAPTER SIX

Eventually, my mind still on the leasing sign for the apartments that replaced my father's hardware store—SMART. SEXY. STYLE.— and the hipster I saw whizzing by it on one of the motorized scooters that seem to be everywhere, the car crosses into Cooper-Young. Once, it was an African American neighborhood, but now it screams its gentrified wokeness, with signs in nearly every yard reminding me that LOVE IS LOVE and that SCIENCE IS REAL— nothing about gentrification, of course. Only reminders I suspect most people driving through this neighborhood don't need, but again, what do I know of this city?

My earliest memories of Cami are set a few short miles from here, where I grew up in Midtown, of her whispered, lulling voice in my parents' room. No light peeked under the door where I lay outside like a locked-out dog, until I crept out of their hallway and back up the stairs to my own room.

With Cami there, the air in our household loosened, and my mother's mind uncoiled. There was music; there was dancing. There was patience; there was fun. There was cat's cradle and *American Idol* and singing old songs they used to know before my mother begged off to bed, saying we could stay up, Cami twirling me in the living room, teaching me Spanish words, me wishing my father would never return from the store and tell me to go to sleep.

I rolled those same words over in my mind after my father said goodbye and patted my shoulder twice at the gate in Memphis the summer I was seven. The *palabras* felt like a mantra to me, a spell, a hymn I repeated for comfort. I smiled, brave, to reassure him that I would be fine down in Florida and hoped that Cami would understand how much she meant to me, that me storing these foreign phrases would tell her everything for which I didn't have the language.

"How was the flight, Mamacita?" she said to me then, in an adult voice.

"Good." I cleared my throat. "*Me llamo Lex. ¿Cómo estás, Cami?*"

"*¡Te acuerdas!*" she said. "*Eres una chica muy inteligente.* What do you want for dinner, smarty-pants?"

I smiled.

Slowly, at Cami's, I stopped tiptoeing as I crossed the hallway at night, afraid to elicit my mother's screams. (The greatest offense was to remind her of my existence. "Alexandra, please don't upset your mother.")

Cami taught me how to cook my first meals—pancakes and grilled ham-and-cheese sandwiches. She bought me colorful clothes and dresses to wear instead of the khakis and polo shirts my mother made me wear to school. That was the summer I fell in love. With Cami. With language. With a dream for my life: to travel and gather items and stories like Cami did.

"*¡Hola!*" I yelled when my father picked me up. I was a portrait of my summer, sporting a tan, a beaded necklace from one of Cami's friends, and a shirt with warrior Mulan that Cami had bought at Disney World.

"English, please," he said.

"Hello."

It was those Spanish-filled memories that made Mexico City so comforting when I studied abroad there. I looked at the colors, the bright-pink houses, the loud music, the dancing, the weak beer and thought, *I could stay here.* That trip showed me that language couldn't be confined to textbooks, that despite the ease with which I impressed my professors—the word "polyglot" always within reach—I still had so much to learn. Those undiscovered words were worth the inconvenience of living.

I didn't say that to Cami, though, when I called her from Houston a few hours after ditching her and my father at my would-be college graduation. Graduation being a generous term, since although my father and Cami didn't know it, I had failed one of my classes and wouldn't be graduating.

I assured her that I hadn't been abducted. I said the decision had been fast, a whim, but in reality, once my mother died, my brain couldn't hold the relief and guilt and fear, grew anxious at the thought of explaining it. Those fears made me chuck my phone out the window, made me leave the address and phone number for Grant's air base crumpled up in my jean jacket, hanging on the back of my dorm-room door.

I didn't tell Cami how easy it had been to get in the car, to turn the key, to drive across the United States, stopping only for bathroom and coffee breaks, to cross the border and show up outside my host family's door. They welcomed me warmly, until their next student showed up and they realized my return wasn't sanctioned by Vassar.

Somehow that road trip seemed quicker than the drive from

the Memphis airport to the front of Cami's Victorian house today.

I make myself get out of the car. The house's dormer window fills most of the available space on the second floor. A tower looms over a small balcony on one side, which reaches up to a loft entered only by a spiral staircase in Cami's bedroom. Each window is decorated with a lush flower box.

The address, the wraparound front porch, are still fresh in my memory, but there's a black cat I don't recognize snaking through the railings with their gingerbread house–like woodwork, and the house is bright purple with mint trim. In my childhood, it had been salmon and yellow, then pink and baby blue. "*Azul turquesa*," Cami corrected.

I knock cautiously on Cami's door, gathering my new sweatshirt around me against the February chill. Inside its fabric, I'm seven years old, seized with anxiety about seeing Cami again.

I crack open the door, and the cat darts in. I assume he knows more than I do about where he belongs. The smell of seafood and garlic drifts from the crack where the cat has disappeared, and I can see a slice of the small table in Cami's foyer, decorated with artfully arranged pink, white, and lavender hydrangeas in a vintage mason jar. The presence of flowers never changes here, but the arrangements, colors, and species tend to shift daily.

"Cami?"

CHAPTER SEVEN

The door flies open and Cami reaches out to hug me, squeezing my foreign-feeling body against her own. Because of my height, I curl toward her, relaxing into the embrace.

The tension from the past days and months and years melts away into memories of my ear resting on the most comfortable part of her thigh, Cami running her fingers through my hair as my parents whispered deep in the house. I always lapped up Cami's warmth, the feeling of her soft skin. My mother would only ever lay her hand on my cheek, pulling it away and turning around before I could react.

"Lex… You're here!" she says in my ear. She still smells like coconut oil.

It feels like a punch to the gut that she didn't call me "Mamacita." Maybe she thinks it's too close a reminder of what I lost.

"How do you feel?" she asks carefully.

"Fine," I spit out, breaking away from the hug.

She gives me a pity-filled smile I recognize from childhood and hands me her glass of red wine. She heads toward the cabinet in search of another bottle and to dry her tears in secret, leaving me in the foyer.

Next to the flowers is a picture of Cami, my mother, and me

on my first day of school. The contrast between the adults is so evident with Cami's hippie-looking pants and my mother's frumpy jeans and Henry Hardware shirt.

The photo has always been here, but I'm surprised it remains. Part of me figured that Cami was trying to forget me the same way I was trying to forget her and my mother, forget everyone I knew here, forget this town and all its memories. But even after all those languages and apartments and jobs trying to drown them out, this house feels so familiar.

I get closer to the photo to examine our faces. I haven't seen a picture of my mother since I left five years ago. Her nose is different than I remember, but she's beautiful despite her best attempt not to be.

My stomach growls, and Cami laughs, hearing it as she comes up to clink her glass with mine. I haven't had a real meal since I ate (and then threw up) all those oats at the hospital.

"*Salud*," she says, which I echo. This is my first drink since my (second) missed period. I try to think only about the taste of the wine on my tongue.

When she opens her mouth again, I'm relieved that I won't have to speak next, but all she says is "Why don't you set the table?"

She goes to check the shrimp in butter and garlic on the stove, and the mofongo I know is in the oven, my favorite dish. I follow her into the kitchen, past the stainless-steel fridge with the iPad-looking gadget on the front that's replaced the white fridge Cami had since she moved here when I was in sixth grade—an American innovation.

"I'm glad you're here," Cami says when we're seated.

I'm not glad to be in Memphis, but I still say, "I'm glad to be here with you." Because it's true.

Cami smiles a thin smile, noticing the wording change, and goes to spoon the plantains and shrimp into our wooden mortars and pour broth over the top.

The dining table's glass is cool against my skin, and I miss the beat-up, carved wooden one she used to repaint every six months in different colors. Perhaps she's had it the entire time I've been gone, and in reality, this table is broken in as much as I've been broken in these last five years.

These are the types of changes I've come to expect from Cami. Either things change, like the color of her house or her hobbies, or they don't, like the length of her hair or her strange accent—southern from her childhood in Memphis mixed with Puerto Rican Spanish from her parents and the first ten years of her life, which she spent there. The accent is present in both English and Spanish, something I loved to try to untangle, even as a teenager.

"Why don't you start with you running out of graduation. What happened next?" she says now.

I shake my head. Not yet.

"Tell me about this," I say instead. I run a finger over the silver candleholder in the center of the table. The lit candle inside makes the gray strands in Cami's hair sparkle. Pheasants fly up the sides of the carved silver.

We watch each other, both afraid of some sort of hidden rejection.

She finally says, "You know that story."

"But I like it when you tell it."

She sighs and smiles with joy, as if deciding that it's really me after all, that my body isn't still back on an operating table in Bali.

As she launches into her story—"Well, this was"—she looks off into the distance, trying to remember, and the realization hits me.

I left Cami. I meant to leave this town, leave my father, leave my mother's memory, but I left her too. Others as well, but I don't want to think about Grant right now either.

"Nineteen ninety," I volunteer. Before she met her ex-husband while traveling in Peru.

"Nineteen ninety, yes! I took the train to Wakayama City to see the castle there. I've been walking on this tiny road for an hour, with Vespas speeding past, when I realize I can't see the castle anymore."

"What did you do next?" I prompt. But even still, I'm thinking about the castle and Japan, how the places Cami talks about in the stories I've heard dozens of times are places I've never been. I wanted to always think of this story when I thought of Wakayama, didn't want to write over her memories with mine, like recording over that VHS tape of *Mulan* we would watch over and over.

"I stuck my thumb out, not sure if hitchhiking was done in Japan. One man pulls over. I point to the castle on the map, but he only pats the back of his scooter."

I laugh, loving this version of Cami. When I heard this story as a child, I would think, that's the type of woman I want to be, not like my mother, who often reminded me that "crime is everywhere."

"I think, what the hell? I'm lost anyway, and climb on. We drive in the opposite direction, and eventually, I glance behind us, and what's back there other than the castle? I start to worry, even though Japan was known as a safe place for women traveling alone. Finally, we pull into a neighborhood."

"His son, who just came home from university in England, is inside, and he speaks English! They serve tea, and then the son takes me on a tour around Wakayama, including the castle. At the end, he takes me to his grandfather's silver workshop. I wasn't old then, not like I am now, and he said I was the most beautiful woman he had ever seen."

"He takes me back to the train station where I'm going to go back to Kyoto, and as I'm saying thank you, he gives me that candlestick to remember him by, from his grandfather's workshop."

"And it worked," I say, as always.

"Yes—almost thirty years later, and we're still talking about him." She takes a sip from her wineglass and then continues before I can squeeze in another word. "Did you go to Japan?"

Instead of answering, though, I ask about the framed postcard on the wall of workers constructing the Eiffel Tower, then about the jade box where she keeps her napkin rings, and the dish by the living room where she still keeps coins. She tells her stories, the same type I had hoped to tell the baby about my own adventures one day.

Out the window, dark clouds pass over the trees and bungalows that eventually lead to my father's house. Maybe it will storm. Then Cami and I could sit on the porch and watch the rain and lightning coming down on the cafés and shops and restaurants in Cooper-Young, the young people smoking on their porches, like we did after my mother died, each of us trying to piece together in silent concentration whether her death was a blessing or a curse.

But the weather holds off.

I listen to more stories from the couch, the cat curled at my feet. I remember so many childhood nights falling asleep to Cami's voice telling these stories in these rooms. So different from my parents' house, where I'd fall asleep to the sound of my father watching local news in the living room and my mother blaring sermons on tape in her bedroom, as if she could exorcise her demons while she slept.

I drift off to sleep on the couch, full of gratitude for this night of peace, that Cami is letting me evade questions for now. I know, whether or not she agrees, that I'll be back on the road in a few days, headed as far away from Memphis as I can afford.

CHAPTER EIGHT

I worked out a plan when I woke up in the middle of the night—tell her I'm leaving tomorrow and ask for a few hundred dollars. The plan formed while I counted the money wrapped and rubber-banded around my useless credit card, listening to the soundtrack of Cami's ankles cracking and the groan of the sixth hardwood board from her door as she paced in her bedroom. The rhythm was the same as when I was a kid, though this time, rather than brainstorming how I could convince Cami to let me stay here forever, I wanted her to let me go.

I go to the bathroom and sit down to pee. The position reminds me of having my feet in the stirrups only days ago, of everything I've lost. Where to go next, I think as I look at my tan face and freckled nose in the mirror, the purple-and-pink bags under my eyes like the sunset in Bali.

Not Germany. Anywhere but Germany. And no beach towns either.

French Canada? I've never been to Alaska, and I know that some people still speak the native Inuit languages, despite Americans' best efforts to squash them. I crave the hardness of Eastern European language; even the word "butterfly" sounds frightening in Russian. That's what I feel like right now. Ice and tundra and stresses on letters and endless rules to memorize. Not the Spanish flowing effortlessly at Cami's.

When I hear Cami walking down the hall, I follow her into the kitchen. From years of working for her in high school, I know the schedule of her store well. She'll need to leave soon. The daisies will be piling up at the back door, wilting, though maybe she has another me to take care of them. A less problematic, less rebellious employee.

"Why don't you sit down?" I say gently.

She sits at the kitchen bar next to me with a stack of what look like old envelopes, tied with a ribbon.

"What are those?"

"Do you want to tell me something, Mamacita?"

Somehow Cami is always one step ahead of me.

"Okay, yes." My eyes bounce around to the kitchen's knick-knacks before I go on. I hope she won't cry; I don't need another regret to mull over as I fall asleep tonight. "I can't stay here."

Instead of looking hurt or creasing her forehead like she does when she's surprised, she nods at me, bored.

"And?" she prompts.

"And I'm going to leave tomorrow. I'm sorry I can't stay. You know I'm not happy here."

She looks down at her stack of envelopes, as if she's thinking of what to say, but I can tell from her eyes that she knows exactly, has practiced the words, the intonation, how the syllables will roll off her tongue and into my ears.

I look at her, my life suspended while she takes a breath, and the feeling reminds me of nights waiting for her to play mediator between my mother and me, waiting for the verdict from Cami, the ultimate decider to whom we both ran with our troubles, each hoping she was ours alone.

"I've thought about this a while," she tells me. "And I think it's time for you to stop running. So you'll stay here for now."

"Cami, I'm doing exactly what you did—traveling the world." My mind buzzes with a counterargument I can't seem to form completely.

"No, you're not."

Her insistence bugs me, the way she states her proclamation as fact, and I cross my arms.

"I left college after my mother died and traveled. Your father died, and you left Memphis to travel! I'm doing exactly what you taught me, following your example. Not running."

She jumps when I mention her father. Does she not remember how much I know from one of my mother's lectures about how good I had it? It was one of our only fights that Cami heard—

"Stop yelling!"

"I'm not yelling!"

"You're both yelling!"

I could tell she immediately regretted being present, regretted seeing this side of her best friend, this version that she always knew lurked in the corners of my mother's mind, but which Cami never had to confront directly.

"Don't blame me for your choices," she says now.

"I'm not."

She stops talking and strokes the top envelope. With each stroke, composure reenters her face, as if the mystery envelopes have zapped out the other emotions. "I was heading to something, not escaping something that was too hard to deal with. There's a difference."

"So what, because you found the love of your life, you were running to something?"

"No," she says. "Because, as you brought up, after my mother left, I spent my life watching my father slowly die. Waiting for him to die and hating myself for it."

She pauses, watching me. I don't want her to see the recognition on my face, the relief and guilt I felt over my own mother's death. The relief Otto felt when the baby died…that escaped me. I'm not sure which emotion is worse.

I look away from her, and she continues: "And once it finally happened, I was alone. Everyone I loved was dead or gone. And I took that opportunity to care for myself for once, to learn who I was. To let myself be selfish.

"The difference between what I did and what you did," she continues, "is that I was happy. The happiest I've ever been, actually. Are you going to tell me you can say the same?"

Am I really that transparent?

"You can't make me stay, Cami." *You're not my mother*, I think with a pang. Not that she could control me either.

She tried, though. Policing the clothes I wore ("don't be vain"), prohibiting me from seeing the only friend I ever made, which only made me want to see Grant more.

The more she tried to turn me into the spitting image of what she herself had been in school—the perfect daughter, preparing to be the perfect, quiet, obedient, and never-complaining wife—the more I rebelled, and the more Cami was called to "talk some sense into me," and the more my father whispered helpfully that I might want to "clear out" for a few days. My mother's giggles always followed my father's suggestion. I could hear them echoing happily as soon as I slammed the front door.

"I can't make you stay, but I think you'll want to." Cami pats the stack of envelopes, and I look on skeptically.

"Are you finally going to tell me what those are?" I say, a bit too exasperated.

I feel like screaming, but I play it cool, like all the times my mother would start yelling and instead of yelling back, I'd stay silent, not crying, which seemed to anger her more—that detached calm, floating in my head to some location unknown to her. If I screamed, I always became more afraid; it made me worry I was becoming just like her.

"Lex, there's a lot you don't know about your mother."

As soon as she says the word "mother," I lean back in my chair and angle my whole body away from her, bracing myself for whatever is coming.

"And whose fault is that?" I shoot back at her. Unlike my father, though, Cami doesn't offer defenses.

Instead, she barrels on like she didn't hear me, slowly untying the ribbon around the mystery envelopes. "I think you have a lot to learn, starting with the few years she spent away from Memphis, when she sent me these for safekeeping."

"Mom never left. You know that," I insist, remembering asking her "What about you?" after my father said he had never flown before that first trip to Cami's. As usual when I asked my mother a question about herself, she shrugged as if the answer hardly mattered and told me to go clean my room.

"Is this some sort of joke?" I ask her.

My brain fills with a vision of my twelfth birthday party. My mother was prone to treating my birthday as a day of mourning, one on which she often became sick with the flu—in June. That year, Cami's first in Memphis, my godmother created a story about pirates, complete with a secret guest (Grant) who needed saving from the gang of girl pirates. The plot continued with buried treasure, snaking through my parents' neighborhood in Midtown, to Overton Park, to her recently opened flower shop, and finally down to Cooper-Young. Cami always loved to send me on a good scavenger hunt, but I'm in no mood for games these days.

"This is real, Lex. I wouldn't make up something like this. Your mother never left Memphis…except for this."

"That's not true."

"Every day you stay in Memphis, I'll give you one." She draws the first envelope out of the stack, leaving it on the table in front of me, and slips the rest into her tote. "Why don't you think about it today, make your decision, and let me know at dinner tonight? If you still want to leave, I'll buy you a plane ticket, wherever you want to go. But these stay here."

"You're not leaving me any decision. You're making me stay!"

"Everything in life is a choice, Lex, including this. I hope you learn that, or your life will always just happen to you." She kisses me on the forehead. "I've got to go open the store."

I stare at the envelope, refusing to pick it up.

Its only address is Cami's, at Lauderdale Courts, the affordable housing complex where both she and my mother grew up only a few apartment doors apart. Like many things in this city, the main glamour of the place is its connection to Elvis, who also spent his childhood there.

"And Mamacita?"

"Yes?" I call to her back, hoping that maybe she's about to confess this is a joke after all.

"Take a shower. You smell terrible." She shuts the door.

When she disappears around the corner, I open the envelope and take out a piece of paper, marked with "From the Desk of John Dowell" across the top and filled with my mother's tight block letters. John? I begin to read:

Dear Cami,

I'd like to ask you a favor.

As you know, my journal is important to me. Writing down my thoughts, my dreams, my realities, telling myself the story of my life with me as the protagonist for once—it's been a lifelong habit I can't seem to shake. Until now.

And not by choice.

My ask is this: I will send you my entries in envelopes marked "Do not open" across the backs. Please store these for me. When we see each other next, I will get them from you. I so appreciate you holding on to these.

Don't bother writing me back. We're in Florence now, but I'm not sure how long that will last. Yesterday, we visited the Duomo. It was under construction for five hundred years— makes Memphis development seem quick. The show there is mainly on the outside. The inside is quite disappointing, like a pretty girl with a bad brain.

I'll write more soon,
Margaret

CHAPTER NINE

My hands shake; my mind vibrates with questions. My mother was in Italy? When Cami said she left Memphis, I figured she meant to Atlanta or Nashville, not Florence. I assumed she'd never been farther than the Mississippi.

And who the hell is John? I heard my father recite their "love story" in church every anniversary, my mother listening to him with a smile and tears in her eyes as if she still loved him as much as that first year. I can picture her pulling his face toward her when he sat back down, the goofy smile that he always gave as she did, so happy to be showered with her attention, other men looking on, comparing my mother's looks to my father's and thinking, how did he manage it? *Oh, he pays for it*, I'd always think.

I tell myself not to believe the letter, not to believe Cami. Nothing in her story makes sense. Why wouldn't my mother be able to write anymore? Why would she be in Italy? And why the hell would she come back? Her letter, not even two hundred words, prompts the same number of questions.

In the absence of a better idea, I follow the plan Cami laid out for me and walk upstairs to the hallway bathroom. I avoid the room I'll always think of as my "real" childhood bedroom, though I slept there fewer nights than the room at my parents' house. A litter box now stands in place of the caddy that used to hold the makeup I kept at Cami's—contraband in my own house—with a small mirror above it that I'd used to apply blue mascara in high school.

Mirrors. I'd only discovered them after a man at church called me beautiful. "Were you admiring yourself in the mirror?" my mother yelled later. The next day, she took ten-year-old me to have my hair cut short and jagged and ugly. I cried the whole time, and the hairdresser commented that I had the bone structure for a pageboy cut, information my mother took in with narrowed eyes. I can count the trims I've had since on one hand, and the dark-brown, almost-black mane hangs down my back, full of tangles I don't want to think about getting out.

When was the last time I washed it? Does it still hold the sweat of the labor, still have remnants of the kiss Otto gave me on our way to the hospital?

"It will be okay," he'd said, though I already feared the worst.

Was Otto planning on leaving even then, hoping the baby would be gone so that he could be too, despite my clarity with him from the beginning that he didn't have to help? As the man, he had a choice, something a woman never has, especially in this country, in the South. My mistake, perhaps, was expecting that when I showed up at his apartment, Otto would write me a check and I'd be happily off with my fatherless child. Instead, he threw his skinny arms around my neck with a smile.

I shut the bathroom door now, but Cami's cat meows outside it, as if called to the room by the sound of it shutting, so I let him in too.

On a little stool in the corner is a pile of clothes, a comb, and a new toothbrush. I squirt toothpaste on the stiff bristles, trying not to count the hours since I last did this, and stare at my face in the mirror. The brown eyes I always wanted to replace with my mother's blue ones, the full lips I've finally grown into, the bushy eyebrows that I never plucked. In high school, the choice felt subversive, but now they're back in style.

I turn on the water, and while I wait for it to heat, the cat stares at me in concentration while laying down an impossibly large shit. Cami told me last night that she found Edgar nestled in her car motor one cold morning. Another animal Cami's decided to fix, not unlike myself.

When I scrunch my nose at him, he stares at me as if to say, *you're one to judge*. Cami was right; I smell terrible. I step inside the shower.

Thoughts of cat poop quickly lead to thoughts of poop in general, which makes me think of how some women poop on the delivery table when they give birth, how apparently some women are mortified by this. You're about to push a freaking human through your vagina; who cares if your husband sees you shit?

"*Meow*," Edgar says with increasing desperation, before transitioning into a full-blown yowl.

"What?" I yank open the shower curtain to ask him, and Edgar takes his paws off the edge of the tub, staring at me like I kicked him. "Thank you for your concern, but I'm not drowning."

Thanks for your concern, just like Cami with her insistence that I "stop running." Thanks, but no thanks. I'm fine on my own, always have been. It's a fact I've come close to forgetting these last few months, believing that I needed the baby. I'm determined not to forget again.

Edgar looks at me sagely, like a cat in India that my downstairs neighbor was sure predicted flooding. The neighbor gave me an update each morning as he ate a mango like it was an apple, peel and all. When the cat didn't show up for her food, you knew disaster would soon come in her place.

I wash my body as quickly as possible, avoiding my stomach, which still seems weirdly small, like when you wash your hair after getting a haircut, finding only air where the ends of your hair used to be. When I turn off the water, the yowling thankfully stops.

I dry off, thinking that Cami has been hoarding my mother's notes and waiting for the call saying I'd finally given up on my new life. Was her timing right, or did she expect to have this conversation years ago?

While my mother seemed shocked by my "random" rebellions, Cami always knew. She seemed able to anticipate my actions, from what I'd think about those clues at my pirate party to the days when I'd come into work late and hungover. "Came down with a cold?" Cami would offer helpfully.

One day in particular stands out because of Cami's sixth sense. I stormed through my parents' house, looking for my mother, planning to continue our fight from the previous day by yelling the most specific criticisms I could muster. I finally found her in the garage. Instead of her smug face, though, I saw only the puffed-out shell of what it used to be, with her head slumped forward on the steering wheel.

My head turned fuzzy and my legs wobbly, hand reaching toward the car door in a pointless and uncharacteristic dash of optimism, when I heard Cami's voice call my name from the other side of the garage door.

"LEX? LEX!" she yelled, as desperate as Edgar, trying to save me, the whisper of a siren in the distance.

Not me, I thought. *Her. It's Mom. Needs help.* As the knowledge that it was too late for anyone to help her—she was dead—replaced the words I'd planned to scream, my body dropped to the concrete floor.

I woke up lying in the grass, coughing on vomit, with a firefighter and Cami standing over me. Memory is so strange, as strange as language, and for some reason, my most vivid picture of that day is of Cami biting the end of her braid when I opened my eyes.

"Thank God!" she screamed. The garage, where I had been what felt like a millisecond ago, was now visible through its open door.

Had Cami materialized there? How had she known? How had she arrived with help just in time to save my life?

The problem is that she seems to think she's doing it again.

CHAPTER TEN

I walk back downstairs, my hair and body smelling of Cami's shampoo, dressed in loose black shorts and a huge T-shirt that says CENTRAL HIGH SCHOOL WARRIORS, CLASS OF 1988.

The background sounds in Cami's Victorian are so faint without her, but the melody in my head roars loud, and items yell their origin stories at me in different languages as I walk back to the living room. The little plane that Cami and her husband got from a pilot in South Africa on their last trip before they broke up and she came back to the United States. I know he brought her the beaded bracelets from Guatemala, now resting on a wooden hand instead of her own wrist because she would never pick out an earth tone. I consider what to do next when I reach the foyer.

The main hang-up I have about dismissing my mother's letter and the writings that accompany it as fiction is that I already knew my mother kept a diary. I even paged through some of them in childhood, but the readings were brief, because, well, the diaries were boring. Yet another example of why I needed a life of adventure, so my greatest thrill wouldn't be new fabric at the craft store or an outing to LongHorn.

But was her excitement about those things only an act?

I could call a cab or try to summon one of those newfangled scooters, but what do I have to do other than walk? So I grab a large hat and sunglasses out of Cami's closet as a disguise, like I'm a celebrity—which in this town, given how long I've been gone, I feel I am.

I stop at the end of Cami's iron fence with Edgar on my heels, wondering which backstreets to take. I've snuck between these houses all my life, biking through the streets of Central Gardens toward something that felt more like home. I turn away from Cooper Street, with the young people happily sitting on The Beauty Shop's patio or standing in line at the Soul Fish Café.

It's around eleven a.m. Cami is at her store. Or perhaps the girls are at home with their dirty kids (probably multiple), living the type of life I always knew I didn't want.

But does changing the location to Bali and removing the wedding ring change the essence of such a life?

Maybe I am a hypocrite, I think as I walk deeper into Cooper-Young. A family trait, as it turns out. Because I did want it, him.

As I pass Central Avenue and near my parents'—my father's, I guess it is now—street, I whirl around, looking for him. Now that I know he isn't walking the aisles of his store downtown, I feel his presence everywhere. A man ambles down a long driveway with my father's clumsy walk, always a single step from tripping. The boom of his sneeze sounds in the distance, from allergies that relentlessly persisted despite the nose spray he used every morning. He always yelled "Woo!" and clapped his hands once after the final spray, energized as if he were a drug addict snorting his morning cocaine. All characteristics I assumed my mother found adorable.

To think about something other than my parents, I think about the exact words she used in the letter—

dream, related to the German word *traum*—no, let's not go to German—related to the Dutch word *droom*, both with a root meaning "lie, deception, seeking to harm." Old English had it too in words for joy and music. Our English word, the ugly mash of the two roots. A joy that can't be trusted. A joy that can harm.

appreciate, not a word my mother often used—Latin verb *appretiare*, "rise in value," unlike everything she touched. "Favor," though, was one of her favorites.

protagonist, more like antihero. "Pro-" meaning "for" or "forward"—as in "prophet, prostitute, profess, profit, profligate, pro…gress"! I think with a triumph that disperses as soon as my father's house comes into view.

I consider continuing toward Overton Park, named for John Overton, who purchased the land for downtown with his law partner, future president and Trail of Tears enthusiast Andrew Jackson. The park contains a zoo, started with a bear named Natch chained to a tree, the mascot of the Turtles baseball team. Explain that, Memphis.

I force myself to walk toward the short driveway and strain to spot my father's work boots outside the garage door. I shake off the thought that has drifted into my head—that he's gone, that he's dead, that I'll never see him again. Not that I care, I coach myself. *You don't. You're fine on your own. You don't need anyone.*

I breathe a sigh of relief when I see the "dirty work" pair, though, the newer pair presumably on his feet, wherever he is. I veer to avoid the house's side, with the garage and the Redbirds flag and the patch of grass where the remnants of my carbon-monoxide-laced barf lay deep in the dirt..

I look for the trick rock with the key hidden in the shrubs

next to the front door. Before I can worry too much about the possibility of my father coming home, I put the key in the lock and walk into the house's stale air.

The front room is full of pictures, same as always. My parents in front of Henry Hardware. Me on a school trip to the Lorraine Motel with the girls with whom my mother wanted me to be friends. My grandfather and me in front of the miniature circus at the Pink Palace.

My mother isn't in any of the photos, but I can see her still, beyond the frame, looking at me, commanding me to smile. I sense her aura more than my own, see myself through her disapproving blue eyes. I pass the stairs that lead up to the bedroom where I slept and head down the hallway at the back of the house, toward my parents' bedroom and bathroom. I rarely ventured inside these rooms. This was my mother's territory.

The bedroom door is shut, but the bathroom across the hall is open. A pink toothbrush and a single tube of lipstick are out on the counter, and I push past them. Another thing I would prefer to ignore right now. John, and now this?

I open the door to the last room in the hallway. It never had a name, but my mother was often ensconced in its walls.

A chair and footrest sit in one corner, and a new table is wedged into another, overflowing with mismatched tools. Boxes marked HENRY HARDWARE that weren't here before stack almost to the ceiling. A row of blank baseball scoring books sit on the floor, ready for my parents and their sharpened pencils.

I go into the closet and dig past the outdated clothes to a plastic bin that holds my mother's diaries. I pull it out, just as I did in childhood. First in the bin are three yearbooks, two of mine from elementary school and one from a local high school. My forehead crinkles, but I keep my mind focused on the mismatched notebooks, spreading them out in front of me.

I open the cover of the first one (Volume I, according to the cover), a furry pink notebook with a broken lock.

March 1: I've barely seen Cami between her new job at Goldsmith's, taking care of her father, and piles of schoolwork. After some prodding, I finally convinced her to go see *Terms of Endearment*. If only I could one day write a story like that, that makes the audience believe family actually means something. I believed, for those two hours. Cami didn't like it as much. Next time she'll probably pick *The Karate Kid*. The theater will be packed, with popcorn being thrown by teenage boys who are only there to see the girls. Cami had to go home after. Her father seems to be getting worse every day, though she never says that, just makes up nonsense excuses like the laundry.

August 1: Today I got to help Miss Kosa clean her classroom. Hanging posters on the wall took a while, but it looked perfect when we were done. Miss Kosa let me order the books any way I pleased. I need to garner goodwill with her because I plan to submit to a few literary magazines this year. She's the only teacher I trust to read my story and respect it for what it is, not to tattle because I used forbidden words like "hell."

September 15: Cami has been busy this week. I finally had to agree to meet her at the school library and help her study. When we were young, we'd sit in the hallway between our apartments, her always listening for calls from her father, and dream about the future. She always said she wanted to be a nurse. But now that we're in high school, every conversation about the future is tinged with a more realistic picture. I've stopped talking about wanting to leave Memphis. Every time I do, she stalks around and ignores me for a few days.

No wonder I didn't find these riveting.

I locate the diary from my mother's senior year of high school—"Volume 4." The first page begins the same way.

January 18: I watched the baseball scrimmage today. After much begging, Cami came out to watch too, partially encouraged by the attention of the third baseman. He got hit in the head with the ball while he was watching her, but she refused to look at him. Dennis kept trying to catch my eye from the sidelines. Score was 5–3.

Was she thinking of going to Italy even then? Was she happy with my father?

I flip through to find my mother's high school graduation, realizing I need to go to the next notebook. It's thin, the leather on the outside streaked with fingernail scratches under my mother's name. The elastic holding it closed is down to one string. When I open the book, the pages are completely ripped out. There's tape on the inside binding to keep it intact with the words "Volume 5."

My heart starts racing.

I open the next journal, Volume 6, but it was obviously written years later.

June 2: Baby Alexandra born. Lex for short?

June 6: Showered today.

June 22: Lay in bed with a pillow over my head, listening to the baby cry. I am empty.

I throw that journal back in the box. Instead, I take out the "Volume 5" journal with the missing pages and try to focus on that.

What happened in those pages that didn't fit the rest? Maybe, I think with fascination, they weren't boring enough to stay.

CHAPTER ELEVEN

If there was a part of my mother that she always hid, some missile she never chose to detonate, I want to bask in that pain now. Even when she screamed at me through doors or as I was running away, I couldn't help but listen, just to hear what she would say, hear the truth in her insults. I can't ignore her arrows from beyond the grave either.

On my way out the front door, I rip my father's hunting jacket off a hanger in the front closet and slip my mother's empty journal into one of the pockets. I'm doing him a favor by taking it. He should have thrown this away a decade ago, like most of the crap in this house.

I storm down Peabody Avenue toward Cami's store, sweating in my ridiculous hat and the hunting jacket despite the chill. My mother's writings should belong to me. Daughter trumps best friend, or I hoped it would, though that was never true in my experience. I'm angry at myself and at Cami that she's right about the power my mother's words have over me; she knows my Icarus streak too well.

I'm brainstorming how to negotiate with Cami when the sight of Overton Square bustling in the distance stops me. Last time I walked by, on my way to hear one of Cami's customers at Lafayette's Music Room, the square was still crammed with abandoned buildings. The owners of Chicago Pizza Factory had fled Memphis with such haste that the tables were still set, like a customer could walk in at any time, with salt and pepper shakers on each. I often peeked through the dirty windows of that building as a teenager, understanding the rush to get out.

When I stomp up the steps of Cami's shop, I'm concentrating so hard on listening for the satisfying clang of the bell against wood when the door flings open that it takes me a second to realize that the door is locked. A sign says, WILL RETURN AT: with a little clock that points to three p.m.

I sigh. When I left Cami's, it was ten a.m., and the afternoon is far away. I take off my hat and sunglasses to peek in the window where the flowers sit in their lit refrigerated case. Cami left the house not two hours ago, saying she was going to the flower shop. Where is she?

A lady with whom my parents used to go to church walks by, and I whip around to don my disguise. Memphis always felt to me like a city that hadn't been told it wasn't a small town.

The tube of lipstick from my father's bathroom enters my mind again. A potential stepmother lurks in every passing woman's face. And the last thing I need is for someone to see me and tell my father. Or Grant.

I duck into the coffee shop next to Cami's store and wait behind a man trying to order a venti vanilla latte as an apron-clad barista explains that flavoring is against his philosophy on "minimalist coffee." Glass beakers line the bar, brewing coffee in varying degrees of brown. A woman wearing a shirt with a rainbow 901 draws on a cup with a set of mini Sharpies.

"Hey, can I use your phone?" I say when it's finally my turn.

The barista shrugs with a smile, seemingly happy not to engage in another confrontation over coffee philosophy, and hands over the phone.

I take out my rubber band wallet and peel off a precious ten-dollar bill. "Dealer's choice," I say.

I call Cami's cell, the number floating to me effortlessly, though I haven't dialed it in years.

"Lex? What is this number? Where are you?"

"Where are *you*?"

She pauses. "At the store."

I look out again to the store with its WILL RETURN AT: sign. It's Monday, I remember. The store is never open on Mondays.

"I'm at the coffee shop next door."

"At a client's house, I mean."

"Uh-huh." I'm hoping to catch her off guard, off the plan from which I've clearly deviated, so I jump in. "Cami, why don't you just give me all her letters?"

The philosopher of coffee eyes me as he pours hot water over one of the beakers. I walk to the other window. "Instead of staying, I was thinking maybe we could meet somewhere for Christmas? Wouldn't it be fun for you to travel again?"

"*Lo siento*, Mamacita."

"What if I come here for Christmas the next two years?"

She doesn't say anything.

"Every other year."

Another pause, the sound of a door opening and closing in the background.

"Every year?"

"We can talk tonight, but I need to get back to this...client's floral arrangements right now." You'd think that being close to my parents, she'd have learned to lie with minimum competency.

"What do you expect me to do during the day—hide in your house until all your mysterious envelopes are gone?" I hear something like a finger snap. "That's a great idea!" she says.

"What is?"

"You don't want to be here, bored."

"Right."

"So let's make things a little more fun. You'll get an envelope every day. But to get it, you'll have to do something for me. I want you entertained!"

"You can't be serious!" I remember being at Cami's house as a child, saying, "I'm bored." She would quickly assign me a chore like pulling the weeds in the yard. When I said I was bored at my parents' house, my father tended to act like my voice was the wind, while my mother would respond, "Well, I guess I'm a terrible mother, then. What do you want, arts and crafts?"

"Another word from you, I'll make it two things."

My mouth was open to protest, but I shut it immediately.

"And if you go start on the first task right now, I'll trade you for the next envelope. Let's do the garden today. Tools are in the shed. I assume you still remember how I like the flowers, if you feel up to it?"

"I feel fine," I snap, hating the mention of my still-swollen stomach, the hormones attacking my every thought.

"Cami—" I start again, but she's already saying, "I have to go. Look under the living room rug." Then she hangs up.

I hand the barista back his phone, take my minimalist coffee, and head home toward the living room rug. This time, though, I cut through the road behind Cami's store.

"Hey!" I yell at a teenager hauling a box of fresh delphiniums in through the back door.

"We're closed," she says, not looking at me.

"Where's Cami?"

"She's coming in late today. Come back in an hour."

"Where is she?"

"At her house? I don't know; I'm not her babysitter." She looks at me. "Do I know you?"

I duck away without answering, wondering where Cami really is and why she's lying. Either way, in twenty minutes, my mother's next entry is in hand, and Edgar stares at me like he understands the gravity of this moment. The envelope is sealed and marked Do Not Open on the back.

But I'm not one for following my mother's instructions, even in death. I open the envelope, unfolding a few pages with ripped edges down the left-hand side.

The pages fit perfectly in the empty journal I found with her stuff this morning—the size, the ripped lines.

I start reading.

CHAPTER TWELVE

MARGARET

Let's start at the beginning: the day our heroine (Or villain? That's up to you) first heard of the man she will soon think is the love of her life. But remember, in the best pieces of writing, the heroes and villains tend to be one and the same.

One fine March day in Memphis, Margaret Green, a bright girl with a cute face and a terrible haircut, sat in the bleachers at her then-boyfriend's baseball game with her then–best friend, Cami. No, not boyfriend—fiancé, a term to which Margaret was still adjusting, despite the excitement around her. His name was Dennis, a description that was accurate in every sense.

Our young heroine sat with her ring-laden hand hidden behind the cover of an SAT prep book. As long as she maintained her GPA, she was set to be valedictorian, a goal those around her thought made little sense, given the ring. But she would rather dream of her speech than admire the dead woman's diamond.

She was not ~~dating~~ engaged to the pitcher of the baseball team or someone equally thrilling. The ball boy: he was ~~her man~~ her BOY. The one who could be defeated by the strength of his own sneezes.

She sat on the bleachers, overdressed, for her mother had

instructed her since double digits to wear a pretty dress whenever a boy would be present, and to powder her face, and to mind her manners. Her mother had a Plan—this was the man her daughter would marry! She hoped that others would judge her daughter not for her address's proximity to Uptown Square, but for the "sir"s and "ma'am"s at the end of each precisely worded sentence, à la *Gone with the Wind*, but Melanie or maybe Ellen, not Scarlett.

Her daughter would follow the Henry boy to Memphis State. She would live in the house by Overton Park. Henry Hardware would be hers the way a church belongs to the pastor's wife, which is not at all.

If a few careful forgeries were all that were required for her daughter to live a prosperous life, then Margaret's mother would do it, no matter how many nights she had to spend huddled over copies of birth certificates and family bibles and war registries at the library, dip pen carefully poised. She succeeded too, quickly becoming a fixture at the Daughters of the American Revolution and partners with Dennis's mother during tours at the Mallory-Neely House.

As far as Margaret could tell, her mother's three goals in life were: One, have Margaret ~~marry~~ entrap Dennis. Two, yell at her husband and daughter as much as possible. And three, test how many jobs one person could hold at once. Margaret would have sworn her mother took some sort of drug to stay awake all night, but through years of observation, she was fairly certain her mother ran on the stress of having an unmarried daughter and the belief that any man in possession of a good hardware store must be in want of a wife.

Our heroine's mother didn't watch TV. She didn't read, she didn't cook. In fact, she barely ate at all. Instead, Margaret and her father chatted over dinner alone. She loved listening to her father's stories about his parents growing up in Germantown, of the many houses and buildings he had helped restore as a carpenter before a handsaw stole four of the five fingers on his right hand. His pinkie was all that remained, which Margaret always thought made him look quite refined. He said nothing about the culmination of his wife's decade-long plan.

For today's dress, though, our heroine had her own motives, or she wouldn't have listened to the fashion advice. She normally nodded at her mother's instructions, then changed into jeans behind the rosebush in the back of their apartment building, licking her hand to wipe the powder off her face.

Margaret was in a tense, weeks-long negotiation to convince her fiancé to fuck her, ideally in a more creative position than missionary and for longer than the two minutes she'd come to understand was customary.

She'd developed the plan while he was on one knee, muttering into the ring box. He moved his lips, but Margaret could hear only the low rumble of the Mud Island Monorail overhead.

"Margaret?" Dennis had prompted.

Embarrassed by the whole scene and picturing Cami's and her mother's excitement, she'd smiled, which had launched him into her arms, the ring gliding onto her finger. Once on, it weighed her body down like an anchor, tethering her to a shore she knew frighteningly well.

But they were *seniors*. Shouldn't she be ready to ~~submit~~ grow up by now? Margaret took the question as a promise that her mother would lose patience with her residence in their two-bedroom apartment as soon as graduation passed. She took every opportunity to hide the tips she earned from her job at the Arcade Restaurant.

She prayed for the rise of an unexpected sexual need in Dennis, kept waiting for him to develop some habit other than sitting in her section at the Arcade, sipping his coffee while locals ordered eggs or sweet potato pancakes and tourists ordered the peanut butter and banana sandwich Elvis made famous.

Dennis's lack of interest in sex was unnatural, was what she'd come to believe, despite all his talk about how it would be disrespecting her, disrespecting their marriage vows, and probably even disrespecting God in all three of His forms: Jesus, Lord, and Holy Spirit. Goddammit, Margaret thought when he started to pull the God card. Even Cami was bound to nod at that criticism of Dennis.

"He's a nice guy!" she would say to most any other snub.

"You sound like my mother," Margaret responded once before regretting it, as she regretted any mention of the *m*-word around her friend.

Margaret could feel the bleachers engraving welts along the backs of her thighs, which she worried would damage her sexual prospects. These were her two chief concerns: the fucking and becoming valedictorian. The order was unimportant. Indeed, they were related.

She gamely flipped past the English section of her SAT book. She had already finished most books in the school library and was the best writer ~~in school~~ in the city ~~(probably)~~, and had been, regardless of grade, for years—even Miss Kosa said so—and thus had no use for further English instruction.

She wanted to go to a top college for writing and then become a famous writer—a dream she had only dared tell Cami once and had avoided repeating. The implication seemed to be, "I'll leave you, my closest friend, here alone." To the school counselor, Margaret had only whispered that she wanted to keep her "options open" when she'd borrowed the prep book. As far as the other goal, how could our young heroine write real stories about pain, suffering, and love if she hadn't felt the most common yet exquisite (she'd heard!) love offered on God's great earth?

She started on a math section, her weakest subject—not at all needed by writers, but apparently the College Board entertained other ideas. She put a finger to her temple in concentration and licked her bottom lip as sexily as a virgin possibly could. See? Two goals in tandem.

She paused at a word problem; adding words to math made questions impossible. She listened to two girls—names as unimportant as they were—behind her reading an article in the *Commercial Appeal* and prattling on about someone named John. She'd heard them complaining to each other in the bathroom last week that their boyfriends only wanted "one thing." Some girls had it all.

Margaret looked up from the prep book. The article detailed the discovery of a famous writer, hiding in plain sight at the Peabody Hotel!

Later, she learned the story behind this story: While John had come to Tennessee to escape the relentless fame and accompanying misery of New York City, he quickly grew bored with obscurity. Being ~~infamous~~ unfamous wasn't as fun as he thought. So he tipped the reporter himself that one John Dowell was seeking refuge in the hotel, writing his next melodramatic novel and what was sure to be a groundbreaking poetry collection.

"Let me see," Margaret said, ripping the paper from their grasp.

"Cute, isn't he?" said one of the girls, looking at the picture accompanying the article.

"I guess," Cami answered.

"Cute?" Our young heroine felt the wheels in her pretty, stupid head begin to turn. A real writer in Memphis? Well, the first since Faulkner's jaunt here, and Louise Fitzhugh, who no longer counted since Margaret had grown out of *Harriet the Spy*. While she was confident Miss Kosa had taught her as much as she could about writing, Margaret wanted to learn ~~more~~ everything. And now, a real, published writer had shown up in Memphis, and all Cami (her best friend since she'd moved in down the hall, all the way from Puerto Rico, at age ten!) could say was… *Cute, I guess?*

Margaret was sure he was her White Rabbit, the spark she needed to tumble down into a more colorful and literary life. Should she write to him? Too…epistolary?

Just one word of encouragement was all she needed. Just one person to whom she could whisper what she had wanted to tell Dennis when he knelt there on the grass: *No. Thank you, but I'm actually a writer. Not a wife; not a mother.* One person she could talk to about writing without the tinge of guilt and blame that was ever present in her other conversations, even with Cami.

She didn't have to ponder her approach for long, though, because that week, John walked into Mr. Simmons's English class, looking and acting nothing like she imagined a famous writer would. He wore a faded pair of striped suit pants, thin on one knee, and stood with his hands tucked in the oversize pockets of his worn-in denim jacket, bashful, almost ~~shocked~~ humbled by his success. From his pocket came a pair of foggy glasses, and he began his speech, detailing how he got into writing—how his grandmother set out to culture him. That type of story sounded so fresh to our young writer then, but actually, this is the biography of every trust-fund baby on the Upper West Side. He'd had to leave the North to get some damn originality.

His readings from his upcoming poetry collection took her breath away, though. She eyed her fellow students to see if they were equally enraptured. Betty—the airhead—was ~~literally~~ styling her hair in a hand mirror. The rest of the gaggle slumped over their desks, and Margaret presumed them all (for the hundredth time) to be idiots. This school, funded by tax dollars, encouraged her to agree with her father that a free education was a waste for most people, especially when there were buildings to save.

There are so many girls from this neighborhood who would die to be in your position, who would die to be engaged to a boy like Dennis, she heard her mother say in her head. If the relationship stakes were high enough for their story to be set in the Capulet family tomb, then why didn't someone else date him? Margaret always wondered. Probably because the other girls had the luxury of seeing Dennis as he really was—a boy who couldn't eat a meal without earning the badge of a stain on his shirt or walk a mile without a stumble—rather than seeing him as her mother saw him, as some kind of shining beacon of lifelong familial security.

When John left, Margaret asked Mr. Simmons if she could go to the bathroom.

"Mr. Dowell?" she said, breathless, as she ran after the writer, her moccasins sliding on the school's tile floors.

"Hmm?" He spun around.

He was the best-looking man she'd ever seen up close, because she attended school alongside boys. The men she knew were old. This person was in between, and it showed.

He would never disrespect a girl by forcing her to beg to lose her virginity. It was demoralizing! Especially with someone like Dennis, and when she was so ~~hot good-looking attractive beauti-ful?~~ hot, she had to admit to herself, staring at her breasts and flat stomach in the bathroom mirror at night as her index finger found that special spot, gasping as she thought of Ned Nickerson, or how she imagined him when she read Nancy Drew anyway. Tonight, though, she'd think of John.

The thought made her turn as scarlet as Hester's letter, and she stammered, "I wondered, what is your favorite book?"

She watched as he considered the question, half expecting him to say *Lolita* and hoping he wouldn't say *Catcher in the Rye*.

"*Ulysses*," he said before walking down the hallway with the gentle stride of a man who knows how to waltz.

"Wait!" Margaret said.

He turned again to face her.

"I…want to be a writer," she said.

"You either are a writer or you are not a writer," he countered. "There is no 'want.'"

She stared at him dumbly.

"So which is it?"

"I am a writer, sir."

"Sir, huh? Am I that old?" She looked at the hair peeking out from the V-neck of his shirt, unable to respond. "What's your name, honey?"

"Margaret Green," she answered.

"Margaret," he said, rolling it over in his mouth. "Marge. Margie. Peggy? No, too pedestrian. Magariit, yes. What kind of writing do you do?"

"Stories."

"About what?"

She wanted to avoid saying "my life," because that sounded juvenile. She recognized that much like Holden's own, there was nothing original about her life. It would be even worse to tell John that the stories represented what she wished her life would be. So instead she answered, "Everything."

"The best kind," he said. "Why don't you send me a few of your stories about everything?"

"Really?" she said ~~stupidly~~ too enthusiastically. "I mean, if you have time."

He smiled and handed her his business card, flipping it over to write his room number and the address of the Peabody Hotel on the back, which she found so endearing—like everyone in town didn't know where he was staying and what the address was.

That moment was the ~~end of~~ tipping point away from the girl she used to be.

CHAPTER THIRTEEN

LEX

My brow crinkles with confusion. The story is in my mother's handwriting, and the characters are the same as the history I know—my mother, my grandparents, my father, Cami—but the plot is different. This woman (the academic, the thinker, the striver) is unlike the one I knew.

My mother was almost valedictorian? She never showed any interest in my schoolwork. When I needed her signature on a report card, she'd tell me, "Stop smiling. Getting straight A's doesn't make you special. And neither does taking fancy honors classes."

The "heroine" about whom my mother wrote was desperate to escape Memphis, to be a writer, but when I wanted to flee this town, when I wanted to follow my own (different) love of language, she called me naive. She spent her life judging me for wanting something more than she had dared dream for herself. "What's wrong with you, Lex?" she asked so many times, calling me ungrateful.

Yet all her life, she had memories of her own time in Italy… with a mysterious man named John. Memories that she could turn over in her imagination to supply her boring days with some bonus tension.

Did my mother take pleasure in pretending that she couldn't understand me? That my desires were unreasonable, when at my age, hers had been more outlandish?

I head outside and trudge through the too-tall grass to the shed, wondering why Cami let it grow so unruly. I've spent many days with the tools in this shed. I always sought to make myself useful to convince her that I deserved to stay. Now, the roles have reversed, yet the treatment is the same.

Under the lawnmower's hum, I murmur to myself about secrets and requirements and all the things I hate, all the wrongs I've seen.

I can picture Dennis patiently drinking his coffee while my mother waitressed, apparently dedicated to his moral high ground. And even from that pedestal, she didn't love him. Or didn't love him yet?

I replay the story I've heard my parents recite many times: boy sees girl in cafeteria, boy asks girl to prom. First comes love, then comes marriage, then (reluctantly) comes baby in a baby carriage! Couple lives happily ever after, dancing to "Love Me Tender" on anniversaries and major holidays and any night they could pretend they hadn't produced offspring, especially one as frustrating as me. The circumference of the circle they formed together was so small that there wasn't room for me. No wonder I didn't have a sibling, I used to think.

Now, though, I'm not sure what to think.

I discovered long ago that my father's actions didn't live up to his Mr. Honest, Mr. Noble, Mr. Innocent act, but in this entry, my mother appears not to know that yet. That was the secret I thought they were hiding, the one I had felt charging through the air of our house. The narrowed-eyed exchanges between my parents in answer to a simple question, the loaded silences, stretching on at dinner until they snapped. Maybe I wasn't thinking big enough.

By six p.m., when I expect Cami to return, the grass is mowed, the flowers are watered, the weeds have been pulled, a bowl of radishes and cauliflower from the garden sits on the kitchen counter, and I've run out of tasks to keep my mind busy. But instead of the door opening, the home phone rings. I wait for the machine to catch it, a reminder from my own childhood of waiting, praying that it wasn't my father summoning me back to what he called home.

"Hi, Lex, sorry to do this, but I need to stay late to finish an arrangement for a wedding this weekend. I ordered you a pizza. Don't wait up for me. I'll see you tomorrow."

The message beeps off, and I'm still puzzling over Cami's words when the doorbell rings. It's the pizza.

Is this her answer to me stepping off her carefully laid path, laden with her confidence that I would make the choices she expected? I left the house when she thought I would stay, busted her for lying about being at the store, and earned the first entry a day ahead of schedule.

I suspect Cami has spent her life engaged in wars of attrition with the people who surround her, trying to fix them. She started with her father, whom she could never heal, and my number has simply come up again for another attempt. Another failure incoming.

I carry the pizza to the kitchen to eat by myself, all the while thinking about Cami, where she is, and what her absence means.

Cami and my mother talked every day of their lives, it seemed to me, often multiple times a day. Yet my mother described her as her "then–best friend." The way she talked about Miss Kosa is also surprising to me. I can only remember my mother avoiding her in church, though she did that to most people. Any agreement with my mother encouraged anxiety, but we both sat stiff-backed in our chairs when the pastor called for the meet and greet.

Once I've eaten and drunk enough to sleep soundly, I stare at the couch, wondering if I can get away with sleeping there again, but my hip hurts from scrunching up my long legs to fit the available space last night. I grab my meager luggage from where I dumped it the night before and bring it upstairs.

When I open the door to what used to be my bedroom, I gasp, again confronted with Cami's vision for my expected return. Last I saw this room, the walls were white, with pothos spilling down them from hanging planters. Now, color bursts from every corner, reminding me of my time in Mexico. The bed's patchwork quilt is Cami's mother's, lugged all the way from Puerto Rico, made from hundreds of pieces of fabric. I begged (unsuccessfully) to take it to college with me. Did Cami know how thin the rope was that tied me to this place, to her, even then?

The rug looks like someone stole a child's paint set, then trampled the primary colors into white shag. My favorite reading chair, which I've seen upholstered in more colors and textures than I can count, is bright orange. A silver floor lamp lights the space where my books will soon go. I take them out of my plastic bag and stack the volumes on the empty bookshelf. I put my rubber band wallet on top. There—unpacked.

Cami has decorated the bedside table with my favorite pictures in stained-glass frames. No doubt to remind me of the good times I've had in this city, for everything in this room has a purpose, everything in Cami's life corresponds to her higher goals, even me.

The pictures show me standing between my parents at my high school graduation. Me the first time I visited Cami. We're dancing the tango, and she's dipping me. My head is thrown back, laughing hysterically, one of my feet off the floor. Grant is there too. Grant and me, with the new bridge "M"-ing behind us. Grant and me making duck faces with the duck master at the Peabody Hotel.

The frame closest to the bed holds a picture of my mother and Cami sitting knee-to-knee, looking at each other and laughing with my little body strewn across their laps. I'm wearing a party hat and a streak of blue icing from my birthday cake. It's my third birthday. I'd met Cami a month earlier, when she'd come back from her travels, and sometimes I fool myself into thinking I remember that day—my parents, Cami, me, happy. The best birthday I've had, lost to memory.

I crawl under the quilt and white sheets with yellow embroidery that used to be mine, kick up my feet to loosen the covers at the end of the bed. The sheets once had a bloodstain from when I got my first period, but surely that's gone now.

I grab my friend and constant companion, *The Dictionary of Word Origins*. The spine is held together with duct tape, the pages crinkled from humidity in India and Bali. My name is written on the front with red marker, then crossed out with Sharpie from a (failed) experiment with the name Martha while traveling.

I flip to a random page:

emetic, see *vomit*.

émeute, see *emotion*.

eminent, someone who "stands out." Latin participle. "Stand, project," see *imminent, prominent*. Possible relation to Latin word for mountain, source of English *mount*.

emir, see *admiral*.

emolument, originally payment to a miller for grinding corn, much like salary referred to payment for salt. Latin, *ex-* meaning "out" and *-molere*, "grind," relative to English *mill* and *meal*.

Before I can read **emotion**, I'm asleep.

CHAPTER FOURTEEN

Sitting next to Cami in a matching rocking chair, I close my eyes in the morning dew that's distinctly southern, distinctly from my past. I've been all over the world, but there is no feeling like this, like watching the sun make its way across the damp grass, the rays playing with your skin on a perfect Memphis morning, the sounds of Cooper Street just beyond the garden gate.

We don't talk about my mother. We listen to Memphis waking up. Cami lets me finish my coffee before she stands up and pats my shoulder. I had hoped to spend today indulgently holed up in her house with her cat and her plants and the chill seeping through the old insulation. But Cami has other ideas.

"I thought you'd come with a suitcase!" she says, taking my empty coffee mug to the sink. "Your task for the day is to get some damn clothes!" she says, bustling me to the bathroom as she once did before school, into the old T-shirt I washed last night and the hat/disguise from yesterday.

She rushes me, the cat, and her credit card past the flowers on the entry table—now white lilies, some half-budded, filled out with tufts of lavender—and out the front door, wanting me to leave at the same time she does. She's still spouting directions to Urban Outfitters when I turn toward the backstreets to Central Avenue.

"Another envelope when you get back!" she shouts, right after I lose her from my vision.

I pause, breathing, calming myself, and watching Edgar, who seems equally surprised by our sudden exodus from the house. My mind returns to the girl—I have to think of her that way, since nothing about her reminds me of my mother. Who is she asking not to judge her anyway, to call her a hero or a villain? It seems like she's asking me, but I know that can't be. This girl doesn't know that I exist. Herself? Could be, considering my mother was the most judgmental person ever.

Make one mistake—take a wrong turn, arrive a few minutes late, chew in an annoying (to her) way—and she could explode.

I think back to myself in middle school, sitting and judging students in class, many the daughters of the same people my mother thought so terrible. Betty ("the airhead") is a federal judge now, I think.

The Urban Outfitters comes into view. It had been a gym, or was it an antique store? But now it's a teen haven, deserted during school hours, the plaster on the walls left off some of the bricks, the old laths peeking through. So hip, so industrial, so...loud. Why is the music so damn loud?

I walk toward the men's T-shirts, all of which seem to proclaim that the wearer resides in another location—Los Angeles, New York, West Coast, Mountains, London. I linger over CIGARETTES AFTER SEX (?), a Star Wars shirt with a tiny Yoda, a shirt that says I WAS ADOPTED BY TIERRA WHACK (who?), and settle on one that says MENTALLY GONE (true) to add to a pile of plain tees in various colors.

I add a black hoodie and am looking at the women's jeans,

wondering what the hell size my body is now, when a toddler begins to scream, holding one of the cheap key chains by the register. He's having a meltdown, and his mother is trying to reason with him logically. Seeing that almost makes me want to cry myself, thinking how lucky he is to have a mother like that. When I screamed, my mother shrieked; when I cried, my mother sobbed, and eventually, I learned to do neither. A tradition I vowed not to repeat when I thought I would become a mother.

Despite the apparently squashed dreams of the girl in the letter, I don't feel bad for her. I don't. You made your own choices. Take responsibility for them, like you always told me to do.

I rip a few jeans off their hangers and take them into the dressing room. Even though looking at my new reflection in the brightly lit mirror is the last thing I want to do right now, I pull down my shorts, unbutton the largest pair first, and try to slip them over my thighs.

I return to words as I button the pants to avoid thinking of anything else—my mother's writing, the last pair of jeans I wore, with the stretchy waistband that held in that baby, which brings me back to my mother again. Ugh. It's weird, I tell myself, how a pair of pants is one piece of clothing. So two jeans would be a pair of pairs of pants? What's the history of that phrasing?

In the dressing room next to mine, a college-aged girl is trying on clothes with her mother. Just another day shopping in Memphis. Something I never did with my mother, and apparently, something she never did with her own.

But my grandmother doesn't seem that bad! She's a woman unknown to me, dead before I could walk. Like my mother, I have great memories with her husband, my grandfather—those same rants about buildings in Memphis, but with even more material. That slave-fueled cotton money had to go somewhere, though that's my own addition.

The girl in the hallway shuffles toward the bigger mirror, and her mother comments, "It doesn't do you any favors, does it?"

The language of American women in dressing rooms is unlike that in any other place in the world. I sink into it to distract myself from everything in my head.

What favor is a dress going to do, get you a cup of coffee?

On the other side of me, a woman takes a sharp breath—"It's not you! The zipper is stuck. I'm trying to... Ooh!" The other woman lets out the breath. Her friend chuckles.

How is this a script we all seem to know, passed down from one generation to the next?

I pick up the first pair of jeans, a.k.a. the ones that are as loose as possible without sliding off my hips, the hoodie and T-shirts, some boy-short underwear and men's socks, and bring my haul to checkout.

I hold my breath like that woman waiting for the zipper to close, and hand over my credit card, hoping I won't need to use Cami's. The limit on my card is fickle enough that charges can bounce if you look at it too hard, and the bill has been accruing interest ever since I started buying things for the baby.

It goes through. This time.

I bask in my brief luck as I walk back through the streets of Cooper-Young, the plastic Urban Outfitters bag reminding me of my slipshod luggage. I know my mother's next entry will be waiting for me at Cami's.

CHAPTER FIFTEEN

MARGARET

Our heroine had just met the man she was sure would change her life. But before the life changing could commence, she needed to add an additional flourish to her academic career: she needed to ace her SATs.

She fidgeted in the line to take the test, next to Dennis, who looked too calm for someone sure to score in the bottom 15 percent. Even his grocery lists were a form of entertainment—razzberrys, quecumber, brokoly.

She reached her hand around his back and slipped a finger down his waistband, feeling him jump. Ever since their fight, he'd been acting like she was a sex siren, able to hex him into penis-based submission with a simple touch.

"If you do that again, I'm not going to stand with you."

She turned her head away, not acknowledging him, but kept her hands to herself. She didn't want to stand alone. Cami hadn't signed up to take the SAT—"I'm not ready for college," she'd said, which Margaret understood had to do with her father's various cancers.

The test was easy. Child's play, for her. She filled in her test-book bubbles to a perfect gunmetal, picturing poor Dennis sweating in the next room. His clear tell of nervousness seemed to happen frequently, often in church since the sex negotiations began.

When they finished at noon, Dennis dropped her off at the Cossitt Library, her favorite place to write. She couldn't help but consider the original building a symbol of Memphis—the city that built a tower of knowledge to rival those of Europe's greatest cities, but let it stand empty for a year because there was no money left for books. And then, later, they replaced the beautiful castle with the ugly box in which she stood.

She sat at her favorite cubicle, morphing her jeans and T-shirt into a scribbling suit, falling into the vortex in which she often ~~trapped~~ ensconced herself at night. Until her second warning that the library was closing, she sipped a Coke from the machine, perfected her two best stories, and even wrote a third about a young girl bent on seducing a neighborhood boy before she realizes he's an angel and he sends her to hell. No relation to reality.

She stayed deep in the world of her stories while she dropped the envelope with John's name and room number at the Peabody Hotel's front desk, marveling at the lobby. Her father liked to remind her it was a "hell of a wedding gift," since that was the purpose for which the building was originally constructed. A father's present to his daughter. When she trudged home, tired and hungry, her mother was standing at their apartment door.

"Where have you been? I thought you failed your SAT and threw yourself off a bridge! Dennis said he took you to the library hours ago!"

Of course she assumed her daughter had failed. Not that it was even possible to fail your SAT, but her mother didn't know the first thing about college. Insulted, Margaret walked right past. Dillydallying, her mother would say if she was in a better mood.

"Have you been smoking again?" she called after Margaret.

(Yes.)

Our young heroine kept walking, cringing over her ~~debates~~ ~~fights~~ arguments with her mother and picturing Cami listening a few walls down, so desperate to have a mother that she couldn't see the pain in it. Margaret nodded to her father at the stove, wearing what was allegedly her mother's apron with the untied strings hanging loose at his sides. Allegedly, because he had been the only person to don the costume for six years. She walked until she reached her bed, where, without giving her mother or Cami or Dennis or the poet another thought, she fell into the deep sleep she had yearned for the night before.

Once she woke up, got dressed, smoothed things over with her mother, and returned to school, two life-changing events transpired.

She walked out of school, and there was John, smoking a cigar, with her writing in his hand. He moved his index finger to beckon her over, and she left Dennis's side without a word and practically ran to him, like Simon in *The Grapes of Wrath,* stumbling to the mountaintop of knowledge and his own doom—"Close! Close! Close!"

"These," John said before he blew smoke into a neat ring, "are excellent."

"Really?"

"Well, they'll need some tweaks, but excellent, especially the one about the angel. You're a regular Virginia Woolf, perhaps a dash of Flannery O'Connor, and none of that Danielle Steel bullshit."

Her heart beamed with pride.

"I've also contacted one of my good friends in publishing, and he thinks he could get one of these in a literary magazine."

"Wow," she said, letting the news sink in. "What do I do next?"

"Well, you keep writing. Never ever stop, no matter who demands that you do." He stroked the perpetual beginning of a beard, thinking. "Why don't you meet me at the Top of the 100 Club tomorrow night, and we'll get a drink and a bite to eat and look your story over?"

She'd never had a drink in her life, but still, she rushed to confirm.

"See you at eight p.m.," he said over his shoulder as he headed to the sidewalk that led downtown.

She watched him go, and then, forgetting Dennis kicking the grass in the distance, she rushed back inside to tell Cami.

"But we were going to see a movie with Dennis tomorrow," was all she could say.

"What?"

They'd planned it weeks ago, since preparing Cami's father for a night without her seemed to take that kind of forethought. Dennis's presence was for her own mother, but Cami liked him, too, laughed at his jokes and defended him whenever Margaret detailed his faults.

"Do you have something you want to say?"

She could see Cami looking at her carefully, maybe even judging her. Like Margaret's mother, Cami saw Dennis as nothing but a ticket, a tie between her friend and this place. A promise to Dennis, and to her, that Margaret would never leave Memphis.

They loved each other, she and Cami, they did. But each knew she could never truly understand the other.

"Can you just give me a ride?" she asked, and of course, Cami said yes.

You, dear reader, are not a naive teenage girl, so surely you now know where this story is going, something our young heroine didn't when Cami dropped her off at 100 North Main. In the elevator, she tried to distract herself from the ascent to the top of the highest building in Memphis by smoothing her black slacks and striped button-down. She'd bought the outfit for college interviews with her ~~sparse~~ precious tip money from the Arcade, ~~most~~ some of which was courtesy of Dennis. Even though he was saving money, he always reminded her, for his future, their future. Together.

They had an account from which she only withdrew and never contributed, financially or emotionally, despite hints to do so.

She'd borrowed the portfolio now clutched to her chest from her father, from a time long ago when he had searched for a job with some sense of seriousness. Into the flap, she had slid her stories. She clicked the red pen in her pocket, waiting for the first opportunity of her sure-to-be-storied career.

When the elevator pinged at the top, she tiptoed to the hostess stand. She had never been to a restaurant like this before.

"Is John Dowell here?" she asked the hostess. She had the air Margaret imagined came from losing your virginity, the easy, graceful way her hips swayed as she disappeared, never to answer the question.

After fifteen minutes of staring nervously at the Memphis skyline out the floor-to-ceiling windows, she worried he'd forgotten her, forgotten their ~~dinner business meeting date~~ BUSINESS MEETING. She jumped when John touched her shoulder and pointed to the back in explanation. The private room from which he had come had already spun slowly away on the restaurant's famous revolving floor.

"Margaret," he slurred. "The writer."

"Yes," she answered, gleefully happy.

He was drunk, but she didn't know that. Neither of her parents drank, and she hadn't yet read *The Sun Also Rises*.

"Allow me." John offered her the crook of his arm, and she slid hers through it, as instructed by her mother when Dennis escorted her down the church aisle on Sundays, her mother sitting happily with his in the (upgraded) third row ever since they'd bonded at those DAR meetings.

When John and Margaret sat down, a waitress appeared immediately, greeting John by name, and he ordered "another round."

Our young heroine tried to convince herself that the floor couldn't possibly spin fast enough to make her carsick—it was all psychosomatic, like Hamlet tossing and turning and seeing his father's ghost. Meanwhile, John stared at the hopeless ~~girl~~ woman in front of him for a long time, eyes narrowed, and she began wondering what she had done wrong. Did he know she could throw up on him? Not that she would, just that she could.

But then he said, "A pretty girl like you has nothing better to do than hang out with the likes of me on Friday night? Have a boyfriend?"

She felt her cheeks turning red. *See, Mother, no need for blush.* She fiddled with the engagement ring on her finger under the table, wishing she had taken it off. She'd have "lost" it already, if it hadn't been Dennis's grandmother's.

"Um."

The waitress saved her when she came back with martinis on a full tray that seemed destined for the room from which John had emerged. When the waitress extended one overfilled martini glass toward Margaret, she quickly took it with both hands, eliciting a rushed "Thank you!" from the waitress.

John slammed his glass down, and at the shock of it, Margaret splashed some of the martini into John's lap.

"Excuse me, fiancé!" he exclaimed, with the same exaggerated pronunciation as her mother. "Let me guess: pastor's son?"

To her confused expression, he barreled on.

"Quarterback of the football team? Richest boy in the class? Drives a BMW and wears those shirts with no branding that everyone knows are expensive… You know the ones."

She didn't. ~~She didn't even know what a BMW was.~~

"Too Emma Bovary? What about the boy next door?" he tried hopefully before gulping down what was left in his glass. "Well, give it up, then."

"Um…his dad owns the hardware store? He's…sort of on the baseball team?"

"How is someone 'sort of' on the baseball team?"

"He manages the equipment."

"No, no, no," John said, shaking his head solemnly, as if her story reminded him of Sydney Carton's death in *A Tale of Two Cities*. "No, no, no, that won't do."

Margaret didn't know what to say, so, as instructed by her mother, she said nothing.

"We'll get you sorted out, then. Righto. Yes," he said, with his hands on his knees like he was in a huddle. Dennis didn't even participate in the team huddles, she'd noticed. John stood. "Where are you going?" She breathed out in a rush. Had he forgotten he was meant to help her with her writing? "To see some friends. Ah, forgotten something, haven't I?" He laughed to himself as he reached into his back pocket and pulled out papers folded as small as the fortune-tellers kids entertained themselves with at school, when Margaret was busy listening, kicking a dozing Cami under the table.

He unfolded the pages, wobbling a bit with the effort, then straightened them on his thigh and handed them to her.

She froze at the sight of her words, crossed out and bleeding red ink, the *Handmaid's Tale* "smile of blood," which had always defined her. Arrows pointed this way and that, surrounded by marks she didn't understand, entire paragraphs crossed out and stars next to words that seemed randomly circled. No one had ever criticized her writing ~~except for her mother~~. Even Miss Kosa's praise of her last essay rang hollow in her ears now: "Illuminating!" Did he think she was a good writer at all? Did anyone?

Heart racing, she stood up. She meant to thank him, but her mouth was dry. "I'll just—"

"You've got work to do, silly goose. Stay!"

She sat back down.

"I presume you have paper and pen?"

She nodded.

"Well, get to work. I'll be back." He turned briskly and disappeared around the restaurant's circle.

She allowed herself a few ~~crocodile~~ very mature tears as she choked down the rest of the sour-tasting martini. The candlelit room turned darker and louder by the minute, making it more difficult to read his notes scrawled in the margins of her story about the girl and the angel. Memphis illuminated the page from beyond the windows. She could see Mud Island and Jefferson Davis Park, the seven flags of the governing bodies that had laid claim to Memphis. In the distance was Robinson Crusoe Island.

She turned to the second page, which was entirely crossed out with a big X.

This!—a note snaking around the top corner of page three proclaimed—*is your story. Cut the throat-clearing.*

Some paragraphs had numbers, some had letters, and as her empty martini glass was replaced magically by a full one, she realized they represented a new order.

More here, another note said on page five.

More. More. More.

Less.

Boring!

Vivid.

I see it.

I do not see it.

I feel it.

I do not feel it.

Stars were good. Circles could be good or bad. Checks seemed to signify little. One page had "succumbed," circled once in the first paragraph and once in the last on the page, a huge line drawn with fat, red marker striking through the other words and connecting the duplicate.

Let good words breathe.

She ~~sipped~~ surrendered to her second martini, which tasted better with each sip, as she undid the stupid portfolio, turning the top page, where her father had written, then scratched out, a list of potential employers and phone numbers. She started writing, from where John had marked the number one on her paper.

Third person, another note said, and she obeyed.

She wrote. The alcohol made her handwriting sloppy, made her forget what she had written a paragraph ago so that she constantly needed to reread, but the words came faster. Before, they were afraid and self-conscious. The martinis and darkness and couples whispering made the girl, the seductress—*siren!* a note said—more daring, risker, unabated; made the boy more than a Gilbert Blythe, the typical boy next door from Anne of Green Gables, gave him random qualities that twisted him, coiled him in specifics that made him real. Christopher... No, that wasn't his name, she decided. Symbolism, a warning, an albatross. Jude, to remind readers of Judas.

As she started on page three, a plate of steaming spaghetti and meatballs arrived. She twirled the noodles around her fork sloppily, left-handed so she could write with her right, reminding her of her father. She shook her head, not wanting to think of him eating alone or Cami mourning their canceled plans. When she finally set down her pen, the martini was gone. The plate was empty. But the pages were full.

The story was better, she knew.

John materialized, buttoned up now and looking better for the time away. "Dessert?"

Her mind buzzed with the story—with the angel, with the girl, whom she had renamed Ophelia, who drowned in the river in the end, waking up in hell—as she took a bite of red velvet cake.

As he drove her home, she couldn't form the words to say thank you and only smiled. She shut the car door quietly, snuck back into her parents' apartment, and threw up in the dirty toilet her mother had been reminding her to clean.

She crawled to bed, but right before she fell asleep, her chest seized with panic. *My story—where is it?*

All her work for nothing, she thought, before forgetting her fears about writing, the ring, her future, Cami, and everything else and falling into a fitful sleep.

The next day, she woke up, head pounding, eyes squinting at the blinding light. There was an envelope on top of their tiny hallway mailbox, and she peeked at it, curious if her father was sending out applications again. Or perhaps it was simply another bill that would send him back to the calculator muttering about taxes, send her mother into one of her rages, Margaret and her father sitting on the couch side by side and looking at their shoes while she railed and paced, waiting for her to tire herself out and finally burst into tears.

It was a folder with her name on it. Inside was her story, written in a scrawl that got messier ~~and messier~~ as the words stretched on.

Much better, the felt-tip marker said. The page was ~~filled~~ anointed with stars.

At the end, it said, *Another go on Tuesday?*

Before you judge me, think instead—what would you have done?

CHAPTER SIXTEEN

LEX

I finished reading the pages and turned the last one to the back, looking for more. Looking for more, always, as was my habit, but there wasn't more. Another day of waiting.

What would I have done? Not what's coming, because she's right that I know where this is headed. My mind shouts that I wouldn't have done the same, even though I know it's not true. My mother was so narrowly focused on what she wanted, on being a writer, on John, that she steamrolled everyone in her way, even Cami, naively continuing on with a half-formed plan.

I don't want to think of the similarities between me at that age and the girl in the story: her confidence, her arrogance, even her intelligence, intelligence I never knew my mother possessed. Even as I tell myself it doesn't matter, I can't help but wonder if John actually thought she was a good writer or was only trying to get in her pants.

I think about how my mother painted Cami in the entries. Is it possible that Cami has been avoiding her past with my mother as much as I've been avoiding my own?

Cami lived through this time with my mother, but how much of what's in my mother's entries could she guess? I picture the first entry in my room, back in the journal from where the papers came. Should I let her read it? For once, I want to be first to know something, anything about my mother.

Deconstructing my mother's words, dismantling them from a story to paragraphs to sentences to words to syllables gives them less power. Something I already knew at her age. So I go upstairs to my reading chair with my *Word Origins* dictionary.

child's play: Oh, how I love a good idiom. They say so much about a language, about the people who speak it. The earliest reference for this one was in the 1300s in Chaucer—"It is no child's play to take a wife." Indeed.

dillydally: Ironic that my mother attributes this example of reduplication to her own mother, since it was one of her own favorites for me. Hanky-panky, hip-hop, pitter-patter, riffraff ("Street rat! Scoundrel! Take that!")

I read until I hear Cami come in the front door downstairs. Unfortunately, while reading *The Dictionary of Word Origins*— which surprisingly doesn't contain the word **zilch** and only has nine z-words, like the writers grew tired at the end—I came up with...zilch. No master plan for confronting Cami about playing God in my life, about where she went yesterday, about whether she's avoiding my mother's writings. All arguments for which I imagine she's already developed numerous responses.

"Lex! Put on some clothes and come downstairs for dinner," she yells up the stairs over the jazz music she's turned on.

jazz, chosen as word of the century and always unescapable in Memphis. W. C. Handy's "Memphis Blues," Elvis, jazz hands. All that jazz.

When I come downstairs, the flowers in the vase by the entryway have turned pink. Cami doesn't comment on my new MENTALLY GONE shirt or ask to see the rest of my clothes, like I imagine a normal mother and daughter would do, not that we are that. She waits, maybe for some appreciation for the clothes I borrowed this morning, her mother's quilt under which I slept, the room with my perfect reading chair where I've spent most of my day. As if I should say thank you only and have no questions for her.

When I don't comment, she holds the front door open and gestures for me to walk through it. "*Vamos*," she says.

"What? Where?" I'm still running through the five *w* questions when she steps out the door and struts down the front steps with Edgar on her tail. I shouldn't have left her alone. It allows too much time for planning, something at which, unlike me, she excels.

I'm barefoot, since I didn't plan on going anywhere. I'm still zipping my hoodie against the chill and squeezing my too-big feet into Cami's pink gardening Crocs as she rounds the corner onto Cooper Street.

"*Puñeta*," I mutter under my breath. If Cami and I are both playing this game, why can't I shake the feeling that she's playing chess and I'm playing checkers?

By the time I walk under The Beauty Shop's neon sign, Cami is already inside, chatting with the hostess, who walks immediately toward the back room, which holds what I thought of for years as our regular table.

Like always, the place is packed—with people, with clean glasses waiting for their next patrons, with open bottles at the bar, which stand on metal slats across the shop's original bright-blue hair-wash stations. Like all the best places in this city, the relics of the building's previous life (as Priscilla Presley's favorite hair salon) tangle with the new open wooden shelves, iron rods spindling around the bar, and the Memphians (young and old, black and white) drinking sangria around the same counter that once held Priscilla's shampoos.

It's been my favorite restaurant since Cami first brought me here to celebrate getting into the gifted program in fifth grade. Since Cami opened her own shop on this street, she's been friends with the owner, and during high school, everyone here recognized me too. Now, though, the hostess eyes me as I walk past the glass-bubble-block windows toward Cami. I'm not a regular anything in this town anymore.

The back room is dominated by a row of hair-drying stations, each ensconced in its own sixties bubble glass partition. Pushed against each is a small two-top table and another seat. I slide carefully into the salon chair across from Cami, ducking under the bright-blue vintage hair dryer that's bigger than the dinner plates around us, and plop onto its worn white leather.

I lock eyes with the sixties model staring at me from the menu. Amid the noise of the restaurant and my determination not to look at Cami, I'm surprised by the waitress carrying over a carafe of their famous red sangria, which I've never been old enough to drink, and before I can help it, I smile.

"Cheers," Cami says, pouring me a glass. I cough to hide my smile, but clink my glass to hers regardless.

I want to talk to Cami but find it hard to make polite conversation while also suppressing my anger over my mother's writings and the surprise plane ticket and the nostalgia-stirring pictures on my bedside table. My fingers fidget, waiting to feel my mother's smooth cream paper again.

Once I've memorized the menu, I chance a look at the diners next to us, whose appetizer includes a small bowl of edamame. I watch as the man pops one into his mouth. Once, when I was at a Japanese restaurant with a spring breaker in Bali, I saw her eat the edamame whole, and I let her do it. "Yummy," she said, smiling with the pod threads hanging from her overbite. The entertainment was practically payment for having to sit with her.

I chuckle lightly to myself.

"What?" Cami asks.

"Nothing."

The waitress sets down an order of watermelon and wings with blue cheese. I haven't thought about the appetizer since I left— not much BBQ or many chicken wings to jog my memory—but my mouth watered the moment my favorite dish entered my peripheral vision.

We dive into the wings, and after our glasses have been filled again and we've both ordered the chef's special without listening to the description, we stare at our empty plates, splattered with blue cheese and watermelon juice.

"How have—" she begins at the same time I say, "What do you—"

"You go," she says.

"No, you."

"You."

I drain the last of the sangria from my glass and refill it.

"What do you remember about the time before my mother left?"

Although I've considered that Cami's stories may be embellished, she's never shied away from telling them, so I'm surprised when instead of launching into a story of her and my mother, she says, "Oh, not that much. It was a hard time for me, with my father."

She looks toward the mirror, where tonight's dessert specials are written in black marker with teacher-level handwriting. "He died about a year after she left, you know."

I didn't, but I nod anyway, wondering what she's leaving out.

"Did y'all ever talk about it? When she got back? What made you get back in touch?"

Cami looks at her bracelets, gathering them near her elbow and watching them fall down her forearm in a chime of metal on metal.

"We talked about a lot of things," she says, waving her hand to make it clear she doesn't want to go into specifics, "but we never talked about that."

"Sure," I say again, as if it's completely reasonable, working out the sentence that's circling my head. When I catch it, I say, "Don't you think it's a little hypocritical to tell me to 'face' my problems when you seem to be disappearing to mysterious appointments and trying to get out of the house early to avoid what my mother wrote?"

"Well, it doesn't concern me."

"What if you're in it?"

"What did she—" she starts before stopping and saying, "I don't care."

I stare at her like I don't believe a word she's saying, and she regains her composure with irritating speed. She waits as plates of pork chops, grilled peaches, and corn with cotija cheese appear in front of each of us.

"Your mother doesn't haunt me—"

She sees me wince, and unlike my mother, she reacts. When I said something about her choice of language, my mother would say, "You think you're so smart, twisting my words like that."

"I have plenty of good memories with her," she finishes, picking up her fork.

Good memories I've heard my entire life, because Cami telling me about my mother's past was the only defense she could muster. I've heard the story of how my mother and Cami became friends as many times as my parents' (fake) love story, also never from my mother's perspective.

Cami, age ten, arrived at Lauderdale Courts after a rushed departure from San Juan. She had learned only an hour before that her mother wouldn't be joining them. The new kid in school was teased for her accent and had trouble understanding the teachers with their southern accents. But my mother sought her out. My mother thought the foods and clothes and language that other kids mocked were cool. My mother included Cami, invited her over, sat in the hallway with her for hours, other tenants stepping over the friends on the way to their own apartments. My mother liked to sit on the floor and play cards with her into my teens, pretending they were still kids in that hallway and that I didn't exist.

Cami takes a bite of the succotash with coconut broth between us, then continues, as if she knows the memories I'm filling in, "I don't think about it like that. I don't want to know about that time of her life, and I don't think she wanted me to know. If she did, she would have told me."

"Then why are you letting me read what she wrote?"

"Because she haunts you."

"It seems like you're just afraid of what you'll find out," I counter, ignoring her assumption. I find myself wanting to reassure her. I could say, *She cared about you*, even though I don't want to defend my mother.

Cami sets down her sangria a little too hard.

"You give the best advice," she says, uncharacteristically sarcastic. "Maybe you have a future career as a therapist." Seeing the look on my face, she softens.

"Let's talk about something else," she says. "And you should eat."

"Okay."

I fill my glass from the new carafe of white sangria, not caring if the flavors mix, splashing out an ice cube at the end. I want to sleep tonight, want to feel that descent after you've drunk a bit too much, when you feel numb to the world and you wonder whether or not there is a bottle of water next to you right before you fall soundly asleep. It's a balance I've perfected over my adult life. I only hope I haven't gotten too rusty since the baby.

Cami raises one eyebrow but doesn't admonish me.

"Why don't you tell me what you think about your little city now?" she says as I dig into the pork chop with my knife.

We get to talking about parks newly stripped of the Confederacy, the lights I saw at Overton Square, the latest births at the zoo, the development by the waterfront. When I sense she's about to veer into topics I don't want to discuss, like the chic apartments where my father's store used to be, I say, "Let me tell you some of my travel stories." I can feel the sangria unwinding the cords in my brain.

Cami jumps a bit, surprised by my offer.

I don't want to talk about Otto. Or the baby. Or my life in Bali. So instead, I tell her about my students at the girls' school in India, how they would belly laugh with their best friends. "We LOL," the Indian girls would scream through tears, their favorite English phrase I offered that class. It was the kind of sister-like childhood friendship Cami knows I never experienced. My fault, if you listened to my mother. Also my fault when I actually made a friend who was a boy and therefore could not be trusted.

I tell her about every single one of my students in Bali, about the little trailer where I taught English and how they would come in every day laughing and chatting quickly in their various dialects and walk out speaking slow and careful English. Talking about other people instead of yourself, I've learned, is one way to stay safe. That and talking about the weather, or the news, or sports. I don't know much about the news right now, and Cami doesn't care about sports. The life experiences of irrelevant strangers will have to do.

I tell her about the naming system in Bali and the confusion it caused in class. I tell her about how English shortchanges us in honorifics. I'll always mourn the Bahasa and Balinese words I've lost, the four choices for politeness that immediately clue you in to your conversation partner (or adversary).

I drink and talk, and eventually, we (I) stumble back across the street, through Cami's front door with Edgar. I'm getting started on English spelling as I walk up the stairs. "That gets me not *f-i-r-e-y*, but *f-i-e-r-y*," I say, as if that English spelling makes sense. Soon, I'm back under Cami's mother's quilt. Somehow, I came up here with a splash of red sangria on my shirt, and it stains the white sheets with red, just as I did so many years ago. Edgar jumps on my back and lies down there.

Since making up with Cami, my mind searches for people who are easier to hate. Since it's dishonorable to despise the dead, I settle for my father.

CHAPTER SEVENTEEN

My father loved my mother more than he loved me. Loved her with a passion so evident (yet apparently, John lurked in the background all the while, which makes me feel both sad and like he got what he deserved).

Anyway, I said it: he loved her more, or differently? More.

It was this confusion that drove the Greeks to adopt eight different words for love—*eros, philia, mania,* and so on—one of many concepts cheapened in my native English.

Even now, I'm not sure how to feel about the statement. I clearly know nothing of what it takes to have a successful marriage. Maybe a love stronger than all others is a necessary component? Although I didn't love Otto, I can't imagine a person I would want to protect more than that baby boy who started as part of me.

But that's not what I want to think about either.

It was spring, and unfortunately for me, my mother had stayed home from the hardware store to cook for an annual welcome event for new members at the church. My father had been appointed new members director, a position held previously by his own father, and the dinner with church leaders was a Big Deal.

The day before, she asked my father to drop her off at the grocery store with nothing but a cookbook, and she had come home several hours later with more groceries than I had ever seen.

She was in a great mood, listening to the latest news on Paula Jones's case against President Clinton and humming around the kitchen during breaks. She even let me help mix and stir, asked me to read directions from the cookbook, and wanted my opinion on if the sauce needed more salt or not. I wanted to hang on to this mood of hers forever. I watched her constantly, worried about shattering her good spirits.

She'd been this way last week, too, bumping hips with me in church and quizzing me on school—"What are you learning?" "What did you eat for lunch?" "What did you do at recess?" "Do you like your teachers?" "Have you met the principal?"—so fast that I could hardly respond before she was on to the next question. She spent the afternoons circling dishes in cookbooks and fretting about chair placement.

The morning after her cooking spree, I woke to my mother screaming my name. I ran downstairs. The fridge was open, and all the cold air had seeped out. The food was spoiled, and she was blaming me.

"Lex! I told you not to eat anything."

I hadn't.

The fridge had been stuffed shut to the point that you needed to press it closed, which I had done carefully. By then, my father had come in wearing his Henry Hardware polo, as if immune to the screaming. I'd just spied his Coke sitting next to the recliner in front of the television where he usually fell asleep at night before he commanded me to apologize to my mother and sent me to my room.

I never discussed the incident with him, but from the way our eyes met and went to the Coke at the same time, I know he knew what had happened as well as I did. My mother screamed up the stairs that I would be so hungry later I would wish I hadn't done it, that I had done it on purpose, as my father talked to her in a low, comforting voice about how he would call so-and-so from the restaurant and get them to fix something and not to let it ruin the evening.

The same measured agreeableness and half-hearted appeals to logic governed his participation in all our fights, as did his interest in peacekeeping over truth-telling. Those values reigned supreme, too, in our biggest blowout before I went to college, when my mother finally realized I had been seeing Grant for years behind her back. She was the angriest I'd ever seen, even without me telling her that I had met him often at Cami's house, Cami posing as objective Switzerland. Was Cami thinking even then that my mother was overreacting because of her experience with John?

That night, yelling about my lies and lack of gratitude and general ineptitude, my mother chased me out of the house like a banshee. I can't remember the exact words she screamed. My main memory is the luminosity of her pale skin as she ran from the house in her nightgown, skin, gown, and hair glowing in the light of the full moon, trailed by my father, who was helpfully pointing in the direction of Cami's house. Did my mother know then that the death she was warring against would be her own? Was she already planning to shut the garage door and crank the engine?

When I showed up at Cami's Victorian, she didn't ask what had happened. She never did, which worked for both of us, because I was afraid to tell her what actually occurred in my house when I was alone with my mother, didn't know how to describe our fights in any language, and I think she was afraid to ask. No matter the fight's subject or temperature, my father would be at Cami's shop the next morning, telling me what a wonderful mother I had and how I should pray for patience and did I have to set her off like that?

Only for me to end up back at the same house I'm taking refuge in this evening.

CHAPTER EIGHTEEN

I lie awake and listen to Cami getting ready, talking to Edgar, who's disappeared from my side, and to her plants as she waters them—a secret she's always claimed helps them grow.

When I come downstairs, Cami is standing at the sink drinking a cup of coffee and eating a piece of toast with honey on it.

"Morning," I say, and she jumps. "Is the next envelope on the table?"

She nods, her mouth still full, and tosses the rest of the toast in the trash. After seeing me approach the little table with the purple flowers, she glances at her wrist, though she isn't wearing a watch, and says, "Running late!"

She bustles toward the door, taking her mug of coffee with her, and grabs the car keys.

"Going to the store?" I ask suspiciously.

She only nods at me again and escapes from the house as I pick up the next letter, leaving me to wonder why she's in such a hurry and where she's really going.

MARGARET

We left our young heroine on the precipice of an endeavor, a covert caper that she needed to lie to keep up. She told anyone who would listen that she was spending long hours at the Cossitt Library, cramming to maintain her lead as valedictorian.

Since her mother would be more pleased with her seeing Dennis, for her, he was Margaret's chief excuse. For weeks, she filled her time with imaginary outings with Dennis, though she hadn't seen him outside of school, the Arcade, or his library drop-offs since that first dinner with John. To Dennis, she begged off, saying she was hard at work on her college applications and not to tell her mother if she asked because her mother didn't want her to go to college. That part, at least, was true.

"Don't worry," he'd say over his coffee before she ~~went~~ ran to another table. "You're the smartest person I know. You'll be fine."

She puckered her lips so that he could barely touch his to hers as a goodbye. Then she snuck off to an abandoned parking lot and into John's waiting car.

In order not to exhaust the Dennis excuse (or the library or studying or working on her writing with Miss Kosa, all standbys), she sometimes told her mother she was hanging out with Cami or helping around their apartment. The only person to whom she felt bad lying was Cami herself.

In precalculus the day after her dinner with John, Margaret had whispered the play-by-play to Cami and the open invitation ~~that came~~ delivered with it, even though she knew she should be listening in case she needed to take the SAT again.

"Are you sheltered enough to think dinner dates with John will make you a famous writer?" Cami had said.

Margaret preferred her friend's looks of skepticism over out-right admissions of it. She had turned away, though they both knew the answer was ~~yes~~ obviously yes. They had always been able to communicate the strongest feelings without exchanging words.

"Then good luck," Cami had said, turning her head in the other direction.

"I never said 'date,'" Margaret hissed back, earning a rebuke from the teacher.

Was it so difficult to believe that another writer would be interested in her writing abilities? Reluctantly, Margaret added her closest friend to the list of people to whom she needed to lie about her whereabouts. The only person who had never heard her lie.

And day by day, excuse by excuse, Cami stopped creeping the few doors down to put on makeup together and compare outfits in the morning. Margaret stopped running over leftovers from the Arcade and knocking on Cami's door after their fathers went to bed, when the friends normally sat in the hallway and ate a slice of ~~almost~~ stale cake. Cami stopped lingering outside the school door to get rides from Dennis, as if she was so disgusted by her friend's deception of her fiancé—the person Cami herself saw as merely means to an end!—that she couldn't stand to see them together.

Other than partaking in her new hobby of lying, Margaret wrote. She wrote and wrote and wrote and wrote and wrote and wrote. She wrote until her wrist ached and sweat pruned her fingers.

She wrote with John, without him, and about him. After an hour of writing, she was one of Huxley's soma-fueled characters in *Brave New World*, blissful in the wave of time that had no meaning, day and night blending into one. At night, she sat cross-legged on her bedroom floor with her stories ~~spread~~ cast around her in a circle, writing a few sentences of one before switching to the next. She'd skip sleeping for days and not even feel tired as long as she had time to write, finally falling into a coma-like sleep, the onset of which she ~~couldn't~~ didn't want to control.

She always wrote with the intent of showing her work to John, of earning those messy stars in red felt-tip marker, of him calling her "silly goose" and saying, "Here, try this," or "Look at this."

They wrote next to each other in his hotel room, though he shielded his own paper from her when they did. She only asked, "Will you write about me?"

As she waited for the worst outcome—"no"—a knocking of anxiety started in her chest and marched down to her right foot. "No" would mean she had no impact, that she meant nothing to him. That their time together would pass as quickly as books passed across John's desk.

"Yes," he finally said. "Though women usually don't like what I write about them."

She smiled, triumphant. "Do your worst."

Until one night at his hotel room, two months before graduation, when he interrupted her scrawling with the Parker Sonnet fountain pen he'd bought her—"Helps with the hand cramps."

"Today is the day to submit to publishers." He closed the lid on his typewriter and set his glasses on the growing mountain of pages she hadn't dared investigate. "Just one detail we need to fix first."

She clutched a pillow to her chest, waiting. Anything.

She had given him the most recent copy of his favorite story that morning, the one with the girl and the angel that she had rewritten more times than she could count. He held out page five to her, which she could recite from memory from all the retyping.

"Well, this isn't quite accurate, silly goose." He pointed to a key moment when Ophelia gives herself to Jude, when her seduction is successful moments before she is condemned. Margaret blushed at the words each time she read them, and she blushed now, looking at the red circles that littered two paragraphs.

"Sex is never about sex. Other things are about sex, like food," he had said once, otherwise leaving the paragraphs untouched.

"You're a virgin, aren't you?"

She jumped at the accusation, even though it was true.

"I can help you with this."

He clucked his tongue, staring at her words intently with the pen in his hand.

She watched him and thought of Dennis rejecting her sexual advances, her mother rejecting her dreams, Cami rejecting her opinion of John, thought of it all as she scooted toward him on the couch.

At her movement, he looked up, stared as she turned toward him. Kept his eyes locked with hers as she slowly, carefully kissed him.

He kissed her back, hard, desperately, furiously, tumbling over her so that she was on her back on the couch with him on top of her. She felt warm and yummy ~~and sexy~~ all over. All the feelings she had been kidding herself that she would feel with Dennis.

He jerked away as a siren went past on the street below.

"Are you sure about this?"

She nodded quickly, wanting his lips back on hers.

"Well then, take off your clothes."

She tore off her shirt and bra and kissed him again with the same urgency, each competing for pressure until he pulled away from her.

"The rest."

She obeyed, quickly shimmying out of her pants and underwear as she would in the dressing room at Goldsmith's, trying on clothes she couldn't afford while Cami worked.

"Socks too," he demanded.

She obliged, and he dove down to her feet, licking each toe, stroking the bottom of each foot until she laughed because it tickled.

He kissed up her calf, then her leg, to her stomach, then breasts, then neck and back down again, creeping down her inner thigh until his tongue was on her, surprising her with a feeling she couldn't name.

The next morning, as she lay in his bed still naked, he brought her coffee while she edited the pages. The girl started with kissing each of Jude's toes and worked her way up and back down, as John had done.

They had sex again before walking out, together. He popped the stamped envelope in his bag as she went to tiptoe to her own bedroom, across the narrow hall from her parents', as she had done so often recently, back to real life and away from the story of her nights.

She exhaled—safe—as she closed her bedroom door.

"Where have you been?" Her mother sat at the desk in her work uniform—one of them anyway—yellow legal pads filled with Margaret's writings covered her lap.

The library was the first excuse that came to her mind, but that was moronic, so she barreled on. "With Dennis," she said.

Her mother crossed her arms but said nothing.

"I know I should be more careful about people catching us before the wedding, but I had to see him."

"Dennis came by this morning with breakfast since you called in sick to work."

They stared at each other.

"Who were you with?"

Margaret, still giddy from her night, erupted into hysterical laughter. It was all so funny. First Cami, then Dennis, and now her mother. She ~~didn't want to~~ just couldn't control herself.

"Stop it."

She kept going.

"Stop it!"

"I can't—"

The slap, the shock of it, surprised Margaret so much that she fell to the floor.

Still, though, she continued laughing at the odd turn her life had taken, remembering how a few days ago, when John had sliced his finger while cutting an apple for them, he had watched himself bleed until Margaret got him a bandage from the front desk, only shrugging and telling her, "Remember, what doesn't make a good time makes a good story."

"You ungrateful little whore." Her mother spat at Margaret who was rolling ~~back and forth~~ with laughter as she and Cami had always seemed to end up doing while playing cards on the floor between their apartments, in Margaret's past life as a child with childish hobbies and childhood friends. "I don't care who it was as long as it stops. Today."

Her mother waited, but Margaret kept laughing.

"You're going to ruin everything." Her mother started crying, which only made Margaret scream with laughter, her face was hurting so much.

Her mother slammed the door so hard a plate on her wall fell and shattered.

Margaret laughed until she became too tired, then finally got peeled herself off the floor, reapplied her makeup, and headed (late) to another day of school.

CHAPTER NINETEEN

LEX

As usual, I agree with Cami: sheltered doesn't even begin to cover my mother's boundless naiveté.

Despite the similarities between us that I can't shake, that's one I don't see.

I wasn't allowed to be naive, never got the chance to learn how, because I had her. Because I already knew something she doesn't seem to know yet—that life, at its purest core, is a fucked-up game you'll always lose. Every time. And the purer your intentions are, the faster you'll want to give up.

I feel a glimmer of pity for my father, because if this is my mother's story, it's his too. I can picture him sitting at the Arcade and standing beside her in line at the SATs, escorting her down the aisle at church—equally naive—thinking he's headed toward the quiet life of which he's dreamed.

Suddenly the guys I dated briefly in high school don't seem so bad. "You should focus on school. You're too young to date," my mother said. Though mostly she was focused on convincing me to avoid Grant.

The sex I don't want to think about, so I look at Cami's note next to my mother's pages. I pick it up to read, but her words make me throw it back down. "Go see Grant." Underneath is an address, a phone number, and no additional explanation.

Grant. He's here, alive. It's the question I've been too afraid to ask, though I'm sure I would have felt his missing presence by now if he wasn't.

Even in that relief, I'm furious. Now I know why Cami wanted to flee the house before I read this. She's finally crossed a line into playing-God territory that I won't permit her to pass. She must be getting me back for being high and mighty last night.

Filled with visions of beating Cami at her own game, I speed upstairs to change my clothes, brush my teeth, grab my *Dictionary of Word Origins*, and head outside, toward the flower shop, again with Edgar behind me. I intend to catch her in a lie again and force her to come out with it, tell me where she's been sneaking off to.

Emboldened, I charge down Cooper Street, past The Beauty Shop where she sat last night, knowing what task she planned to ask me to complete today.

Because of the prospect of seeing him, the memories of Grant and me flood in, the memories I've been most avoiding. Walking along the same streets we did for years, all I see are images of the two of us, swirling together, like the feeling you get when you've drunk too much and all the embarrassing things you've said, all the mistakes you've made, spin around you and vie for your attention when you lie down, until, as if on a ship, the rhythm of it all finally rocks you mercifully to sleep.

At the street leading to my middle school, I see a younger Lex, eyes rimmed with black eyeliner, neck decorated with a black choker—that's how you tell people you're choosing to be alone—sitting in her assigned seat at a citywide summer camp for gifted students. I see Grant writing a note and passing it to her: "This is dumb." Oh, what poetry. I see the notes grow into letters slipped between those summer classes. Slipped and slipped and slipped and slipped until she forgets what his voice sounds like, only hears it in her head like he writes, and hears herself telling him everything as he listens.

I see that first meeting at Christian Brothers, where Grant's father went to school, the place we considered our own between my parents' house in Midtown and his house in Chickasaw Gardens. I remember waiting for him by the bell tower while he waited for me on the other side, each of us about to give up. After we found each other, we walked through the fields where college students hit or threw or kicked balls of various sizes, feeling content.

Those days morph into every day and those minutes into hours, until that girl forgets what it's like not to have him by her side.

I see Cami moving to Memphis, perhaps the biggest break I ever got, and Grant helping her hang her art, her smiling and saying, "I'm glad you finally found a friend."

I see my mother grow furious when I wave hi to him one day downtown. "How do you know that boy?"

I shrugged. "We're friends."

I see young Lex in her room with a pen and paper, writing the next note to be slipped, about how she's grounded for the next month and they have to be careful.

For years, through grades, through textbooks, through half-hearted boyfriends and hair colors and styles and outfits, my handlebars steered toward Grant's house. I see myself sneaking through his backyard where inevitably, the bay window perfectly frames him and his parents gathered around the upright piano, practicing for church choir, Grant in the middle like they're in a commercial.

The type of life, the type of family, I would never have.

I see myself standing outside, feeling the jealousy burn in my chest, jealous of his parents and jealous of their time with him. His mother stayed home, which meant their house was always spotless and had fresh sweets, which she'd offer to me before she vanished. His father did something with real estate. A perfect, normal American family.

I see myself not belonging. How his mother would freeze whenever I was around. How even she, with her sunny disposition, could see that I brought bad luck to everything I touched.

I see myself tapping at his window, him opening it and climbing through, us talking and talking and talking until eventually one of us fell asleep and the other one punched the sleeper to keep them awake. Usually it was me doing the punching, lacking the safety of sleep. I see myself finally heading to Cami's for the night, tiptoeing up to my bedroom and lying awake, waiting for Cami to wake up.

I see myself hugging Grant goodbye a year before my mother died. I see myself promising to write. I see him in his air force uniform, diploma in hand, ready to take on the world. All to return to Memphis, the prodigal son. Coming back was the one thing on which we never agreed.

Then,

I see

nothing.

CHAPTER TWENTY

I slink past the flower shop and crouch under the side window, looking for Cami.

She stands with another woman at the high table in the middle of the shop. It's splattered with paint and strewn with scissors and ribbons and open bridal magazines, and there's a sample wedding bouquet in Cami's hand. Red anemones, an inappropriate choice for a wedding, but I suppose she wouldn't know the Greek behind it.

The woman says something, and Cami turns toward a row of calla lilies, the flowers she used at my mother's funeral, I remember with a pang—though even then, I had wondered why, since Cami's flower choices always seem to come with some deeper meaning. She walks toward the stockroom, and I duck.

Well, I think, *she wasn't lying this time.* Did she think I would follow her? No, she probably thinks I'll stay at the house today. Surely she knows I won't be following her command to see Grant.

The difference between Cami and me, although I believe we're equally stubborn, is that I have no life, and thus I have all the time in the world. Betting she won't stay at the store, I go to the same coffee shop as yesterday. I order a coffee and sit at the window, listening to the spiel about the lack of sweetener in between looking out at Cami's flower shop and reading my *Dictionary of Word Origins*.

Even after telling myself not to, I find myself thinking of Grant and me again, memories of me telling him all the places I wanted to go and him telling me all the planes he wanted to fly.

airplane, from French *aéroplane*, combining two Greek words: *āēr*, for "air"—the stuff we breathe, not the Old French *aire* meaning "nature," "quality," and eventually, "demeanor." Add *-planos*, meaning "wandering," and you get *aéroplane*, or the more English "airplane." Something that wanders through the air, but like Cami and unlike me, Grant's wandering always seemed to get him where he needed to go.

mayday, again from French, a shortened version of *venez m'aider* or "come and help me." Situation probably full of "mayhem," Old French.

crash,—

I push back my chair too quickly. Out the window, Cami waves goodbye to the helper girl from yesterday and walks toward Central Avenue.

"I have to go, can you…?" I point to my coffees and the plate with the remnants of a muffin. The barista looks at me like I'm insane (maybe I am), but I don't bother to wait for the response. I rush out the door and behind Cami's shop again, waiting to see which way she'll turn across the street.

I know the back alleys of Memphis well from many nights of darting between my house, Cami's, and Grant's, hiding from the glow of the streetlights, sneaking quietly as a mouse and listening to the hollerin' and blues-tinged rock flowing out of doors along with waves of smoke.

I watch as she turns on Cooper and heads toward the Urban Outfitters where I bought the shirt I'm wearing.

Despite the weather, I'm sweating as I make my way around Peabody Park, following her path along Central Avenue. I tail her so long I start to get winded, scurrying this way and that around the backs of houses and along side streets.

I'm not sure where I imagined she was going, but seeing her disappear off Central Avenue and into the Cathedral of the Immaculate Conception shocks me. Is this her secret? She's no longer a lapsed Catholic?

I watch her through the stained glass on the side of the church as she kneels in the pew, as she crosses herself with a naturalness I've never seen, as she goes to the front to take communion with the other people there. When she walks back, though, I lose sight of her. I look through the next window and the next, trying to find her long, floral jacket.

"Feeling religious?"

I jump.

Cami is standing behind me, and even though I achieved my aim of catching her somewhere other than the shop, is it a lie if it's…church-related? My cheeks turn red. Somehow, catching someone praying on their knees feels more personal than catching them having a secret affair or doing shots at a bar.

She doesn't bother to hear my answer, though. She keeps walking while I'm frozen in place, back on Central Avenue.

"Looks like rain. You better head home," she says as I watch her turn away from her store.

When she gets back to Clanlo Hall, my grandfather's greatest and last project, I watch her climb into the passenger seat of a Honda CRV.

Whose car could that be?

I jog back to the street, intent on catching up with the mystery car, but when I reach the light, they're already gone, turning toward the highway that leads to Nashville.

After the worshippers exit the church, filing past me with my dirty jeans from hiding below too many windows, I realize I left my *Dictionary of Word Origins* at the coffee shop.

Ugh.

I race back there as the sky rapidly turns to gray. Cami was right...again.

The barista doesn't say anything when I shuffle through his door again. The table where I spent most of the morning is clean of my cups and crumbs, and someone is rapidly typing what they probably think is the next great American novel. The barista simply hands me my book and turns back toward the espresso machine.

I walk out, past the flower shop, where I notice Cami's car is still in the driveway. As I pass by, the girl from yesterday runs out.

"Are you Lex?"

I whip around, struck with fear that she knows my father or Grant or anyone else in Memphis other than Cami and strangers.

"Maybe?"

She narrows her eyes at me.

"Cami said to give you this and tell you she won't be there for dinner tonight."

She holds out an umbrella.

"Okay," I say, when she turns around, looking at me, judging me, I'd guess. "Thanks."

CHAPTER TWENTY-ONE

I'm so sure Cami hasn't relented about Grant that the next morning, I don't bother checking the front table for a note. Instead, hearing her in her bedroom, I tumble onto the living room couch, still dressed in the Central High School Warriors shirt, and turn on the television, content that at least Cami will have to witness how miserable she's making me. The television is turned to the Weather Channel, reminding me instantly that Grant is the only person under seventy whom I've seen watch the Weather Channel without irony. He always eyed the radar in preparation for when the moving blobs would overtake the fluffy clouds surrounding his little plane.

Cami comes down, fully dressed, on her way out the door, and watches the television behind me for a moment.

"Oh, snow in the Northeast—that must be nice for them. I wish we got more snow here."

Without looking at Cami, I retort, "Blizzards lead to more domestic violence," and turn off the television.

I don't look at her, but I know she's rolling her eyes that way she does, like she's humoring me. I refuse to acknowledge her planning or the smirk she surely wore last night when she changed the TV to this channel.

"Are you going to sit around here all day, or do you have another secret mission up your sleeve?" she says.

"Well, I'm not going to see Grant."

"Why don't you come to the shop with me?"

I stare at the blank television, remembering my years of watching Al Roker (the fat version), as if I'm committed to never-ending suffering.

"It will be easier to spy on me from there."

I look at her now with my own eye roll, even as I'm thinking she's not wrong.

As usual, when Cami commits to changing my mind about something, she succeeds. I relent because I don't want to be left alone with my thoughts, with all these memories of Grant. And, I think, uncharacteristically full of hope, maybe if Cami witnesses my tortured attitude up close, it will make her realize the impossibility of this next task.

Part of me wonders too if going with her might be a trap. If Grant showed up, at least I'd be free from making this decision. Cami's forcefulness would be a relief at this point.

At the store, the girl from yesterday is gone, and Cami sets me up in the stockroom with the shears. I fall into old routines, listening to Cami talk to clients in the front while I sit in the back trimming piles of lilies and lavender, evergreen moss and roses.

I'm shocked at how much I remember about my duties from working at the flower shop in high school. I thought that space in my brain had filled with new words and languages. Hindi. Bahasa. Russian. More, everywhere. But apparently, under all those new words, the correct length to cut a monstera leaf stem so that it will propagate in water has been sleeping, waiting to be unleashed.

Eventually, Cami comes back and picks up the next batch of lisianthus flowers, working next to me.

"Why don't you want to see him?" she asks, still not looking at me.

In answer, I cut another stem a little too forcefully.

"You know, he doesn't have a girlfriend," she continues.

I drop the scissors, and they clang on the table.

"That has nothing to do with it," I yell at Cami, who narrows her eyes at me.

"Big words for someone who hated every girlfriend the poor boy ever had."

"Did not!"

"What about Lizzie?"

"She cried every time she got her hair cut."

"Erika?"

"She spent most of her time talking about horses."

"Jennifer?"

"He bought her the sweetest, most thoughtful gift for Christmas—a vintage board game she played when she was young—and she was mad because he didn't get her an iPad. An iPad, Cami."

Cami looked at me like my explanation does all the talking for her. I sigh and go back to cutting flowers.

"And every one of those girls dumped him, by the way, so maybe I was right."

The truth was, I wasn't only jealous of Grant's girlfriends, I was jealous of every single person with whom he came in contact. I was jealous of the suck on his time because I wanted all his time and all his attention and all his secrets, and when he started dating, that time chipped away, his girlfriends always giving me the side-eye when he introduced us and stated confidently that he thought we would be friends. As if.

For me, spending time with him always held more allure than being with any boyfriend, but despite what Cami seemed to think, it was never romantic between us, and I never wanted it to be. There was too much at risk.

He was...safe. Beyond the nucleus of my crazy family. Normal. Consistent. Forever.

"Well," Cami says, finally changing the subject. "How about some lunch? Think you can stay here and (wo)man the register?"

I nod skeptically as she chuckles at her joke.

This is it: her moment, her plan. My hand shakes as I write down what I want from Central BBQ. I walk to the front of the store, as unsteady as those first few steps out of the car in Bali, toward the plane that would take me here. What will I say to Grant when he walks through the door?

To fill my head with words, I flip through my *Word Origins* dictionary, letting some catch my eye—

companion, Old French and Latin form a compound noun from *com-*, "with" and *pānis*, "bread." Someone with whom you share your bread. Companion in *companionway*, meaning "stairway on a ship," is of similar origin.

elbow, meaning "arm bend," goes back to the base *el-*, *ele-*, which itself means "bend," so at the deepest level, "elbow" tautologically means "bend bend."

mosaic, derived from the Latin word *musaicum,* work of the muses. Also, the Greek word *mouseion*, meaning "shrine of the muses." Origin also for the word *museum*.

At least it's something to discuss if I run out of other things to say, though he's heard plenty of linguistics from me over the years.

The shop door is open to the cool Memphis air. Every mild

gust trills the bell on the door or ruffles the banner above the store's awning, and my head darts up with terror over and over before I snap back down to look at my book again, hating myself and Cami and Grant and…everyone.

My head flies up again to see two women waving to each other on the sidewalk. "I'm just going to steal another minute for myself," one says, walking up the few steps to the shop door.

As I'm wondering why southern women always say that— like they don't own their own lives and spending time on something they want to do is stealing. Stealing from whom? I register that the woman is Haley, one of the most popular girls in my high school. She had the gift of being both pretty and smart. We were in most of the same classes, and even now I can feel the look of judgment radiating down from her in Spanish and history, eyes fixed on me and my black shirt with the ribs on it. I was sure she was watching me, waiting to hear what I said in class when called upon so she could snicker with her friends.

We were graded on how many comments we made in class, a system I despised. But since I needed to keep up my grades for college applications so I could get the hell out of Memphis, I relented to it. Haley's green eyes always studied me as I interjected. And then she would speak again, so confident, watching the teacher put a tally mark by her name with triumph.

Before I have time to dodge—there's nowhere to go, after all— she's upon me, with those same intense green eyes that studied me in school.

"Hi."

"Good af— Wait. Lex?"

I smile a half-hearted smile, and she pushes her sunglasses

deeper into her perfect blond hair before coming over to hug me. She smells like vanilla, I think, as I succumb to her hug, my arms pinned at my sides.

"How are you?" she says with what seems like genuine interest and excitement. I'm overwhelmed; I don't like being the center of attention.

"Oh, I'm…I'm fine. How are you?"

"Good! What have you been up to?"

"I've been traveling. I was teaching in Bali for a while."

"Teaching what?"

"English, to businessmen there."

"That is so cool! I bet you were really good at that. I still remember when you'd help me with my Spanish homework in middle school. So patient."

A flash of my younger self—"No, not *cómo se LLAMA*; say it like *ya-ma*." Not at all patient.

"I'd love to hear more about it. Cami tells me you've been quite the traveler." Haley puts down her wallet on the counter, briefly sidetracked by the tulips behind me. She points to them. "I'll take those," she says before continuing.

"I always wished I had your brains. Remember how Ms. Roberts always kept track of how much we talked in class? Ha-ha, that was terrible, wasn't it? Thank God they've mostly gotten rid of that kind of crap. Embrace differences and all that."

Because I don't know what to stay, I start punching numbers into the register.

"Anyway, I'd love to get coffee sometime. How long are you in town for?"

"I'm not sure."

She picks up the flowers and leaves a twenty-dollar bill on the counter, and before I can say anything else, she's talking about how she has to go to Target to buy new underwear for one of her kids because he's become obsessed with the environment and therefore decided not to use toilet paper, so she'd thrown out his underwear. "Kids!"

"Honey, ready?" The other woman is back, poking her head in the shop door.

"Yes!"

I stare dumbly at them both as Haley bustles out with a friendly goodbye. I am watching her go, still processing our conversation, as Cami comes in, carrying a bag with our food.

"Was that Haley with Allie?" Cami says, looking behind her.

I nod.

"Nice girls," Cami says as she busies herself with taking out the plastic silverware and scooping pork, slaw, and potato salad onto our plates.

I've always hated the phrase "nice girl." Southerners seem to think it means *oh, she's a sweet girl—you can walk all over her.* While "nice guy" seems to be code for *he doesn't hit.*

Saying nothing, I concentrate on my food, eating and chomping so I can sneak to the back room. I'm thinking of Haley, how I once ran into her in the hallway. She was bent down, turning a penny over so it was heads up. *What the hell*, I remember thinking at the time. *Did she do that to make me trip?* Though when we collided, she came up giggling, saying she was silly.

It makes me think back to my mother doing the same, judging my father and not believing Cami and hating everyone with whom she shared this city. Was I as bad as her in high school? Was

I as bad…after? I think back to my time in India, sitting upstairs with my same *Word Origins* book and listening to the other English language teachers talking and drinking in the pieced-together living room below, a mishmash of random furniture that had been left behind.

When I resume my snipping in the back room, I realize with some disappointment and an illogical amount of annoyance that I was wrong about Cami's plan to spring Grant on me. I wrap up the flowers I've cut in paper so that when the men come after work, the bouquets will be ready. For each man who comes in for one, I think, *What did you do wrong?*

Cami eventually dismisses me.

I nod to show how much it doesn't matter that Grant hasn't shown up and walk back home. Edgar jumps from his perch in the front window and follows me. I'm spinning my wheels here, waiting for the next piece of my mother's writing. The writing that won't come until I do the impossible.

CHAPTER TWENTY-TWO

That night as I lie in bed, asleep again after another evening of wine and Cami's cooking, something makes me stir. I look at the clock blinking two a.m. and at Edgar studying the darkness out my window. That's when I hear them—five taps on the glass in the rhythm of the anthem of the camp where we met, usually belted out louder than necessary, especially early in the morning.

My chest jumps with fear, and I wrap Cami's quilt around me for protection rather than modesty. Before my brain can think too much, I'm up, stepping on the color-splattered rug with my bare feet, then the cool hardwood floors. My hand trembles as I open the window's latch.

We stare at each other, taking one another in. He looks different, older, with a mustache that I would never have imagined would look good on him, yet it does. He's wearing a Bluff Flight Center T-shirt, and I can see the tail of a tattoo he didn't have before snaking down one forearm. We used to talk about getting our first tattoos together. Another promise I ruined.

I dive over the windowsill and into his chest, at the same moment he opens his mouth and says, "Hey, stranger." His long arms envelop me, and I keep hugging him, staying in this position if only to avoid pulling away, to avoid thinking of what I'll have to say next or hearing what he'll say next, to avoid him seeing the look on my face. The hardness in his muscles from those photos taken in basic training is still there, the pudgy kid I remember from middle school no more. The image of him now and him the way he was when we met war in my mind.

When I pull away, he sees my lost look and helpfully nods to his backpack, urging me to continue pretending the year is 2008.

"What'd ya bring me?" I say, wiping my eyes, which have begun to water.

He smiles at me with pity and reaches into the backpack to pull out a bottle of rum and two mugs.

We don't talk again until we're both settled on the roof, looking out at my work in Cami's garden, the neat rows of flowers and the freshly mowed grass and vegetable garden free of weeds. The lights are still on at the high school baseball stadium in the distance. The roof is sharp under my feet, and I tug my large T-shirt down over my ass to keep more of my skin from its splintery surface.

I take a big sip from my cup.

"What did Cami tell you?"

He shrugs and takes his own deep sip. "Nothing. That you were back. Is there something more?"

"No. Not right now."

I lie back and look at the stars, marveling at how different they are from what I saw last week. I don't know what Grant has seen. Don't know where he's been, what languages he's heard, what coastlines he's spotted from the cockpit of whatever plane he flies these days.

Did he go back and finish college, as he said he would when he joined the air force? Is he still a pilot? Cami said he didn't have a girlfriend, but how many have I missed since I left? What life did I miss that I'll never get back? All these questions feel too big to ask right now, too big to talk about. These are the questions you ask a stranger, not the person you used to know better than anyone.

The reason I don't know the answers: me. But he left first, scribbling an address I was afraid to write to, a phone number I had trouble dialing and eventually left behind in my deserted dorm room.

He left, then my mother left in her own way, and just like Cami all those years ago, what reason was there for me to stay? Unlike any similarities with my mother, parallelism with Cami I welcome, especially with leaving Memphis, if it allows me to share the blame. The excuse rings hollow, though, even to me.

I've said nothing through several gulps from the mug, so I finally offer, "Do you remember that time you fell off the roof?"

He laughs. "Thinking about it makes me sore." He rubs his left shoulder.

He fell into Cami's patch of sunflowers, creating a Grant-sized hole there. Thankfully, they cushioned the blow, but many sunflowers died in the process. Grant was up the next morning trying to piece them back together.

We go on like this, conjuring safe memories and avoiding everything else we need to say.

He takes a pack of cigarettes out of his pocket and lights one, passing it to me, like we used to do when one hidden cigarette and a half bottle of rum were prized, hard to come by.

"There's just something about a smoke and a drink, isn't there?"

"A certain je ne sais quoi?" I retort, and he smiles at me.

"Like a good aioli on a sandwich."

"A beer and a great accent to study."

"Oh, sure, totally," he says sarcastically. "How about a bay leaf in rice? You don't think it will do anything, but it adds. It does."

We fall into giggles, rolling on the roof like we used to do.

We catch our breath, and he pours another round, the number of which I've lost count.

"Did you know that we almost had to answer the phone with 'ahoy' instead of 'hello'?" I'd consumed the right amount of rum to start slurring about linguistics.

He laughs and, emboldened, I continue. "Imagine how different the world would be."

"Ahoy?" Grant says, picking up his phone like he's answering it. "Pirates would be decriminalized!"

"Wait! What is that?" I say, batting at his hand and missing, and we both fall into hysterics again.

"What?"

"Your phone. An iPhone! You swore you wouldn't!"

He had a flip phone when I knew him, one he insisted he would never get rid of because he didn't want to be easier to contact and never wanted anyone to ask him why he didn't comment on new Facebook pictures.

"You want to hear a funny story?"

Of course I do.

He launches into a story of Jennifer, the last girl I remember him dating, the one I was afraid he would marry when he deployed.

"She broke up with you?" I slur, though I already know she

did. He was madly in love with every girl he dated, from that first girlfriend in middle school whom he waited six months to kiss. A serial monogamist, as I'd become prone to calling him over the years. I suppose when you come from a home like he did, everyone feels safe.

"Well, she said we should break up, and I quickly got on board, so according to her it was mutual."

I remember many such conversations. Us on the roof exactly like this with him detailing his breakups, me muttering apologies and trying to hide my smile. "Anyway, she stole my phone number!"

"What?"

"We were on a phone plan together, and I couldn't get my number back. I had to get a whole new phone and new number. So I decided to join the twenty-first century and get an iPhone."

"How is that even possible?"

He says "ahoy" again, and we both laugh more, like the old days. Even my interactions with Cami had an air of anguish, of memory, since we were ultimately united by the pain my mother caused. My relationship with Grant was all my own, though, with no tinge of darkness, and I loved it for that.

When the laughter dies down, we both look out at the lights. Grant finishes another cigarette and extinguishes it against his boot, holds the butt until it's cool enough to slip into his pocket.

"Lex?"

I brace myself for what's coming. A threat. An indignation. Blame. My tongue is looser from the rum, but the only stories that come to my head, rushing past me, seem to have no purpose, no meaning, and I know they aren't what he wants to hear.

I swallow. He takes my hand and rubs it between his like it's cold. I am kind of cold, but I've forgotten because of the rum. "I'm glad you're back." He's slurring his words too now. He takes my hand and lays it on his chest. I can feel his heart beating there, like so many nights of pressing my ear to this spot and listening to the beating, to remind myself that I wasn't alone in this world.

"Bedtime," he says, then pats the tops of both his thighs, like he used to do. He leads me back through my bedroom window by the hand, yanks up the bottom corner of the comforter and sheet, and crawls into his side of the bed, the one by the window, burrowing under the covers with his head at the footboard, feet at the headboard. I hesitate, watching him, until he's asleep with his bare feet on top of the pillow he forgot to move.

When he starts snoring, I turn out the light and lie down next to him, letting one leg stray to his side to feel the warmth of his arm with my toe. The only person next to whom I've ever slept soundly. I fall right to sleep, like I always used to when I would beg Grant to sneak over so I could sleep without nightmares. They all seemed to be about my mother dying, but once she actually died, they turned into dreams about her living, coming back from the dead of that car like a ghost determined to always haunt me.

CHAPTER TWENTY-THREE

The next morning, after promising Grant I'll join him for a late lunch, I force him, hungover and all, to sneak back out the window, even though I know the ruse is pointless.

Downstairs, Cami perches on the couch, drinking her coffee smugly and waiting for an apology.

I sit down next to her. "Cami," I begin.

She taps my hand once.

"It's okay."

She gets up to pour me a cup of coffee, and as she does with the cat and a treat, she gestures toward the door to the porch, coffee in hand. I sit under the roof where Grant just dangled, where the sunflowers used to be, replaced now by the newly pruned squash.

"How did you know he would forgive me?" I ask.

"Friendship like that, like y'all have, it's as strong as blood—sometimes stronger, because you choose it."

I nod.

She taps the sealed envelope from my mother on her knee, and I wonder again if Cami is avoiding her friend's words.

"Is that why you forgave her?"

"Margaret was family to me."

"Why, though?"

Why, when she was so terrible, when she was so terrible to you, I think, but I don't ask. Why would anyone choose to be family with my mother? Even her childhood memories surely outweighed everything that came later?

Instead of answering the question I did ask, though, Cami answers the one I didn't: "I waited too long, you know. She was too trusting, had never experienced what I had—a loss, being abandoned. I was waiting for John to leave her, waiting for him to use her, so for once I could be there to pick up the pieces. But, as you've probably read already, that's not how it happened."

She hands me the envelope and kisses the top of my head before I get another word out. Before she heads back inside, she turns to me once more, my hand lingering over the envelope's seal.

"Admit it," she says. "You missed us. Grant and me."

I smile at her, realizing for the first time that maybe she needs to hear it. And I need to say it. Because it's true. I have missed them.

"Yes. I missed y'all."

"That was your task for the day. Congratulations."

"My mother missed you too," I say, because I know it's true for the girl in the letters. But I'm unsure if Cami hears it, because she immediately spins on her heels and is gone.

CHAPTER TWENTY-FOUR

MARGARET

Well, that's enough of that, isn't it? Quite Parisian, or perhaps Margaret's story is more American than *Huckleberry Finn*, than *Their Eyes Were Watching God*, than *On the Road*. As John counseled, sex is never about sex, and it isn't in this story either. Plus, the silent treatment doesn't make for fun reading—dialogue! The life of your story!—and Margaret was now facing silence from Dennis, her mother, and Cami (all for different reasons, some true).

So ahead our story skips, like a rock along the Mississippi. We skip past a night when Margaret saw Cami struggling with laundry and helped her carry it, without speaking; past the next week, when Cami showed up with a cake for Margaret's eighteenth birthday; past a few card games in the hallway when they felt each other's presence, apologies, and absent words but were too afraid to speak any, until a few weeks before graduation.

Our ~~young~~ heroine had been up all night. Not with John, but on her own, refilling the bathtub from eight p.m. until past midnight, despite her mother's ~~screams~~ reminders to stop wasting water. She ignored the pounding on the door until her mother finally retreated to bed. All that soaking, and Margaret had finally come to a decision.

She had savored her last meal with her father earlier that evening, concentrating on how he said "won-da-ful" while he slurped the soup she'd made to go along with his main dish. For their Last Supper, they'd cooked together in the small kitchen, each humming to themselves (her: "Hey Jude," him: "Folsom Prison Blues"). Her father was the only piece of matter she would miss in this entire apartment.

She would miss Cami too, but she couldn't justify her choices to her best friend. When she told Cami her plan, whispering in the hallway between their apartments as they often did, she could hardly contain her excitement. John was leaving, and she was going with him. Tomorrow.

"What?" Cami had said, clearly surprised, like Margaret's olive branch and Cami's truce meant that John had ~~gone away~~ evaporated.

"I just…" Cami had continued, eyes darting back and forth, mulling, rationalizing, like Margaret had seen many times. She did the same gesture on the rare occasions when Margaret beat her at cards, as if she could hardly understand her loss. "I didn't think…"

As Margaret tried to formulate a response, Cami's eyes had narrowed in a way she had never seen. "You won't do it. I don't believe you," she'd said in the hallway, loudly enough to elicit a few open doors. "I'll tell him. He'll stop you," she had said pointlessly, looking like she was on the verge of tears, as if Dennis ever had control over his fiancée. Cami had slammed the door in her face, and Margaret had heard Cami's father asking a question in Spanish. She'd waited outside, but the door didn't reopen.

Let her tell Dennis if she wants to. Fine.

The next morning, Margaret entered the baseball diamond, cocky smile plastered on, again wearing powder and her pretty dress, to find Dennis, if only to show the poor guy what he would spend his life missing. Surely ~~eventually~~ he would realize what an idiot he had been, wouldn't he?

The conversation was short. He stood there holding three baseball bats while the team's stars played catch in the outfield.

"You don't have to say it," he said in a way that made her unsure if Cami had carried through with her threat.

He held out his hand when she ~~slipped~~ tugged off the ring, saying only that she didn't belong here, never had. She hadn't expected Dennis to ask questions. He had been agreeable from the moment his mother suggested he ask Margaret out. (Oh, how his mother would regret that decision.)

She wouldn't be at graduation, not that it mattered. Her grades had slipped, and she wouldn't be valedictorian anyway. There was no point to any of it; she realized that now. Education was what she was getting every night with John. This building, the signs reminding her to stay away from drugs, the books most kids would never read—they were nothing to her. She only needed to say goodbye to Miss Kosa.

"If you really want to be a writer, this is the exact wrong way to go about it," she said.

"Since you've been so successful with your own strategies," Margaret ~~pointed out~~ said, smiling sweetly.

When our young heroine turned to leave, her teacher had only this to say to her back: "You'll never be a writer now."

Margaret stopped, but she knew the old hag was wrong.

To her parents, she said nothing. Her mother would hardly

know she was gone with how much she had been working recently and only saw her daughter (through an alliance with Dennis Henry) as a ticket to retirement. Her mother hadn't picked a husband for her daughter; she had picked a son-in-law.

Margaret didn't own a suitcase, so she made a few trips to John's hotel room with her purse and backpack. No books—too heavy, and there would be plenty in her future literary life. She left the cracked spines of *The Secret Garden* and *I Know Why the Caged Bird Sings* and *The Prince of Tides* and shut her bedroom door.

As she left the apartment, she grabbed an envelope from the College Board off the table—her SAT scores, surely. Her mother would have loved for her to leave this behind, if only for the chance to prove her daughter wrong about her college prospects.

She walked past Cami's apartment door that last time, straining to look in any direction other than that of her dearest friend. She didn't want to give her the satisfaction of watching out the peephole as Margaret carried by her meager possessions.

Before Margaret could change her mind, she threw her SAT scores away, sealed, in a public trash can.

"I'm so glad you came, my little muse," John said when she arrived again at the Peabody. She beamed with pride when he called her that.

They held hands all the way to the airport, Margaret watching the sun set across Memphis, a knot in her stomach about the plane ride.

She fidgeted so much in the car, despite him reminding her to relax, that he gave her a small white pill, taking two for himself.

After, she glided through the airport with not a care in the world, the ~~buzzing~~ stricture in her chest from the past months of secrets finally loosening, past all the sights of Memphis that she had never seen from the sky. He had shown her a new Memphis, and now, this was the end of a world that looked anything like the one she knew.

They were going to New York City, then off to London and who knew where else, all to end at a little house in Tuscany.

The plane was high and new, but hardly memorable now. A rising in her stomach as it took off, and then she was flying, giggling at something John whispered in her ear before she tumbled into sleep, waking up only when the pilot announced, "Welcome to New York."

Within two hours of landing at JFK, our young heroine lay under the softest sheets she'd ever felt, next to John, in a hotel overlooking Central Park, the lights from the taxi still a blur over her vision that seemed to Margaret like a dream already beginning. The next morning, though, she woke up first and went downstairs to the hotel restaurant with her notebook, intent on proving Miss Kosa wrong. Proving people wrong—the hobby to which she'd been most dedicated in her lifetime.

"Room number?" the waiter asked, for the check. And when she told him, he answered, "Certainly, Mrs. Dowell."

She jumped, because she'd never ~~thought~~ known to ask if John was married. She pushed the idea into her stomach. *No,* she thought as she swallowed another cup of coffee, *I'll use it.* So she wrote it.

New York passed in a flurry, days spent holed up in the hotel, scribbling in this same notebook, happy to be out of Memphis, for New York beyond her window. John visited his agent, they went to dinner, to get an emergency passport and an even more urgent emergency diaphragm, then to another airport for another flight with another little white pill.

In London, they saw Big Ben and the London Eye, ate bangers and mash, spent a night in a hotel overlooking Buckingham Palace, and your young heroine can't remember the rest. "We were together," as Walt Whitman wrote. There was a trip to Harrods, where Margaret let her benefactor follow the sales associate around the store, pointing out different clothing, into which another sales associate zipped her with increasing speed. Every ten minutes, John circled back to give a simple yes or no, like an assembly line.

Another flight and pill took them to a hotel in Rome on a tourist-filled square next to the Pantheon. There was a hilltop overlooking the city where a guitar player strummed for coins and, in either Florence or Venice, a large church with horses on top and a bar rumored to be a favorite of Hemingway, where John developed a habit of dropping Margaret off with a wad of bills and her notebook while he went to meet friends for early-afternoon drinks that frequently turned to dinner and then to nightcaps.

It wasn't until they made it to the ~~abandoned ruined~~ cottage outside of Tuscany, their new ~~shelter~~ home for however long it took John to finish his book, that Margaret began to wonder if she'd made a mistake.

She started noticing things. For one, John took a lot of pills "to keep up with her," and each time, he swallowed them dry all at once like some sort of monster. Disturbingly, he did this even when he stood merely a foot away from a glass and a sink. Who would do such a thing? Why? She didn't know this dry swallower of a man.

Was Cami…right?

Still, time passed pleasantly enough in the little cottage where John flitted in and out without a schedule, reminding her of the time she'd spent living with her mother.

There were nights when the car was gone, the store too far to walk, when Margaret scoured the fridge, then decided to go hungry. On those nights, she found herself ruminating on big questions such as: What is the purpose of life? Is God real? Or, chiefly, am I in love? The answers seemed more reasonable the less she ate and the more she drank.

She could go days without talking to another human being. In fact, that was how she liked it, staying up all night writing by the lone lamp. She would study John as he slept or watch a neighbor attend to his goats in the early morning.

She lived in her stories and talked only to the characters belonging to them. If ~~left alone~~ shunned long enough, if she sat very still, she could sometimes see them—the boy who would become Jude telling her about his creation or the ghost of a little girl from another story who was killed on the train tracks in Memphis while chasing after her father. "I wanted to help," the girl told Margaret, and she knew the feeling of good intentions gone wrong.

She and John read to each other. She always applauded after he read and said his writing was wonderful. He always delivered some stars and a page of suggestions that were never enough for Margaret. When she could sleep, they slept until noon, wrote for a few hours, had sex, ate a meal—the timing of which no known meal designation explained—took a nap, wrote until late in the night, and then slept intertwined and sweaty in the summer heat before waking up and doing it all again.

In the absence of groceries, bourbon was always plentiful, and pills when she couldn't sleep for several days, and a chaise lounge John got from somewhere. Our young heroine lay out in the sun in the backyard, slathered with oil, naked the first few times, since she didn't have a bikini, until John said nothing turned him on like tan lines. So she started wearing underwear and a bra, and then arranging clothes around different ~~parts of her body~~ ligaments and limbs to create hearts or cutting out pieces of paper to write his name.

She thought about her friend Cami and her father often, even Dennis sometimes. But when she sat down to try to use that emotion—something resembling longing—and to write about Dennis, all she came up with was a first line: "He never wore a shirt without a stain."

Cami, though, Margaret could go on about for pages that made little sense when she read them back later, observations interspersed with random memories from their shared childhood. When the pages reached an unbearable number, she'd write Cami a letter about all the fun and amazing things she had done with John over the month, ignoring their fight, willing the letter to turn from fiction into the truth, willing the happiness of the girl in the letter to be her own. She never gave her friend an address, though, because she couldn't bear to hear what Cami was going through in Memphis, couldn't take the guilt.

Writing about her father was the antidote to which Margaret turned when she was tired but still wired, kept awake by snacking on her wooden pencil. Writing about him always put her straight to sleep, as if her brain knew it would self-destruct if allowed to think about him too long. As soon as the thought occurred to her that he couldn't survive without her, she'd nod off wherever she sat.

CHAPTER TWENTY-FIVE

LEX

I sit on the porch with my mother's entry until my second cup of coffee has gone cold and Edgar has tired of terrorizing the chipmunks rooting around in Cami's garden.

The Margaret Green in the letters—the determined, smart, assertive, playful one—is not a complete stranger to me. Indeed, that version of my mother was my favorite. She would emerge in fits and starts, like a creature trying to surface from beneath some terrible ocean, giving me hope each time that only hurt more once she'd been dragged back under.

The first week of summer seemed to bring her out. My mother would bask in the sunshine like a plant that needed light to survive, and that first week, she cannonballed into the pool while other mothers sat on the edge, oiled legs beading with the water she splashed while they glared at her. They judged her audacity in wearing only one of my father's large T-shirts over her swimsuit, showing her bare, pale legs. My father was often along on these days too, sitting in the shade by himself, unreadable, self-contained and not participating, until the time when he stepped in to say "that's enough" when my mother lapsed into bouts of the same giggles that had annoyed her own mother so much.

It was the Margaret Green from her entries who marched into the elementary school on 9/11, found me hunched over, sheltering in place in the hallway, and over the protests of the teacher, dragged me out into the too-bright sunlight. She made me roll down a grassy hill with her until neither of us thought about the video looping on the news. It was that Margaret Green who took delight in getting the daily count from my time as a hall monitor. I was in charge of roaming the school halls with a paintbrush and painting over the penises that people drew on the walls with Sharpie. It was that Margaret Green who could be thrown into hysterics by the sight of the DARE shirts we were required to wear each year at school.

On those days, I'd come home from school to see my parents happily scoring baseball games together, my mother's brow furrowed in concentration over her pad, both pencils poised and both parents shushing me if I tried to say something.

I lived for that version of my mother, but knew I would eventually plunge her back under the water to a depth that only monsters roamed. Maybe today, maybe tomorrow, maybe next week, but the breaking point would come—some screwup of mine that would leave me feeling stupid and guilty and make me plot desperately to avoid the mistake next time.

She wants to go out to dinner? This is a good sign! Don't make suggestions; the smallest suggestion can throw everything off-kilter. She's asking for a suggestion? No, don't! It's a trap! She's staring, this can't be good.

"You better answer me, Lex."

"Italian? Maybe?" I would say, holding my breath.

"Hmm, maybe."

She'd turn away and I'd sink into one of our living room chairs, relieved.

On those good days, I'd retreat upstairs while my parents hugged and kissed, so there was no chance of me being difficult. Any bit of difficulty could subvert the whole endeavor. If I had only danced a little lighter or run through the sprinkler a bit differently or said something more complimentary about the food, that would have been the key, that would have done it. If only I hadn't come home a minute late or interrupted my father while he was talking to a customer who would have bought something, she was sure. Once my mother left a squeezed lemon slice on the counter, which I threw away, attempting to clean up in order to drag out her good mood. "Now I can't have a second cup of tea. Did you do that just to spite me?"

I think about the young Margaret Green seducing John, heading forward in life with all her positivity and wrongly placed good intentions toward something she doesn't know, toward a life she will hate, a family she will hate. Since the first entry, I've wondered what happened to make the curious and playful girl from the stories into my mother.

I fear I know the answer, what spoiled all those summer days, what torched this fantasy with John, what broke everything, even our last conversation—me.

CHAPTER TWENTY-SIX

I'm so busy feeling sorry for myself that I almost forget Grant is picking me up at two p.m.

Even deep in regret over my mother's words, I smile when Grant pulls up in the Buick from his grandparents, with the tape player that broke before either of us was born. There's a map light in between the driver and passenger seats, perfectly placed for rolling a joint on the front middle seat, something I can't understand why cars don't have anymore. Who doesn't need a little help deciding which direction is best?

"How can you still be driving this?" I say as the car comes to a stop.

He gives me the "one second" finger from behind the glass and then rolls down the driver's window. I can see the muscles in his left arm pumping as he turns the lever.

He looks so pleased with himself that I bust out laughing.

He reaches over to pull up the lock under the passenger-side window, and I creak the door open. About twenty-five empty cans of Coke Zero litter the floor under the passenger seat. I laugh again, realizing I've laughed more in the hours since Grant knocked on my window than I have in so long.

"What?"

"Nothing," I say, because I can't explain it to him. How life

is so different now, but also so similar. Kind of like déjà vu, borrowed from French, like cul-de-sac and carte blanche.

"There's nothing wrong with this car—I still like it. My buddies at work tease me too, but what can I say? I'm a man of habit."

I look at him carefully. His mention of work has crushed the
fantasy that it's just us two in high school again, in this car, driving in circles around my problems.

"I'm a pilot for FedEx now," he offers.

I only nod, not wanting to get into real life. "Where are we
going?"

He turns toward Overton Park.

"I decided to show you what you've been missing in the Bluff
City."

"You're taking me to Graceland?"

He laughs. "No way."

"Riverboat? Only a few hours until the Peabody duck walk."

"You'll have to wait and see."

As we drive toward Uptown, I watch the determined look of
concentration that shows he has something to prove. I'm not sure
it's a state of being I feel up to fulfilling.

"Love Me Tender" comes on the radio, and I flick it off.
Grant doesn't say anything. I can remember so clearly my parents
dancing in the living room to that song each anniversary. I'd
sneak downstairs and hide by the banister to observe the perfor-
mance every year. On that day, my mother always wanted to go
around the table and say what we were grateful for, like it was
Thanksgiving or something.

"We're here!" Grant says to break the silence.

I was so consumed by the song that I've lost track of where he was taking me—into what once was a seedier part of the city. I gasp as the old Sears warehouse appears through the wide windshield. Instead of the graffitied behemoth full of broken windows that I remember, the building buzzes with activity. I'm still staring as he pulls into the packed parking lot.

We're not far from the building, now dotted with outdoor shops and restaurants with open doors, but it takes us twice as long as necessary to reach the front. I didn't remember that Grant can't pass a dog without petting it. Every single dog we pass, he bends down to make sure it knows it's a good boy. Even worse if the dog is waiting outside a restaurant for its owner.

"You know, some of those dogs have to be girls."

"It's an expression." He continues in a dog voice, petting a dog in front of a coffee roaster: "Lex should know that since she loves words so much, shouldn't she?"

"Have you ever noticed how distressed small dogs look when they're shitting?" I say as we pass a Yorkie waiting outside a hair salon with a bright-green neon sign. "Like they don't know what's happening?"

He ignores my comment and proceeds to tell the dog it's a good boy.

This habit would annoy the hell out of me with anyone else, but I only smile and keep walking past the cupcake shop. Another reason I love Grant—I love who I am when I'm with him, or at least I used to.

"Is that a juice bar?" I say as we pass a line of teens with floppy haircuts and women in yoga clothes.

"That's what I wanted you to see." He turns to me. "Does that convince you to stay?"

"Not quite."

Even though I'm trying not to be, I'm impressed when Grant opens the door to the atrium. Strings of lights start at the first level and float up countless stories to a center point, a glittering disco ball hanging down from the ceiling. A staircase made of teal metal and wood dominates this part of the atrium, and one floor up, I can see the plaster-scraped and peeling columns from the old Sears building. The skylights and windows illuminate the hoppers that used to be filled with rust, the same ones my grandfather showed me through broken windows. "Damn shame," he would always say. It's where my grandparents met, I know. My grandmother worked here; my grandfather needed some blue jeans.

"Hungry?" Grant says, and I nod, still taking in all the people and eateries and shops filling this once-empty space. And without warning, I wish my grandfather and even my mother were here to see the marriage of their memories and this new city.

We pass a piano in the lobby, where a woman dressed in scrubs is playing "Great Balls of Fire" for several scrub-clad singers. Grant leads me down a hallway while I marvel at the framed photos of the deserted building and a wall of clipboards, each with an old photo of Sears. I strain, looking at the women in the photos for any family resemblance; any one of them could be the grandmother I never knew, the one it seems my mother never really knew either. Another family legacy, it turns out.

We pass a man carrying a tote bag of groceries and wearing a shirt that says CHOOSE 901.

"Want to hear a funny story?" Grant asks.

"Always."

"My mother went to a party a few weeks ago where they served a drink she liked, so she went to that store," Grant says, pointing in the direction from which the man came. "She asked them if someone could help her find the Percocet."

He looks at me like he expects me to laugh, but I'm still stuck on the spiraling art of old EMPLOYEES ONLY and STEP UP signs on the wall and the mention of his mother. Did he tell her I was back in town? How did she react?

"You know, she got it confused with prosecco?"

"Oh." I laugh like I just got the joke—not quite homophones. "How are your parents?" I say, because it seems like what I have to say.

"They're getting up there. But still good. My dad had a knee replacement last year. Still live in the same house. It's nice to be nearby."

Grant leads me into Global Café, looking self-assured. There's an NPR article on the wall—HOW A MEMPHIS FOOD HALL IS TRANSFORMING REFUGEE LIVES AND THE COMMUNITY—and the menu is full of Syrian, Sudanese, and Venezuelan dishes. All places I've never been, but offering that information would give Grant too much credit, too much confidence that his quest to make this city impress me, bewitch me (for the first time), has any hope. So instead, I order asado negro and a cocktail called Venezuela de Noche, wave off Grant's offers to pay with one of the last twenty-dollar bills in my wallet, and go sit down.

We sit at a table by the glass wall, and even though I'm starving, I continue to study the commotion beyond the window. Once I've taken in the kids reading on the steps and the girls with their phones taking photos in front of a red spiral staircase and the visions of my grandmother in this same space, I take my first bite.

"Can I ask you something?"

"Shoot," he says, smiling like he's not even afraid of the question. The type of carefree trust in the world I could never muster.

"Why don't you fly anymore?"

"I fly at work."

"No, not like that, like you used to." I'm picturing Grant looking at books of small planes and watching them in the sky and tracing out flight routes with his fingertips, not transporting someone's latest order of toilet paper.

He looks away immediately, then catches me watching him.

"What are you doing here?" he says kindly.

Now I do the same. I look past him, back toward the red staircase.

"Trade?" he offers. I snap back to him with what I know is a horrified look. "I'll go first."

He takes a breath.

"I went through basic training okay, and I even shipped out, but when I got in the plane, I couldn't do it."

"But you love flying."

"I just…I got overwhelmed with all the choices. I kept thinking about all the things that could go wrong, all the mistakes I could make. And then I couldn't see anything."

Why? I almost ask, but I know as well as anyone that sometimes you just don't know the answer to that. Sometimes when you get the urge to run, you have to run. So I only look at him, waiting for him to continue, not saying anything.

"I can't explain it. It was all these images." He looks down at his hands. "I'll tell you what it was," he says as if he's only now figured it out. "You know how my parents have that ten-seater dining table?"

I can picture it so clearly from my nights peeping through their windows, much like spying into these windows with my grandfather: Grant and his parents sitting at one end, chatting happily with each other or playing rummy.

"I couldn't stop thinking about that table. How they bought it when they were newlyweds. How they wanted to fill the whole thing up with kids, have me grow up in a big family like they both did. But they couldn't have more kids. Us three and a lot of names my parents couldn't say out loud without finding each other's eyes, wherever they were. And I thought, one wrong move, and the number at that table goes down to two. It's like I took all those names of would-be siblings on, and if I died, they would go along with me, truly go. And I thought about the boys around me, all of them on the ground, and all the dining tables that would need one less chair with one break in my concentration, one bad flick of the wrist."

He looks down at his beer bottle and twirls it between his fingers. An old party trick from high school, I remember. Demoted to a nervous tick.

"My copilot had to take the controls." He smiles at me, despite the tone of what he's saying, as if he's worried someone is watching and he has to continue to play the perfect son. "Panic disorder, they called it. I got discharged after that. And I came back here. Been working at FedEx ever since. Packages never complain about turbulence." He smiles again, though his voice doesn't match his expression.

"And you haven't flown at all, like you used to?"

"Sometimes I move planes around at the airport, but no, nothing like I used to. And no passengers."

"Why not?"

He shrugs.

"Your turn."

I can only handle one part of the story at a time, I decide. That's fair, I think, since Grant's story is missing details too. So I start with Cami.

"Cami got in touch with me," I say. "She found some journal entries written by my mother. So I came back. But she's been making me do something every day to get one so that I'll stay longer."

He jumps at that. "What?"

"Yeah, it's crazy, right? Every day I stay, she gives me one."

I can see he wants to say something, but if I don't say the rest now, I'll lose my nerve. So I tell him in a hurry about my mother and father, about John and Italy and Cami's mysterious outings, how she's avoiding my mother's writing. I recite the details as quickly as possible, and when I'm done, I take a few sips of my cocktail because my throat is so dry.

"Does that mean you're going to leave when you get the last one?"

I stare at him, and he stares back at me, meeting my eyes like only he and Cami ever dared to do. I see the panic that must have overtaken him that day in the cockpit. Panic I've never seen in him before. Only in myself. In my mother.

I shrug, trying to lighten the mood, and smile as a reminder that he did the same when I asked him a tough question.

"I need you," he says, suddenly serious.

"You don't need me." *I need you*, I think. I've always needed him. He's the one with all the people waiting in the wings, always has been.

"Why do you think it was you I always cried to?"

"To whom you always cried," I correct, because I can't help myself, hiding my emotions with words. My fingers rub together, wishing they had the pages of my *Dictionary of Word Origins* to distract me from whatever he's going to say.

He barrels on like he didn't hear me: "You're the one I can be myself around. I don't know, with you, I feel…"

Safe, I finish in my head, but before either of us offers an appropriate adjective, we hear, "Grant!"

A few people stream through the doors, one patting Grant on both shoulders and looking at me curiously. We're both surprised, blinking in the new light from the darkness of our conversation. "We're going to the brewery! Do you and your…lady friend want to come?"

"You know who this is!" Grant says, recovered now, all smiles. "Lex Henry!"

I strain and squint to match the faces before me with those I knew in high school and earlier. These are the same people who dotted the walls at parties I attended with Grant, who I always imagined whispering about me under their breath while I walked around, muttering to myself in Italian and waiting for Grant's date to ditch him.

"Oh shit!" The person says, someone Grant assumes I recognize, though I do not. "Then y'all have to come!"

Grant shrugs, never able to say no, and I curse him in my

head, following diligently as he walks down a hallway with his shoulders hunched, unwilling to check behind him for my reaction, to the Crosstown Brewing Company. Inside, people fill the bar and living room setups and the wooden tables with their red chairs.

Grant hands me a drink as soon as we walk in, and we join a circle next to someone who looks suspiciously like Rhett, who managed to play on the football team (second string) and be at the top of our class and the darling of the gifted program.

He's telling a story about his eye exam.

"And they're like, one or two? One or two, right? And I'm like, well, what if I get it wrong—I don't know! They all look the same."

The group laughs, and Rhett, seeing me on the edge, asks me, "You ever have that, Lex?"

I laugh in spite of myself at the ridiculousness of it all, at the ridiculousness of this situation—seeing these familiar strangers and feeling a bit tipsy from our lunch cocktails. "No," I say, and take a sip from my beer.

A girl with whom I once measured liquids into a beaker laughs and says, "Of course not! You were always so intimidating—knowing exactly what you wanted."

Before I can respond, Haley grabs my hand, dragging me away from Grant and the group. I'm not sure which emotion is strongest—my fear over Grant's absence at my side or my pleasure in reducing the number of eyes watching me.

"I guess we'll have to settle for a beer instead of coffee," Hayley says before launching into a conversation about her work as a real estate agent and all the foolish things people say, like the wives who look into the walk-in closets in Germantown and ask their husbands, "Where will your clothes go?" and the husbands who judge basements based on their functionality as "man caves." In the South, a room of one's own for women means the kitchen. At that thought, we both decide to get another beer.

I listen until people start making their way to a table in the back, and I follow Haley there, plopping next to Grant. No one contests the seat, which I consider a good sign, a wave of that old jealously rising in me. But despite myself, I'm having fun, listening to a girl I once sat next to at a baseball game, whose name I think starts with a D—Deidra? Desiree? Destiny?—talking about how she's studying for *Jeopardy*.

I always thought these people hated me, judged me, but maybe I judged them? Just like my mother. Maybe I have more of her in me than I care to admit.

They grab another round, saying "Thank God it's Friday" as they clink glasses of the Traffic IPA. Drinking leads to eating, which leads to shuffleboard on the indoor courts, which leads to corn hole on the patio, which leads to more drinking to warm up, and pretty soon, the party is starting to filter out, and my head is feeling deliciously hazy.

Grant gives me *the* look, asking silently if I want to leave, but I decide to do the crazy thing and stay—watching all these strangers drinking, talking, and having fun, and maybe having some myself—until the only people left in the taproom are a few older men in the corner with beers. As tends to happen in this city, they've started talking about Elvis.

"I once saw him buying some hair grease," one says.

Grant grabs his keys and taps me on the shoulder, nodding toward the door. I follow him.

"You still want to ride with me?" he asks. "After what I told you earlier?"

I'm so confused by what he's implying that it takes me a beat too long to respond.

"I'll call you a cab if you want," he jumps in.

"No way, I'm fine. I trust you. And before I leave, you're flying again. Like you used to—small plane, passengers, no toilet paper."

He stares ahead, not saying anything either way, which I take as a yes. But I can see his shoulders riding up to his ears.

CHAPTER TWENTY-SEVEN

Before I even wake up, Grant is knocking, at my door this time. While I blink at the sun coming through the windows where I forgot to pull down the blinds, he juts a coffee thermos through the door crack, followed by a to-go bag from the Arcade Restaurant. I wave him in, and he puts the bag on the bedside table.

"I feel like I can't let you out of my sight!" he says, only half joking.

He studies the flipped-over picture frames for longer than makes me comfortable. I don't want him to see that I turned over his picture.

"How many are left?" he asks instead, kicking off his shoes and lying on top of the covers on his side of the bed.

"What?"

"Your mother's entries. How many are left?"

"Cami won't tell me."

He stares at the ceiling with that look of concentration he gets. He's wondering if he can get the answer out of her. Cami has always had a soft spot for Grant. Despite the complication of his gender, he was the friend she long wished I would make.

I watch him as he puzzles out the likelihood. His face turns nervous, like he was last night, and he taps on his knee like he's a drummer with terrible rhythm. Did I cause that?

I think back to the girl in the story, saying goodbye. Her

bravery is perhaps the only quality I'm sad I didn't inherit. We both chose to leave, but instead of running off without a word, she faced my father. She faced Cami. She faced Miss Kosa. I never had bravery when met with someone else's pain.

"Grant," I say, and at my tone, his head snaps back to look at me. "I'm sorry."

His face softens.

"I shouldn't have taken off without saying anything to you, without letting you know how to reach me, without saying good-bye. I can't promise I'll stay, but I promise I won't do that again."

He holds up a pinkie, and I take it with my own. Pinkie promise, like we did as kids.

The front door closes downstairs, and I say, "Come on." I lead him down to the little table where, during my period of captivity in Cami's house, I've become accustomed to getting my daily portion of my mother's writing.

Suddenly feeling embarrassed to read the entry in front of someone—what would it say? How would I react?—I grab Cami's note first.

Master bathroom repairs:

- Bathtub tile
- Door sticks
- Cracked ceiling plaster

It's written without preamble. Why is there so much stuff anyway? And this is only her bathroom—what could tomorrow's list bring? *Ugh.*

I hand the list to Grant, who whistles.

"You'd think she'd have a handyman for this stuff. Why does she want you to do it?"

I study the perfectly curated list of tasks.

I laid the tile in her master bathroom alongside my father, running out with chalkmarked tiles to the tile saw he set up in the yard. The sticky upstairs door reminds me of my father dampening ours without a word so that one day when my mother and I slammed them, they only whiffed. The cracked plaster reminds me of my father slowly going through our own house, patching up holes left behind hanging art that had once belonged to his father, me next to him as he talked me through the steps. With tools, he was always friendly, advising, inclusive.

The tasks fit my memories so well, I wonder if the similarities are coincidences, because how would she even know about those things? I never told her, and I'm sure as hell my mother didn't.

Because she's Cami, perhaps.

"She's trying to get me to go see my dad."

Every second I spend thinking about my father and his bright-orange toolbox and the smaller pink one he bought for me at age five, Cami is winning this little game of ours. Avoiding him is easier without remembering days like those, without remembering his pride when I helped a customer select the right drill bit, before I began restocking shelves with my headphones on and then transitioned to working at Cami's shop.

So instead of dwelling, I open my mother's next envelope. I gesture to Grant so he'll read over my shoulder. I don't want him watching my face for clues while I read, and I don't want to explain what the pages say. Besides, secrets have always been shared between us. Secrets that were once my mother's feel no different.

Since she's gone, I suppose they're mine now. Inherited. Mine, Cami's, and my father's.

Secrets belong only to the living.

CHAPTER TWENTY-EIGHT

MARGARET

Days and nights continued much the same until John announced they would host a dinner party for some of his friends, including his editor, who were all in Europe for a book festival in Munich. Margaret figured she'd be ~~gone~~ expelled for the night; she'd never met John's friends. But, no—she would be cooking!

She tried to remember her father's cooking lessons over the years, but still, she buzzed with anxiety and excitement that John would allow her to host. That they would host *together* as a Real Couple, that they would break out of the routine they'd developed as writers first and become lovers above all else. She would be more than the wife hidden in the attic, as she had been in New York, listening to the echoes of his real life below.

While he went to buy extra dishes and silverware and mugs and wineglasses and highball glasses—previously, they'd each had one fork, one plate, and shared a spoon after the second one disappeared—he dropped Margaret (his muse, soon to be acknowledged for what she was!) at the tiny grocery store thirty minutes away in town.

Margaret circled the rows, looking at the mysterious ingredients. Spices she had never heard of and types of squash that seemed ~~foreign~~ neoteric, especially in Italian. She finally amassed what she thought was a complete basket and checked out, right alongside the Italian women with their fresh breads.

She started cooking as soon as she arrived home, while John rushed to finish edits on his book before the famed editor arrived. The Editor—that's the only name Margaret knew—would leave tonight with a copy of his next book, and the pressure was high.

Margaret fretted over her outfit and her hair—was it muse-worthy?—loading on the one blush she had. She hadn't worn it since leaving her mother's high standards in Memphis. Her mother would have advised her to bring makeup and a flattering dress if she knew her daughter was moving in with a man.

She applied the blush in different configurations, hoping to give her sunken face some dimension. For she was the portrait in *Dorian Grey*—as John became more creative and beautiful and ageless, she absorbed his sins behind the curtain.

When the doorbell finally rang, the table was set with glasses with gold stickers still on the bottoms and John was still locked in his study, so the hostess skipped to the door, the woman of the house and a fellow writer, no less.

She flung open the door and offered a little curtsy to the group. "Welcome, y'all! Thanks so much for coming! I'm Margaret."

They stared at her in the dingy dress with blush smudged on her eyes and ~~a little~~ a moderate amount in her eyebrows to fill them out. She had hoped the color would be brown enough.

"Aren't we quaint?" one man snickered, not ~~bothering~~ deigning to introduce himself, as John came to the door. "Where did you find this gem?" he said to him. Another man shook John's hand. The older woman, who Margaret assumed was The Editor, looked on sympathetically, then peeked toward the stack of pages by the typewriter. Two wives stood in the doorway with wine bottles, unsure how to proceed. Another man, younger than the rest, lingered behind the women.

"Come in, come in, and I'll pour drinks," John said, and they gathered around the newly purchased bar cart while Margaret retreated to the tiny kitchen, embarrassed. As she finished preparing the meal, she poured herself a glass of bourbon neat. She checked the temperature of the ancient oven, unsure if it was really on. Even her parents' oven was better than this one. And the selection of spatulas and wooden spoons and pots and pans was even worse than what she imagined Dennis would procure for himself in his bachelor apartment, now at Memphis State, she guessed. Perhaps some other girl now filled the space she had once ~~planned~~ succumbed to occupy, as her mother had threatened.

When she returned, John was in the middle of a story about his time in Memphis.

"It's such a small place, and they still have the cotton exchanges where they used to price out cotton flowing up the river from everywhere in the South. Well, I had a quiet existence at first, though the library was lacking and there wasn't a bookstore in sight. I had to get dear Laura here to send me the latest releases!" he said, hitting The Editor—whose name, it appeared, was Laura—lightly on the arm in a way that seemed to indicate they knew each other in a biblical sense.

"It's true!" Laura said, laughing, and the table laughed along with her.

It was not true.

Margaret listened as he continued his story about how he

introduced some much-needed culture into her little downtown, how the streets had flowed with country music and banjos and rolling plantations and few stoplights.

She studied him, trying to commit to memory what he looked like when he was lying his ass off. With a pang, she realized that he was dancing his thumb between the fingers of his right hand, a nervous tick she'd seen him do often. Had he been lying every time?

John's story had reached New York, where he described with great enthusiasm how violently Margaret had trembled on her way to the gate for her first plane ride, how he had lectured her on the physics of planes and reassured her that they were safer than cars.

The man on one side, to whom she still hadn't been introduced, laughed. "Is that how it happened, Margaret?"

"More or less," she lied.

Before additional questions could be asked, John announced that dinner would be served. Margaret got up from her seat at the other end of the table, a proper hostess, and went to fetch the salad course.

After a few trips to the kitchen to distribute the salads, which now looked sad and wilted, she turned toward the man on her right.

"How do you know John?" she asked casually before taking a bite of the salad. The dressing was horrible. Had that not been cream she'd used? Who could even tell in Italian?

Though Margaret hadn't thought she'd asked the question loudly, the entire group froze, looking toward John.

"Um," the young man said. "I'm…his son."

John stood abruptly to clear the still-full salad plates while she watched him, too shocked to move.

The wife of the "aren't-we-quaint" man saved our young heroine by commenting, "I hear you're a writer too?"

"Yes." Margaret swallowed another bite in defiance before John could whisk away her salad.

They got to talking about writing and about her own job as an editor, though her husband wrote short stories. She said she'd like to read something of Margaret's, so ~~she~~ the hostess disappeared around the corner to retrieve the story about the angel, handing it to The Other Editor as John plunked down plates of the store-bought spaghetti noodles, drenched in sauce fresh from a jar that she hoped was tomato. She had mixed in some freshly chopped onions for good measure.

She had wanted to remind John of their first meal, when he ordered spaghetti and meatballs for Margaret while she looked out over all of Memphis from the Top of the 100 Club, while she worked on the story now in The Other Editor's manicured fingers. Instead, though, he just slurped at the noodles.

The rest of the group did the same, and the conversation turned into one-word answers to basic questions, slipped in among the sound of forks on plates, instead of among the voices of John's friends. His mystery son had disappeared, Margaret noticed. His seat didn't even have a pasta plate.

The dinner progressed rapidly, with both couples ~~saying~~ claiming they didn't have room for dessert before ~~leaving~~ evacuating.

Margaret sat surrounded by the still-full dishes on the table, mulling over whether she should hand-wash them or throw them away, since she didn't anticipate John having a dinner party again in the near future.

As soon as the door shut, though, John came in thundering, "How dare you?"

"What?" she said.

"You embarrassed yourself. And worse than that, you embarrassed me."

She thought immediately of the terrible cooking and the "y'all," and her face turned as red as the tomato sauce she wished she knew how to make. How she craved to trade her Memphis accent for one more refined, like John's. Were there lessons for such skills in real life?

"The rain in Spain stays mainly in the plain," Margaret muttered to herself.

But he continued on: "Throwing your story at her like that. Desperate. Terrible."

Margaret stared at him, confused. "I thought she wanted to see it!"

"She said that to be nice," he spat.

Her stomach sank. Tears welled in her throat. "Really?"

"I sometimes fear you're only here for my connections, for my writing advice, and that apart from that, you don't love me." He stormed to the bedroom, and while he did, Margaret stared at the logs in the fireplace, which the weather had never been cool enough to light. He came back, waving her journal manically.

She watched him holding the monogrammed, leather-bound notebook her father had somehow bought for her sixteenth birthday. He had slipped it under her covers so she found it when she went to sleep that night. When she'd left him and every other person she knew, it was that notebook she took. That and a tube of her father's ChapStick, which she'd been rationing like a sailor would a vial of his sweetheart's perfume.

Why?

Why anything, she wondered pointlessly.

"Listen to how you describe me," he said, clearing his throat as he always did before reading a piece of his own writing. She stared in horror at her notebook in his hands. She hadn't let it out of her sight for more than the twenty seconds it took her to pee. But she hadn't brought it to the grocery store.

She went over everything in the book, everything she hadn't read to him, because she offered him such a small slice of what she stayed awake writing, scribbling after he went to bed.

"'A man whose most original quality is how much time he spends talking about how original he truly is.'" He flipped to a page that hadn't been dog-eared before. "'She was the muse, but she also knew that she was stronger than him, for she didn't need a muse other than herself.' You think you're better than me?"

"No, John," she said, watching as he lit the logs at which she had been staring a second before. The flame caught the dry wood, and instantly, beads of perspiration fell down her face like they did when she and John ~~made love~~ fucked in the warm afternoons. The heat, thick with smoke now in the dirty chimney, made the air feel heavy, much like Memphis, the ~~place~~ hometown she suddenly wished she had never left. But where could she go now?

He tore at a clump of pages with such force that they popped off the spine of the notebook, still bound together with glue in their own little book, the book that contained stories and journal entries that not even she could remember. Her writing always felt like a fever dream of which she had little memory.

He threw the pages into the fire.

"That's not about you!" she said.

The sound of another clump of papers ripped over the roaring fire.

"They're only characters!"

He looked at her, eyes dancing with the flames, and said, "There are no characters. There are only people. Or there are no people, only characters. You should know that."

She sat, watching him, as he ripped and threw and burned until the only pages in the notebook were blank. Even in her devastation, even with the tears streaming down her face, she couldn't block out this latest writing lesson.

Was it true? Were characters and people one in the same always?

"You are nothing to that editor. You're here only because I want you here." He stormed out into the night, taking the car with him.

She sweated in front of the flames, eventually falling asleep in front of the fireplace like the cat on the Christmas card Dennis's mother had sent last year.

The end result—after the fighting and the not-fighting and the flowers John brought the next morning and her apologies and the tears and holding each other and the makeup sex—was that Margaret would stop writing.

CHAPTER TWENTY-NINE

LEX

I've always read more quickly than Grant, so as I turned each page, I handed it to him. Now I watch as he finishes the last page, waiting until he reaches the end, at which point I'm sure he's going to start watching me. I'll let him read my mother's writing, but I don't want to discuss it.

When he hands the last page back, I cut off his pity-filled and expectant look with, "Let's go look at these," holding up Cami's list.

Grant lists the supplies we'll need on his iPhone as I walk through the house's projects—hammer, nail set, electric hand planer, measuring tape, pencil, ruler, painter's tape… The list continues.

I don't know where I'm going to get everything. Cami and I both know she has…maybe the pencil, but with her scripting habits, perhaps she only owns calligraphy pens. She always knew she could borrow tools from my parents, and my father and I would often come do little jobs at her house and her shop. You don't watch both your parents working in a hardware store for over a decade without learning the difference between a box wrench and a socket wrench.

While I look at the missing tiles around Cami's bathtub,

which look suspiciously like they were removed with an electric chisel, and Grant's hand is poised over his iPhone waiting to write down the next item we need, like in all those scavenger hunts Cami sent us on, I can't shake the feeling that stubbornly refusing to seek help from the obvious source is exactly what the girl from the letters would do. The girl I still can't admit also happens to be my mother.

I think of her, spending all that time alone in the cottage, and it reminds me so clearly of me in India and Ecuador and Bali and even here, burrowing under the covers with my *Word Origins* dictionary, not caring if I talk to anyone all day—indeed, preferring not to.

She said all she needed was writing to be happy. But when John asked her to host, she was so excited it hurts even me, so excited that I feel the rage in me turning inch by inch away from her and toward this unknown person who burned my mother's dreams. But she still gave up her writing to keep him. All these emotions can't be true at once, can they?

I've spent the last five years assuring myself of the same myth: words are all I need to be happy. Myself, and no one else. But is it true? Was it true for her? I think about her with my father or playing cards and laughing with Cami on the porch, me lingering at the door, and I think she was happy.

But still she ended up in that car.

I've never thought seriously about killing myself. Never considered that type of running away. Even after my mother did. I always wanted to know the destination to which I was running. Beyond this world, there are too many unknowns that can't be explained by language or new foods or learned songs.

"Grout saw," I say to Grant now.

I think about the baby. That was the first time I let myself think someone else could make me happy. Even better that it was a baby, to whom I wouldn't need to explain my past. Yet here I am, asking that of my mother, even in death.

And somehow, without me noticing, Grant and Cami have snuck into the spot where I expected the baby to fit, where I thought Otto might eventually fit. After yesterday's adventures, even Memphis has joined my memories of colorful, wonderful places.

And each day I stay, more of my grandfather's stories come back to me: the Veterans Hospital they built without irony on Shotwell Road during World War II—eventually the road was renamed Getwell Road. The courthouse's brass doorknobs with the seal of Shelby County, complete with a brass spittoon. Ashlar Hall's castle-like fortress and the stories of the building as a (highly effective) haunted house.

How the clocks never seem set to the right time and the whole town smells like bacon and the water tastes more refreshing than normal in a way I can't explain.

I can lift Cami's toolbox with only my index finger. It's mostly full of those pointless little wrenches that come with IKEA furniture. The ones no sane person would ever use, yet here I am trying to use one to unscrew the hinges from the bathroom door, with Grant holding it steady.

Am I happiest by myself? I've always thought not getting attached to anyone was the easiest way to remain unharmed, to keep people I loved from being harmed, but now I wonder if it's true. I look at Grant as he sets the door off to the side, with my pencil mark at the bottom for when we get the planer. I feel him lingering behind me while I study the twists of cracking plaster on Cami's ceiling, thinking for no reason about a famed day in Memphis when it rained snakes. I think of Cami on the day I returned to Memphis, the tears in her eyes, and realize maybe it's not true that I saved them by leaving. I even think of my father, of how lucky my mother was, though she doesn't know it yet, that she's ultimately heading toward him and away from John.

Maybe I hurt them all, even trying not to, by not saying goodbye, which I thought then would be more painful. More painful for them or for me?

Hurting those you love is sometimes easiest when you're trying hardest to avoid it.

Grant stands on the ladder now, carefully cutting around the broken ceiling plaster with one of Cami's kitchen knives. I try to chisel out half of a bathtub tile that's hanging on by hitting my *Dictionary of Word Origins* against the back of a butter knife.

I've talked to Grant. I've apologized. I can feel that hurt melting away from him, feel myself becoming lighter with every item on our list that we accomplish. And tomorrow, I need to talk to Cami. I'll make her listen. I'll make her see.

And somewhere, my father still lurks, further down on the list, but on it all the same. Even in spite of myself, I want to read more of what my mother has to say. I want to know the answers, how they came back together, want to feel a stronger urge to forgive him before I consider it. Can you forgive someone whose sins continue to haunt you, to dictate your life?

I'm not sure, yet here Grant stands next to me, in Cami's house.

When we stop and stare at the mess we've made, lacking the tools required to put everything back together again, Grant finally breaks the silence. "I think my parents have a drill. Let's go there and get it. They probably have some of this other stuff too."

"Okay." I say, because I can't think of a reason that won't work. It's so obviously the perfect solution, but I'm still kicking myself when we turn on Central Avenue toward Chickasaw Gardens and hoping his mother isn't home.

But of course she is.

CHAPTER THIRTY

When we get to Grant's house, his mother comes to the door in an apron, the hallway smelling of chocolate chip cookies like she's Betty Crocker.

"It's so great to see you, Lex!" She hugs me, even though we both know she does not in fact want to see me.

Grant smiles like seeing us hug is all he desires from this lifetime.

"Hey, Mom, we came to get some tools. Doing some repairs for Cami."

"You know where your father's tools are."

I linger in the doorway, thinking maybe I should tell her not to tell my father I'm here, but they've never said a word to each other. My father has never set foot in this neighborhood, I'm sure of it.

"Did you figure out about John?" his mother asks innocently.

My head immediately snaps up to look at Grant, and he lowers his eyes to his shoes, blushing.

"Mom!"

"What? Can I not ask?"

"No!" he says.

"Oh." She looks toward the kitchen. "Let me get you some cookies."

"You told her?" I hiss at Grant. One of my only complaints about him is that he's such a damn mama's boy. A personality trait to which I obviously can't relate. People who are close to their parents... Something I'll never understand. It's unnatural, though of course I thought it would be different with my own son, had hoped that he would be just like Grant.

Grant doesn't offer a defense because it's obvious he told her.

"Why?" I say as he leads me to the garage.

I look at a pegboard of completely new tools, many with the stickers still on. "Oh, this is good," I say, briefly diverted from my questions.

"Sorry," he says. "She was asking what I've been up to, and she's been so worried about me that I told her a little bit. Only a little. She was interested!"

I look at him skeptically, then step forward to grab a putty knife off a hook.

"She thinks you should Google John."

"You Googled him?" I say, because I know if he's suggesting it, he's already done it.

"He has an event at Brown University not tomorrow night, but the next. I was waiting for the right time to ask if maybe you wanted to drive up together and see what he was like."

"No! Why would I want to see that asshole?" I'm so surprised I can't even say anything else. "No," I finish. "He's nothing to me."

He's the man who ruined my mother, I think, a tantalizing lie I know is only that.

I hand Grant a hammer and a new drill with bits, still sealed in its case.

"Do you know where grout would be?"

Grant points to a cabinet with a printed label that says BATH-ROOM REPAIRS.

"Is that everything?" he asks me, five minutes after I've figured out that it is not, as if Cami called ahead to make sure they didn't have enough power tools.

"Not quite," I say, shrugging. "Maybe we leave it and have her call a handyman?"

"We can't leave her house like that!"

Thinking back to the state in which we left her bathroom, I have to agree, especially since I want her in a good mood when I talk to her tomorrow about my mother's writing. We could go to the hardware store—well, not *the* hardware store, since my parents' is closed, but a hardware store. Imagining the cost of a tile saw immediately surpassing the credit that's left on my credit card and the conversation that would provoke with Grant, I discard that idea.

"Okay, okay," I say, defeated once again by Cami. "Let's just drive by my father's house. If he's not home, we can run in and get the last few things."

I can't help it. When we turn the other way on Central Avenue, my heart starts racing, and I wonder again if his work boots will be by the garage. It's broad daylight, so I hunker down in the passenger seat when Grant pulls up to the house.

"I don't think he's there," Grant says.

I pop up.

"Wait."

I pop back down.

"Look," he says.

I rise up slowly, my nose at the peeling seal on Grant's car window, until I can see the driveway clearly.

What the fuck?

Before I can say anything else, what comes out of my mouth is "DRIVE!" And Grant slams the gas pedal to his stained floorboard and squeals down the street.

It was Cami. Coming out of my father's house.

My mind goes back to the lipstick and the pink toothbrush in my father's bathroom, the potential of another woman's possessions occupying the space where my mother kept her glasses cleaner.

But…Cami? Cami is the owner of the pink toothbrush, the new woman in my father's life? No, not new, I remind myself. I've been gone long enough for nothing I've missed to be considered new.

How long has this been going on?

She told him I was here, I realize. If they really are together, she told him, of course she did.

This game—I haven't been playing with Cami alone. Was she only the front, the figurehead, with my father behind her, pulling the strings?

I stay slumped in Grant's passenger seat, feet on the Buick's wide dashboard, processing, unable to think clearly.

"Are you going to ask Cami about it?" he says after a few minutes.

"No!" I say. "That's exactly what she wants me to do." I kick my feet off the dash and straighten up. My mother used to say I'd break my legs one day sitting like that, if the airbag went off.

"You sure?"

"No." I'm not sure about anything anymore.

Could this be why Cami has been avoiding my mother's

letters? Was she sleeping with my father back then? Was she sleeping with my father while my mother was in Italy?

No! No. I tell myself not to spiral, always the first clue that I'm spiraling.

Her defenses of "Dennis" in my mother's writing return to me fast and clear, and all of a sudden, I'm on my mother's side, as suspicious as she was of all the people in her life.

John we'll never agree on, though. That asshole. And the stupid girl who allowed him to prey on her. Okay, off her side again.

My brain is a very confusing place to be.

"Let's get a drink." I decide to leave Cami's bathroom in a state of disrepair after all.

Grant takes me to a bar above an Italian place that only has four barstools, a couch, and a few armchairs. He whispers to a man at the door like we're going to a speakeasy in the seventies, before Memphis allowed alcohol, and once we're seated at the bar, the bartender insists that there's no menu and that he's going to "craft a cocktail attuned to my unique flavor profile."

"Strong," I say. The only other person in the bar orders something extremely complicated that requires a ladder to reach bottles on the top shelf.

We drink, then move to the Italian place downstairs to eat. Grant shows me a Facebook group with alumni from the camp where we met, and we pass the phone back and forth, each challenging the other to match the middle schooler with the mother of two or the grown man in a dirty truck or the teacher in a Black Lives Matter T-shirt.

"That's the girl from my school who Alex McKinley called

a bitch at the football game before he got impeached as class president."

"That's that guy who never left the band room at camp."

"Is it...whoa. He's a jazz singer now? He looks good."

We stay out late, wasting time together, until Grant parks at Cami's house and falls asleep on her couch and I climb the stairs, wanting my toothbrush, before falling asleep in the bedroom.

Did she see us at my father's house? I wonder as I fall asleep to the sound of Grant's snores echoing up the stairs. I'm not sure. Either way, I don't want to see her until I know my next move. I'm sure she already knows hers.

CHAPTER THIRTY-ONE

By morning, I've decided I should act normal with Cami and try to catch her in the act. So they can't deny their relationship. I already know my father shares my mother's talent for lying, and now I suspect even Cami may be a better liar than I gave her credit for.

So when I walk downstairs and see the now-empty couch, I only greet Edgar and pour myself a cup of coffee.

"Is that you?" Cami says, and for the first time, I wonder if she really does mean me. Or if she means someone else—my father maybe.

"Good morning," I say as she comes in, fastening one of her earrings.

Does she not know I saw her, or did she want me to see her? Thinking about the possibilities makes my brain hurt. I take a sip of coffee, studying her expression and trying to work it out.

"So, you were with Grant last night?" she says, pointing to empty couch. "Is something going on?"

I'm so surprised I don't have time to consider how hypocritical the question is, given her own love life. I say too loudly, "No!"

"Really?"

I cough. I almost spat out my coffee the first time, and now I'm struggling to swallow it down. "Yes!"

I swallow.

"Pity," she says, rinsing her own coffee cup in the sink and putting it upside down on a dish towel. "I always thought you two would be perfect for each other."

"He's like my cousin or something."

"Be careful," she says, grabbing her purse off the front table. "I think he's always been a little bit in love with you."

I struggle to remember the direction I planned to take this conversation, unable to even protest.

"The next entry is there," she says, pointing to the table. "Your task for the day is to reassemble my bathroom." She smiles at me like she's just caught me sneaking out.

"Are you going to the store?" I ask as she's opening the front door. "I was hoping we could hang out today."

She stops with her hand on the handle.

"I thought you'd be with Grant again today."

"No, I thought we could, you know, talk…" I let my voice trail off, looking at the table with the next envelope, even as I tell myself not to.

"If this is about reading your mother's writing, I don't want to, Lex."

I see an opening, with her hand on the door handle, so I blurt out, "When she wrote you letters about all the fun she was having in Europe and never let you respond, that wasn't real. She was lying." At least I think she was.

"I know," Cami says, looking at me now.

"You knew?"

"Yes."

Cami figures out what to say first. "I'll go to my meeting and then come back to pick you up. We can have lunch, and maybe you'll want to go by the shop with me after?"

I nod yes, but she's already shut the door.

This is my chance.

I leave the unread piece of my mother's writing and run upstairs to quickly change my shirt and brush my teeth.

Donning my disguise from earlier in the week, I slink out of the house and toward the street I hurried down just days ago, before I read the first piece of my mother's writing. Before I made up with Grant. Before I knew about Cami and my father...

Before I knew so many things about my mother, but what about my life does this knowledge change?

Cami thought it would change a lot—change me, even—or she wouldn't have given me my mother's writing. Was she right or wrong? I'm still not sure.

I expect Cami to be at my father's house, but I'm still surprised to see her car in his driveway. Seeing it, though, confirms everything I've imagined about them, and I storm up to the side door, the one without the glass panel, intent on swinging it open. It will be unlocked; my father always leaves this door unlocked when he's home.

My hand hovers over the knob. Do I really want to see Cami and my father doing anything remotely sexual? No, I do not.

But the element of surprise is my best chance for getting the truth. And I'm sick of the lies. My mother lying to Cami in her letters, then sending these sealed journal entries with the truth. My father lying to me and my mother. Cami lying to me. Cami lying to herself.

I fling open the door, and the handle dents the wall behind it.

Cami and my father are huddled together at the kitchen island, and at the sound, they spring apart, like an Australian couple I saw making out, close to making love, on a beach in Bali.

My eyes meet Cami's first, and from the look on her face, I realize this discovery was not something she was counting on after all. My father's eyes meet mine next. They reflect no surprise about my presence in Memphis.

I prepare to utter some words of betrayal, but I'm still trying to process the scene with Cami and my father before me, mashed together with memories of my mother in this kitchen, with that memory of her cooking away all day and then blaming me for the spoiled food, the fights, the yelling, the tears, dancing with my father in front of the open freezer door to cool down one July.

Cami's sleeve is rolled up, and she has a band on her arm. She's showing it to my father, like she's a death eater in Harry Potter, and my mind fills pointlessly with all the Greek and Roman influences I savored in those books. Clear medical bags litter the kitchen counter where my mother stored her teas. Needles are strewn across the table, and a Band-Aid is on Cami's arm.

My father holds a needle, his thumb looking comfortable on the plunger. I try to concentrate on that thumb, to form a connection to something from my past, to rationalize the scene in some way, but instead, my eyes bore into the wrinkles that form a crevice on his forehead. He looks like he's aged more than the five years that have passed since we last saw each other. His hair has turned white, and his hairline is receding, yet he's wearing the same old khakis and green Henry Hardware polo.

I picture the junkies I saw once in Russia, clustered like my father and Cami around the kitchen counter, but instead around a street corner, then in dark basements in Moscow. That explanation would be easier for me, I think. More comfortable. Yet even as I hope for that version, I know it's not right. And Cami and my father are both still staring at me, waiting for me to say something.

I gulp. "Are you..." I say, not able to get the word out that would finish the sentence. "Dying" is what I was going to say.

Cami looks at me and says only, "Yes." But I don't know what question she's answering. Is she dying? Sick? Sleeping with my father? Sorry? All of the above?

My father stands there watching me, turning back to her and then to me like his brain is out of RAM. Seeing the way he looks at her, full of worry about how she's going to react, reminds me of how he looked at my mother.

He walks toward me like he's going to say something, his eyes full of pity and apology and questions and answers. As he comes closer, I back away a step, then another, then another, and he stops, defeated.

He looks at his watch, the Hamilton watch I know belonged to his father, and says, "We're going to be late" to Cami.

You're not going to be late, I think, though I have no idea where they're going. While some fathers seem to think that if you don't come in first, you might as well be last, my father always preached that if you don't arrive twenty minutes early, you might as well be late. He had a habit of arriving embarrassingly early to appointments, standing outside in the Memphis heat before the doors had even been unlocked.

"Lex," Cami starts, but I walk away, shutting the door to my parents' house carefully behind me for once, the door's trim still chipped from so many slams, my mother's and mine. The marks in the wood have outlasted her, I realize. Is that a legacy?

They don't try to follow me, so I jog to the end of the street and hide behind a tree until the Honda CRV I saw before passes. I suppose it's my father's car because he's driving, though it looks like it was meant for a suburban soccer mom. He turns toward the highway, to where? The hospital?

I strain to remember what illness struck Cami's father. Is it the same? Is it deadly? Does it hurt?

I don't even care that she's sleeping with my father. I don't know why she would want him, but if she does, she can have him, I bargain. She can tell him everything as long as she lives.

I'm not sure what else to do, so I go back to Cami's house to get my mother's entry from this morning.

I should have come back sooner. I should have stayed. I shouldn't have yelled at my mother during our last conversation. I should have done so many things.

I'm tearing up as I walk toward Cami's, trying to force myself to stay angry—at my father, at Cami, at my mother, at Otto, at God, at the framers of the Constitution and at slave owners and at every person who's ever kicked a dog, at child molesters and people who use the word "literally" incorrectly and teachers from my high school and Coca-Cola for inventing soda. At the white men who stole this land from the Chickasaw tribe and the idiots who put fake hieroglyphics on the Ballard and Ballard building and people who pronounce "mature" like "ma-tewer." At the FBI for shooting MLK, at all the ugliness that ruined this city and all the people against its comeback. It doesn't even matter who anymore. All I want to feel is anger. Anger that can drown out this hurt, this sorrow. Anger is always easier.

I land on my father. He doesn't deserve her, I think. He doesn't deserve Cami. He doesn't deserve her last days, if that's what these are.

I don't really deserve them either.

He's here. You weren't, I tell myself. I'm having difficulty summoning more anger, even toward my father, than I have toward myself. Especially picturing him in the driver's seat of the car, picturing him holding the needle, quietly doing what he thinks needs to be done, for better or for worse, like always. That's a type of bravery too, I realize.

Shaking my head, hands trembling, I keep walking.

Anger, even toward myself, is better than hurt. Is preferable to pain. Anger has always felt more purposeful to me. *Stay angry.* I want the feeling so badly, I'm willing to go there. To think about the most anger-inducing conversation I've ever had.

CHAPTER THIRTY-TWO

I blame my father for that last conversation I had with my mother. I blame him for everything that happened after, the garage filled with invisible poison. I can even blame him for my leaving if I try hard enough. Maybe it's his fault that I haven't been here with Cami.

I can pack on even more blame if I think about that morning with my mother. Because the morning of the fight that would be our last started with one of the best conversations we'd had in years.

Vassar, being the hippie-dippy haven that it was, prided itself on teaching "life skills," which essentially meant students got a traditional liberal arts education with a few mandatory skills thrown in that were actually marketable. I chose personal finance. And after some prodding from Cami, who I had finally returned to Memphis to see since she stubbornly refused to visit me, I decided to profile the hardware store for a project on entrepreneurship and small business.

That project was how I came to sit in the dusty, windowless office where my mother hid with the door shut most of the day, gnawing at a pencil she kept either in her mouth or behind her ear, sort of listening to my father's classical music. The music could stop for hours before my father would walk by, notice, and change the CD.

I had become so attentive to my mother's shifting winds that I could tell she was in a good mood from the way her hands bounced over the computer keys, from how her foot tapped to the CD that was still spinning. Helpful, since we would be in close proximity, huddled in front of her computer screen.

I waited until she was ready to start, not daring to talk first. Conversations with her had become even more tense in the last year. At college, I had witnessed enough mother-daughter interactions and overheard enough conversations to know that my mother's anger was not normal. Not only that, but I realized that I didn't have to entertain her tantrums, so I started simply walking out rather than listening, heading to Cami's preemptively before a fight even began.

My mother happily explained the ins and outs of payroll and inventory to me, clicking around her spreadsheets with such speed that I could barely follow. This must be how some of my older professors feel when they watch students navigating PowerPoint, I remember thinking.

I had no talent for finance, but even I could see that the outgoing and incoming expenses didn't add up. I listened carefully while my mother tried to talk around the discrepancy, concentrating too long on how much money the business spent each year on screws and ignoring the fact that seemed obvious even to me: the business was losing money. A lot of money.

Finally, I couldn't smile and nod anymore. I had to ask.

"What's that?" I said, pointing to a number that very clearly indicated the business had spent $230,000 more than it had made last year. It was the rent, it looked like—it had been rising for years since this area was making its comeback, drawing more

people to the daiquiris at Wet Willie's where the old grocery used
to be, drawing tourists to the stadium and locals out of the area,
fulfilling their hardware needs at Amazon or wherever else.

"Oh," my mother said, suddenly shutting down the computer.
"It's nothing. Your father has it handled. He has some other
sources of income."

I knew as well as she did that my father had no other jobs,
that the hardware store was his whole life. Stocks? An inheritance
I didn't know about? What could it be?

"I need to finish this." She held open the door. "Lesson's done
for the day."

When I left her office, the door slammed behind me and the
classical music started up again, causing me to notice that it had
stopped during our conversation.

The store was still closed for the morning, and my father wasn't
in yet, so I went downstairs to the cash register, intent on rummaging in the drawers he used there, similar to what millennials would
now call "a standing desk" but was once just called "working."

There was little need for rummaging, though. As I opened the
first drawer slowly and carefully, listening to the squeaks of its
wheels on the outdated roller, I saw that it was overflowing with
envelopes that were stamped red with PAST DUE or OVERDUE.

What had he gotten himself into, I thought, grabbing one of
them and opening it.

Overdue on $780,000.

Dear Alexandra Henry…

I stopped.

My eyes hovered over my own name there on the form. I
thought back to the beginning of the semester when we pulled

our credit scores in class. Mine had been in the dumps. "Have you ever taken out a loan?" my professor asked.

"A loan? No."

"It must be a mistake. Don't worry, you can get it fixed."

The task was written down on a legal pad somewhere in my college dorm. I had forgotten about it until now, though. It hadn't seemed urgent.

I kept digging.

Alexandra Henry. Margaret Henry. Dennis Henry.

All of our names on loans totaling more than two million dollars.

I stormed back up to my mother's office with the evidence of my father's betrayal of me and of her, intent on showing her what I had discovered, intent on getting one of them on my side against the other for once.

I would not let this betrayal follow me for my entire life. Surely taking out loans with your daughter's social security number is illegal?

I thought back a few weeks, to when my father had visited me at college and handed me five crisp hundred-dollar bills as he left.

Money from the loan in *my name*, I realized now. With interest.

When I opened my mother's office door, she took one look at me and another at the papers in my hand, and I could tell immediately that she was not surprised at all.

"You know about this?"

"I found out last week. I got a call," she said, shuffling papers on her desk instead of looking at me. Calm for once in her life while I was the one yelling.

"What are you going to do about this? He's bankrupting us!"

"He's doing his best, Lex."

"What?"

"I'm sure he's trying to help. He's trying to help keep the business. He's probably embarrassed."

"Embarrassed? You're not mad about this?"

I thought of my next semester of college tuition. I had a scholarship, but would any of this change that? Would I need to take out loans for living expenses I couldn't pay with my campus job?

"I'm going to talk to him about it," she said.

"You're going to *talk* to him?"

"I'll figure it out."

"What? You're going to take the fall for this?"

"I love your father."

"That means you're willing to let him commit crimes? What's next, murder?" Was this fraud? I thought back to the finance class lectures when instead of listening, I had doodled words in Arabic that wrapped around the corners of my notebook. What does good credit even get you?

"You just don't know what love is," my mother told me.

"And whose fault is that?"

She looked at me long and hard. Then, like the flick of a light, I saw the switch go off in her brain.

"I'm sorry that I was such a terrible mother, that you hate me so much."

"You hate *me*!"

"I bet you wish you had another mother."

"I bet you wish I was never born."

"Well, maybe I do."

"Then how would you get a loan?"

She stopped at that.

"And maybe I do wish I had another mother. Maybe I wish Cami was my mother. Or that if I was going to be stuck with you, I hadn't even been born."

I stormed out, leaving the overdue notices in my wake like fluttering tumbleweeds in a gust of wind.

CHAPTER THIRTY-THREE

I stand in Cami's house, looking at the next sealed entry, but right now, I can't take any more. No more words; my brain is full of all the words it can hold, for once. I wait until an hour past the time when Cami said she would pick me up, though I don't expect her to come, and she doesn't.

I sit, staring off into the distance, until I finally decide to do something. It's dark and rainy outside. I pour half a bottle of wine into Grant's coffee thermos, which sits by the sink, and call a cab to take me to the riverfront. I want to see it, as restless as I feel, want to see those same flags my mother saw from the Top of the 100 Club.

But when I get there, the flags are gone, along with the statue of Jefferson Davis. The statue of Tom Lee, reaching a strong arm out of his boat to help people who wouldn't do the same for him, still stands. Since it was added, it's been my favorite.

I sit and drink from my thermos, getting wet with drizzle despite my hoodie, until the wine is gone. I watch the storm approaching over the river, but all I can think about is that last conversation with my mother. I'm not even sure who I'm mad at. Everyone, I think.

That fight was the only time I invoked Cami's name, the only time I said out loud what I'd thought my entire life, and I immediately saw the impact of the words on my mother's face. In conjuring her best friend between us, I could see her questioning everything, could see that name cutting her in a way I had never been able to before.

It was that conversation that finally killed my mother, I've always thought.

But whose fault was it? Over the years, I've blamed myself, my father, or my mother, whoever earned the most scorn from me on any given day. But maybe it was all of ours.

And if it's everyone's fault, does that mean it's no one's?

fault, from the Latin word *fallere*, meaning "to deceive." Fail, fallacy, fallible, false. The word didn't evolve to include the idea of moral culpability until the late fourteenth century.

A teenage couple on the bench in front of me has started making out, laughing as the rain gets stronger.

Is there anything more depressing than being alone with a couple making out, I wonder, trying to drain the last drops of wine. Eating by yourself while people sing "Happy Birthday" to someone you don't know. Walking by a school when parents are picking up their kindergarteners for the day. That's a recent one for me. I had pictured doing that with the baby, taking him to a little school in Bali or Germany and picking him up, smiling, right on time, like Mother of the Year.

I feel the pressure of the girl frozen in my mother's writing. I have to let her go on so she can go to Dennis, so she can come back to Memphis, where sometimes she'll be happy and most times she'll be sad and angry and bitter, and eventually, she'll fight with her daughter, who will throw her greatest gift in her face.

I walk to South Main Street, which Grant couldn't stop

talking about at the brewery when he thought I was in earshot. I hurry out of the rain as I pass the Arcade Restaurant, blinking to remove the vision of my parents there. I dodge a trolley rolling down the street—the trolleys are back?—pass an escape room establishment—only Americans would *pay* to be trapped in a room—and finally slip into Earnestine & Hazel's. The most haunted place in Memphis and the perfect place to read my mother's writing, so many memories haunting us all.

I start reading, hoping that (for once) she has some comforting words for me but knowing, because of that last conversation as much as any other, that she'll haunt me more than the ghosts of the women who used to work in the brothel upstairs.

MARGARET

A few weeks later, our ~~young~~ youngish heroine sat alone at a table in a tiny restaurant and waited for John. He had been disappearing more since their fight. She didn't know where he went and was beginning not to care, enjoying the time he was gone, when, despite her promise, she would extract her notebook from its hiding place and write their story, ripping the pages out and sending them off with the post to Memphis before they could meet the same scorching fate.

She took out the notebook now, fingering the money she had been slipping into its back pocket, perhaps the only proof that she wasn't quite as naive as she once was. But seeing the frayed edges where the pages had been ripped and knowing the risk—it was their one-year anniversary!—she put the book away. The words used to pour out of her, but more often now, she found herself staring at an empty page. The words, the remembrances of how she got here, came to her without order or reason—the curve at the back of John's knee, how Cami drank black coffee and had since they were children, a cat that had walked around their apartment building as if it owned the place. Pointless memories.

She ordered wine by pointing to the menu. She always wished she possessed a talent for other languages, but alas, English was her master, her inspiration. She opened the notebook's front cover and read: "If found, please return to Margaret Green" with her phone number. Written in another time, another place, by another Margaret Green.

"Excuse me?" the man next to her said.

She looked at him, startled, for she had begun to think herself invisible and was surprised when proven wrong.

He continued: "I–I'm sorry, I don't mean to pry, I saw your notebook, and I thought that maybe you speak English?" he said, faltering at the end the way Dennis used to when he was nervous, what she had assumed was a childhood stutter sneaking back in.

Margaret nodded. Yes.

"American?" he continued.

She nodded again.

"Do you mind?" He gestured to the chair destined for John. "I haven't spoken English to anyone but myself in so long. I've been coming to this place every night for three weeks and never seen another American."

"Please," she heard herself saying, to relieve that familiar nervousness. John never had that.

The man (midtwenties, cute) sighed thankfully, like her father did after a big meal, and collapsed into the chair, reaching over to grab his own wine bottle and ordering another glass in perfect Italian.

"I'm Donovan. From LA. What's your name?"

"Margaret. From…Memphis."

"Memphis! What made you venture here?"

They sank into easy conversation, with him telling her about work his company was doing nearby on an old church, which made her think again of her father. He was laughing at some joke he'd made about his recent travels to Austria when he turned to see John tapping him on the shoulder as he would a dance partner.

"John!" Margaret said. "Meet Donovan."

He sized up the ~~strange man~~ unknown adversary.

"I was just heading out." Donovan reached for his wineglass, tipping it to release the last drop. "Thank you so much for keeping me company, Margaret. Nice meeting you, John."

The men shook hands, smiled at each other. "You have a nice evening."

"You too," John answered, friendly enough.

Soon John was in the warm seat, a new glass of wine in hand, telling her about his day and all the other things there were to tell, since they hadn't talked much recently—his students and the drain that wouldn't work on their street and his most recent communication with his agent. She listened and ate and drank without strife until John made the universal sign for their check and the waiter came over, shaking his head.

"No," the waiter said.

"No?" John asked.

"No pay."

"What?"

He pointed to the door and back to the chair where Donovan had ~~sat~~ perched.

Margaret looked on, another game of interaction charades. She'd become used to playing during their months in rural Italy.

"Paid."

John tried to hand the man money in a stack, but he refused it, saying only "paid" and gesturing again to the chair.

"I think he's saying that Donovan paid," Margaret offered.

"That guy?" John pointed to the chair where Donovan had sat, and the waiter nodded forcefully.

"Why would he—" John began as Margaret said, "That was nice of—"

"Nice?"

John looked toward the door and back to the chair. "Does he not think I can pay for myself? Is this some sort of come-on?"

"No, I'm sure it's—"

"Did you give him our phone number?"

"No!"

"What were y'all—"

At the noise, the dishwasher had been summoned, most likely because he seemed to speak the most English of anyone.

"Man paid the bill. Bill is good," he explained again, making the sign that umpires do in baseball when a runner is safe.

"Well, what's his address? Where does he live? Get this back to him, will you?" John shoved the money at the dishwasher, who refused to take it.

After a few more attempts, John abruptly pushed his chair back from the table and stormed out. Margaret struggled to grab her cardigan off her own chair before trailing behind him.

She rode home in the passenger seat while he sped around the road's unlit turns, muttering to himself. When they reached the cottage, he barricaded himself in the kitchen, and she heard the slamming of cabinets.

"If you're going to defend him, why don't you go live with him?"

"Maybe I will!"

"Good! I'd like to see you on your own. Little Margaret, what's an avocado, what does a penis look like?" he said in a little mouse voice. "Give me a break."

"Well, I'm not as bad as Mr. 'I'm better than everyone else.' Maybe you're scared because you think that maybe, just maybe, I *am* a better writer than you."

"You know what? You're not." He stormed over to his bag and took out the envelope, the one containing her writing that he'd ~~said~~ promised he would send off to his publisher friend, still stamped from Memphis. "Without me, you have nothing."

The world started crashing, and she said, "I don't need you!"

Margaret made a big show of gathering her clothes and stomping out. She took her notebook with the ripped-out pages and slammed the door behind her.

She ~~walked~~ treaded carefully along the path with her purse and her thin sweater, back to the restaurant, whispering to herself about how John was probably right during the hours-long journey. But because of her stubbornness, she continued.

When she got to the restaurant, it was late, and she sat on the stoop until the busboy came out. "Train station?" she asked him. He looked her over and said, "Come." She slept in his bed while he slept on the couch without saying much, and the next morning, he drove her to the train station.

She wrote as her companions—a woman and her two children, with whom Margaret fought for space in the shared train car—stared at the unaccompanied girl across from them as if her existence was as impossible and interesting as Wonkavision. She had learned that she was not, in fact, interesting, one of the many lessons from the last year. But perhaps right now, on her way to Paris—the city she'd always wanted to visit, had been told she would get a chance to visit (a lie), had been told was the most magical city on earth—she was. Paris was the perfect place to leave from, if you were about to leave for the last time, she decided.

She checked into a hostel, dead tired, and fell asleep in the ladies' dorm room, even with a woman in the bunk above hers snoring like her father always did—so loud she could hear it through her own closed door, starting and stopping with gasps that always made her hold her breath until he took his next one. Even though Margaret knew he wasn't sick—he was always fine except for his hand, the lone pinkie he controlled with the precision of a trumpet player in Handy Park—seeing Cami's father wither away more and more with each rare permitted entrance into their apartment made her fear nonetheless. Especially when she knew her mother was working another night shift at one of her jobs.

Margaret woke up to an empty room and the Paris sun streaming in. She drank an espresso and ate a croissant and headed for the Seine with her notebook to finally get a look at it, to see if the river had the right energy for her plan.

The ~~energy~~ atmosphere for her last moments needed to be perfect, required a certain je ne sais quoi. She wanted to see the water, to determine what kind of dress would match the calm current as she floated down, down, down. She studied the landscape, trying to decide which bridge would be the most poetic for her last step. Perhaps Pont Alexandre III, all that gold? Or Pont Marie? Less clichéd, more unexpected.

She went to Pont Neuf, smoking a cigarette she managed to bum off an elegant Parisian man without any words exchanged. He lit it for her too. That was the ~~feeling~~ decorum for which people come to Paris, Margaret guessed, that type of old-world class. Her mother would love it.

She decided the dress should be light green with yellow accents. That would truly stand out against the water as it fanned around her. She resolved to look for it today, to prowl around different shops in Paris and spare no expense. She would buy the nicest dress she could afford with the rest of John's money; she had no use for coins and bills anymore.

She could throw herself off the bridge this evening, but the weather wasn't right, and besides, she needed to send these pages to Cami first. She hoped that when she didn't come back, her friend would read them. Margaret hoped her friend would realize what an idiot she had been but that she still loved her, that her departure and John had nothing to do with her, and that she was sorry. Because she was.

Margaret was very sorry.

Her friend had been right. About everything.

She only hoped Cami would forgive her. One could say it was her dying wish.

CHAPTER THIRTY-FOUR

LEX

I finish the letter and order two bourbon shots. I also order the only menu item, a hamburger, because I'm not trying to drown tonight. Unlike the girl. My mother. They are one in the same.

She was planning her death even then.

She was planning it before the fight.

She was planning it before me.

Knowing that makes me so sad and relieved and sad that I'm relieved, bringing back all the emotions from my mother's funeral, bringing back the emotions that Otto must have felt that day in the hospital. Each new wave of emotion is more overwhelming, and I order more bourbon until I've completely run out of cash. My card will get declined for sure this time, I know.

I wait for one more drink, bought by a guy at the bar to whom I don't have enough energy to lie. The Lex of last year would delight in making up a story just crazy enough to be believed, relish in choosing her accent and mulling over her word choices. But false identities hold no allure at the moment.

I pull out the address Cami wrote down that first day and walk the few blocks to Grant's apartment at what used to be the Tennessee Brewery. I find his name on the call box and buzz up, refusing to identify myself. He comes to his apartment door in boxers, looking at me, trying to answer his own questions.

"Bedtime," I say, and he lets me in without voicing any of them. I crawl into his bed on the side that's unmade and warm, laughing at the space sheets, and he plops down next to me. I think of my mother, decades ago, sleeping in the bed of that Italian busboy. What must he have thought of her? I imagine her on that train and checking into the hostel and smoking on the bridge.

Quickly, though, I stop thinking. That's the good thing about southern bourbon and tears in the rain. Even if you're hurting, they put you to sleep.

CHAPTER THIRTY-FIVE

In the morning, I don't wake Grant. Instead, I head in the direction of downtown, intent on talking to Cami before she leaves for the store.

I walk past the Lorraine Motel, where Lorraine herself suffered a stroke and later died after hearing that MLK had been shot. I remember walking between houses at night when I was a teenager, seeing the laser beam from this building, shining from the precise place where he was shot, where the vintage cars are still parked out front. I walk past the murals proclaiming I AM A MAN. During my entire walk along South Main, I see only a few people because it's so early in the morning. These were always my favorite times in Memphis, walking the city before it had woken up, as if it were mine alone.

I pass the Rumba Room, dark and dirty from last night's festivities, and the Hotel Chisca, with lights on inside that I've never seen, past the still-flashing sign of the Orpheum Theatre. Before now, I had only my grandfather's memories of so many of these buildings.

I walk under the BEALE STREET, MEMPHIS sign. A door ahead says SAINT ELVIS CATHEDRAL, and the whole street has the hush of a church, so much so that it makes me want to pray for myself, pray for my mother's soul, but most of all, for Cami. Pray for her health, bargain with God to let her live. I pass the red, white, and blue banners in front of A. Schwab feeling incredibly lonely—as lonely as my mother on that bridge, maybe, though she never would've admitted she was lonely. My only company is the neon lights, still flashing like they haven't been alerted that the theme park is closed.

The buildings feel unreal, and the sidewalks feel spacious without their flippers and singers and tourists and the sound of the blues or rock coming from every door.

I see only a man drinking coffee and sitting on a cement pillar from which steel beams jut, holding up the facade of an old building. An unidentifiable person in an orange vest picks up last night's party trash in the distance.

It all makes me realize that I don't want to be alone. I don't want to be like my mother on that bridge by herself, dreaming of erasing all possible futures when people who loved her were a phone call away. It's not brave, I realize—it's stubborn, a type of stubborn I don't want to be, not anymore. A mistake I want to learn from.

I line up at the Peabody Hotel taxi stand, next to the horse-drawn carriages waiting for the tourists, and use the twenty dollars I nabbed from Grant's dresser for a taxi back to Cami's house.

I ride there with my mother's envelopes on my lap. They hold a final apology.

Her apology, but it also belongs to me. The Henry girls—mother and daughter—apologizing to someone who was always there for them.

Why, though?

Why would anyone want to be with us?

When I walk through the front door, I realize Cami has already gone. Or maybe, realizing that there's no reason for secrecy anymore, she slept at my father's house. In the bed he used to share with my mother.

I place all my mother's envelopes on the little table where Cami left them for me with a sticky note from Grant's desk on top— "She WANTED you to read them. Please, do it for me." Cami can start at the beginning, like my mother would have wanted.

I trade my pile for another envelope, this one with no note from Cami. I had hoped she would ask me to do the most difficult task yet. Some impossible home improvement project—in addition to reassembling her bathroom—that could stand in for the apology I need to make.

I open my mother's writing and read:

MARGARET

Another rainy Paris day over the Seine. Another cigarette. Margaret had always loved the poetry of smoking. It seemed to say, I am not long for this world. And for her, that was true.

She had ~~found~~ spotted the dress in the second shop she visited. She had mailed the entries to Cami, her project was done, and tomorrow was the Big Day.

She walked to the hostel with only her journal, imagining how tomorrow's leap would feel, the chill as her body plunged into the water, the perfect dress billowing around her, helping the entirety of mankind in the process; they would now be free of Margaret Green. A legacy starting with Lady Macbeth, the White Witch, Estella, Abigail—just another misunderstood orphan from Salem.

The weather tomorrow, which she'd spied in icons in a man's newspaper, was meant to be sunny. She comforted herself by picturing how once she was dead, Cami would open the envelopes, cautiously at first. Her friend would hear what Margaret could never say aloud. Like when they could barely understand each other's accents.

But when Margaret opened the door to the girls' dorm at the hostel and went to the trunk under her bed, all her stuff was gone. She hadn't brought her wallet or purse to the river, because she didn't have much money left and didn't want to spend it on cigarettes and alcohol again in case she wanted to buy herself a nice meal tonight.

So the next day, our heroine sat on her bridge, blowing smoke toward the sun rising over the Seine, with only her memories of the dress that would have matched this water perfectly.

Now the entire color scheme was ruined.

The theft was almost a bit of ~~a relief~~ an allayment. She would be able to truly disappear into the water, with or without the dress.

She saw herself standing on the side of the bridge. The wind tickled hair against her cheek, whipped behind her down the river, while she listened to the angel from her story whisper—

Jump

jump

jump.

Jump, Margaret Green.

The pleas were hard to ignore, even though she knew the angel wasn't full of good intentions. She knew because she'd made him up. That Jude could be quite the bastard.

The only tests he seemed to invent were ones he knew others would fail, and what was the good in that? Maybe Jude was the real devil, she realized. Maybe the girl who seduced him was just a girl, unfairly punished.

From that new vantage point, she saw a group of young people with tents and sleeping bags. She could barely pick out a young couple making love with the girl's skirt hiked. Tomorrow, she decided for the second day. Rattled by the loss of the dress, and with a longing look back at the water, she headed to join the group.

They turned out to be mostly American, and they were a riot. They sang and danced and debated how "over" the United States was. She had no idea what they were talking about and didn't want to ask for specifics, so she turned to one of the girls not participating and asked her where she grew up.

"On a commune in South Dakota."

Margaret sat up straight, the wheels in her writer brain turning. Now, *that* was a story. All she needed was one to stay awake another day, to ~~spend~~ toil through another day on earth. One story that still needed to be told.

"What was it like?" She thought about taking out her notebook but didn't want to spook the girl.

"I don't really like to talk about it." The girl rolled over.

"Oh, okay," Margaret said to her back, the beginnings of a story evaporating. She turned the other way too and eventually fell asleep on the shoulder of a woman named Joann with hairy armpits, to the sound of the boys debating the world's future and drinking the last of the wine.

In the morning, Margaret walked off with her journal and

a few bummed cigarettes to resume her vigil on the bridge and write everything that had happened since yesterday, a project she accomplished swiftly.

The sky looked dark. Again, the weather, the environment, wouldn't cooperate with her plan. Perhaps the forecast shouldn't matter, but she'd always loved the sun. Was it such a big ask that her last vision be that of a sun-filled sky reflecting off the water over her head as she exhaled for the last time? Especially now that the dress was gone. Forces were conspiring for—and against—her demise. It was downright confusing.

She found a café with an awning when it started to rain and ordered a glass of wine. A rowdy group of American soldiers came in, all clapping each other on the back and smiling, speaking terrible French, not that she could do much better. The only foreign words she had mastered were a few Spanish curse words Cami had taught her.

She was hungry, so she smiled back at one of the soldiers staring and mouthed "Hello."

"Ah!" Two of them screamed to each other, tapping the table to get the attention of the others. "Are you American?"

"*Oui*," she said, so clever.

A round of applause.

They pulled up a chair for her. She got lost in a haze of cigarette smoke and wine and the food they ordered and the lies she told until she too was more character than person, wondering which was real, and the soldiers pushed in their chairs and headed back to their accommodations for the night.

One tugged her by the hand with a mischievous glance when he asked which way she was going. She was tipsy on wine and

~~thinking~~ reflecting that getting lost and robbed in Paris might be the best thing that had ever happened to her. Maybe tomorrow she wouldn't jump off the bridge.

Maybe she'd give it a few more days to see what kinds of adventures she could turn up. The type of adventures about which she'd always wanted to write. But she didn't want to think about that, didn't want to think about her writing—burned—her possessions—gone—or that the only creative past she had was now in her head.

When they got to his room, she reached back to unclasp her bra while the soldier fumbled with it. Like Margaret starving in that Italian cottage when John would bring food, his mouth flew to her nipples, sucking and slurping, as she shimmied out of her underwear.

When she lifted her foot to his face for inspection, running her big toenail along his lips, he gave an awkward laugh and carefully lowered her leg.

Men were so confusing.

He yanked her thighs toward him as Margaret remembered she had forgotten the soldier's name.

What was it? Something overtly American. Like Robert, but not Robert. Chris? Something biblical—Mark or Matthew?

He entered her, and she smiled, feeling guilty over the name, but perhaps the time to ask had passed, so she called him nothing in her head, feeling his rhythm in her body, thinking the pillow behind her head was comfortable and how happy she would be to curl up in this bed when he was done and fall into a restful sleep for the first night in a long time—since she had left that train car, or since the fight with John, since he burned her writings, or maybe even since leaving Memphis or since meeting John at all.

As his eyes slammed closed and his face squished together in concentration, Margaret thought of her diaphragm, still at the Italian cottage in the bedside table, and then thought back to her period. When was it last? She counted back in her head.

Back, back, and back again.

He gasped a short intake of breath. "Oh God. Oh God." Followed by a satisfied sigh.

Oh God, she thought. *Oh God.*

He rolled off her and nuzzled into her neck.

I'm pregnant, she thought. She knew. *I'm months pregnant.*

The light turned out, and within fifteen seconds, No-name snored peacefully beside her, his arm slung lazily over her bare breast.

CHAPTER THIRTY-SIX

LEX

I feel his blood ping-ponging through my veins before I can even form the thought—

That asshole John is my father!

Yeah, there it is.

John and Margaret's offspring. All swirled together in a soup of the worst human qualities imaginable. This is who I came from. This is who I am. This is what I deserve.

I picture my father—er, Dennis—helping Cami while I accused her. Very John-like behavior. Very much like my mother. I am my mother's daughter. I am my father's legacy.

And now, here I am, not even saying goodbye to Cami, about to ask Grant to do me a huge favor, the one person I haven't yet alienated (again), though given my genetics, it must only be a matter of time.

I have to see John. I have to…avenge! I have to, something.

John, this man, this asshole—he's the easy target I've been seeking, the perfect vehicle for my anger.

My mother, not so much anymore. Even I can't help feeling sorry for her, and I'm sure once Cami reads the full story, she will be putty in my mother's hand, even from the grave, the tool junkyard in the sky. Even Dennis perhaps wasn't fair game. Cami definitely isn't, even if she is sleeping with my former father. But John.

John is easy.

Indefensible.

Yes.

I look at the kitchen clock. Before I can think, just as I did on that drive from my would-be graduation to Mexico City, I grab a few of my belongings and put them in a shopping bag, intending to hit the road to John.

John, my father.

I get a taxi with money from Cami's change jar, passing by the turn toward the house I used to think of as my parents', and my chest jumps, realizing this really might be the last time I see this road.

But it feels right. Feels right that I do not belong here. That I belong elsewhere, that I was conceived in Italy, the itch to leave built into my core by the water of those old Roman aqueducts. *Mamma mia…*

I replay the glances between my parents, my father's disinterest in me, my mother's shame during that last conversation, and now it all makes sense to me. I never belonged with them, and they knew it.

And behind those thoughts is more of my past. That little boy, Otto and me, feeling like my mother when she learned she would soon have me, and something I didn't expect: empathy. For her. Because in that moment, as she lay in bed with that nameless soldier, I know exactly how she felt.

I look at a shortcut that leads toward the highway, that leads to the airport. I could easily go there. I could leave Memphis, go toward John by myself. With only myself to worry about, only myself to disappoint.

But Grant's words ring in my ears—

You don't have to do everything alone, Lex.

The pinkie promise. I will never leave again without a goodbye. And I know I can't disappear on him again. I know too that I need a reason to come back. A reason stronger than my mother's writing, because I don't need her words anymore. I can fill in the gaps—her calling Dennis, him taking us, raising me as his own. It's so clear to me how the story ends, so clear I could write the rest myself.

I need a reason to make myself face Cami's illness. Because again, I know myself, and sometimes it's easier not to know. Not to ask how long, not to count down the days. To live in the mystery where everyone you once knew is both dead and alive, happy and unhappy.

When the taxi drops me at Grant's apartment, I hit buttons on the buzzer until someone lets me in, knock on his door.

But his mother answers.

"Oh, hi," I say.

"Hi," she says, equally embarrassed.

"Is…is Grant?"

"Lex?" He comes out past her, putting his hand delicately on her shoulder, the tender touches between a mother and child that I will never know. The ones I had pledged to have with the baby. *No, don't think about that.*

He leans in toward me conspiratorially, though we're not in high school anymore, whispering, "Did you forget some—"

"I'm going!"

"What?"

"To John's reading." I say, and he relaxes a little. "Do you want to come? It's fine if you don't," I say, already turning back to the elevator. "I'm fine by myself. I know you probably have—"

"Wait, Lex," he says, catching me by the hand. "Let me just grab my stuff."

"Okay," I say, hating how relieved my voice sounds.

I'm tapping my foot and pacing back and forth in front of the building, checking my watch, when he finally comes out, kissing his mother on the cheek as he says goodbye. She stares at us for a long time, as if she's worried I'm going to kidnap her son, before she heads to her own car.

I force my way into the driver's seat of Grant's Buick. "So you can read," I say, handing him the letter.

He nods and starts reading. I don't want him to realize where we're going. Not yet.

I drive through Memphis, a place I haven't driven since my mother died. And my foot presses too hard on the gas. Grant glances at me as he reads.

Finally, I pull up to a stop sign, the last before I can get on the highway. The guy driving the truck in front of me is gesturing to the car at the stop sign going the other way. A pair of steel balls hangs off the back of the souped-up truck, an object whose purpose I've never understood. The driver of the car is gesturing for the truck to go. The truck driver gestures again.

"Someone go!" I scream, laying on the horn.

I swear, if the South could get over its damn politeness, we'd all be better off.

"Switch," Grant says, making the motion with his hand that we would make in high school.

"What?" I say with my hand still on the horn.

"Yup, go."

"No!"

"I'm driving."

Before I can comment again, Grant is out of the car with the door open, standing in front of my door and blocking traffic.

"I can drive," I mutter to myself, unbuckling my seat belt slowly. "I know how to drive." Behind us, a car beeps twice, politely.

I slide into the passenger seat as Grant buckles his seat belt. He turns onto the highway.

"Wait," he says. And I can see him working out my plan. He's always been too trusting, I think. It's both his greatest and most dangerous quality.

"There's no way we're going to make it before the reading," he says, eyeing the clock on the dashboard with its hour and minute hands, not even a digital clock, adding an hour in his head for daylight saving since he hasn't changed it. He's been adding an hour half the year the entire time he's had this car.

He jerks the steering wheel and pulls off the highway onto the shoulder. Another cascade of honks follows us.

"Lex, no," he says, and I can already see that his left foot has started to bounce. He flips off the radio.

"I told you that before I left, we were going to fly!"

"It doesn't work like that. We can't just show up at the airport! There has to be a plane and fuel and clearance and runways and a flight plan."

"Call Bobby. You can figure it out."

He looks at me like when we were in high school and I told him that my mother had kicked me out again, confusion mixed with emotions he'll never understand.

"What she wrote, it could mean anything," he says.

"I know what it means."

"If it's true, if John is your father, it doesn't change anything," he says, finally looking at me. His leg stops jumping. "Your parents are still your parents."

I close my eyes because he's missing the point. "You would say that."

"What?"

"Never mind."

I cross my arms. There's no point in being a bitch to him (it's what John would do, I think, hating myself), but I can't help it.

"You would say that because your parents are perfect. You don't know what it's like. Not to have a family. Not to know who your parents even are! I spent my life feeling like I didn't know who they were figuratively, and now I find out I don't know who they are literally." My use of the word makes me stop, but it's the correct usage. Ugh, damn Valley girls have ruined an entire (useful) word for all of us.

Grant is staring ahead, thinking.

"Are you going to do this or not?"

He nods like he's being sentenced to death as a martyr and makes the switch motion with his hand again.

"Go that way and get off three exits from now," he says, taking out his phone.

"Hi, Bobby... Yeah, this is Grant. Last minute, I know, but..."

I'm smiling so much I don't bother to listen. Instead, I drive and fiddle with the radio, turned down quiet, trying to find a song that he would like when he gets off the phone. I eventually settle on a KISS song, which he starts to sing under his breath, drastically off-key, in between his first phone call and his second.

CHAPTER THIRTY-SEVEN

When we pull into the small airport and flight center where Grant started working and flying in high school, he stops talking and fidgeting completely. The eerie calm freaks me out more than the nervousness. I'm not afraid to fly with Grant. I never would be afraid to do anything with him, but I see us teetering on a line; if I made a wrong bet, he would get us safely on the ground but never fly again.

We pass the open hangar, full of the Memphis elite's private jets. Birds fly manically around the space, desperate to get out, their cries echoing against metal.

Grant walks down the airport hallway, standing straight as I imagine he did in the air force, past the flyers advertising introductory flights and plane tours of Memphis—"romantic sunset flights!"—and the pictures of old men (always men) smiling in cockpits with headsets. A full-size picture of a cockpit dominates one wall with the promise: "Your career path to this office begins here." For Grant, I suppose that was true.

I hurry to keep up as Grant scans a badge, and we go outside to the runway, where planes are parked in spaces with white lines like this is any normal mall parking lot.

I try to think of something funny to say as Grant circles the little plane like he's circling a rental car, appraising it. I hold my breath as he turns the propeller and looks at the laminated checklist he picked up in the office, as he checks the fuel gauge and steps up to the wing to make sure it's right.

He opens the door to the four-seater plane, the seats smaller than the ones in his Buick, and starts flicking switches and turning knobs and plugging things in.

A charter plane is at the end of the runway. The sound of its propeller makes Grant's head snap up, and he watches as it cruises into position, gets a galloping start on the tarmac, and takes off. He only looks away when it's out of sight.

He holds open the passenger door for me. I think about my mother, afraid to get on that first airplane with John, and wish I'd saved one of the nurse's pills for this moment. Grant could pretend I was nothing but a box of toilet paper.

My mother never would have imagined that her and John's child would be on her way to see him in this rickety old airplane.

I climb into the worn leather passenger seat, and Grant shuts the door behind me, the reason for his anxiety. I try to pretend I'm not there so he can too.

The window is cracked open, just like it was in his Buick, and there's a cup holder at my feet. We can pretend we're driving. He climbs into the pilot seat and puts on his seat belt and headset, motioning for me to do the same. He adjusts my mouthpiece in front of my lips and says, "Test it."

"Alpha one niner, niner, Lex here, over." I smile.

He doesn't.

He holds what I guess is the steering wheel and pulls it back and side to side while mine does the same, hitting my knees and making something on the wings go up and down.

"You're too tall," he says with a smile, the first smile I've seen from him today.

He helps me move my seat, and I squeeze into a smaller area so he can maneuver.

His knee starts tapping again as he finishes the preflight checklist and flips more switches. I wonder how different this plane is from the one he flew in the air force. I wonder if he lost someone, if he pondered what it would be like to kill, but now isn't the right time to ask.

Instead, I look ahead while he requests permission for takeoff from the control tower, using the plane call sign and repeating everything back like the professional he is. Ahead of me is a small sticker that says CARBON MONOXIDE TESTER with a skull. It says "replace after" with a date written sometime in 2017. I decide not to bring this up.

A voice comes through our headsets clearing us for takeoff.

"You sure about this?" Grant says.

I nod.

"All right, here we go." He closes his eyes and breathes out long and slow, like I imagine they teach you in meditation.

We start moving, the propeller whirling, taking us to the end of the runway. A family on the side of the grass is watching us, a little girl sitting on her father's shoulders, waiting for the small plane to take off. Maybe a future pilot in the making, I think with a smile.

Grant squares his shoulders and speaks again into the headset. Soon the plane is going, faster and faster, vibrating more and more. The windows rattle on their unsealed hinges, and my seat shakes. His eyes focus on the runway, which is disappearing in front of us. This is the moment, I think, the moment I'll know if I overplayed my hand, like Cami is perhaps fearing now.

The plane lifts off, and my stomach goes to my throat like I'm on a roller coaster. We're lifting up and up and up past the trees and a forest and the highway we just drove on, heading toward John. I don't look at any of that, though. I'm looking at Grant, and he's smiling broadly, showing his teeth, as if he can't believe we're doing this, the look he had in childhood when he would talk about flying. I relax.

A beeping starts, high and fast, and my eyes dart around, trying to figure out where the sound is coming from in the small space.

Grant laughs. "It's okay. We're approaching altitude."

"Is that what you're doing with the steering wheel?" I say as he pulls it out.

He laughs, like this is the funniest thing he's ever heard. If only I was always this funny.

"*Yoke*, Lex. It's the yoke." He shakes his head and laughs to himself. "Steering wheel."

My brain fills in the entry from the *Dictionary of Word Origins*, realizing that we must have had this conversation before.

yoke, Old English noun *geoc*, Dutch *juk*, Latin *iugum* meaning "to join." Indo-European form derived from base *jug-*, *jeug*, *joug*, which also produced Sanskrit *yoga*, meaning "union," acquired by English via Hindi, which denotes "union with the universal spirit."

yolk, see *yellow*.

He explains the steering wheel-yoke. He takes his hands off the controls, like he's a biker showing off—"Look, Mom, no hands!"

He talks me through what he's doing, as I imagined he would with anyone who would listen in the air force, as I remember him doing in high school, carrying around guides on flight equipment and having me quiz him.

"Beep, beep. Traffic, beep, beep. Climb, climb," a robotic voice tells us.

He explains altitude. "We've got to go up," he says, and we do, rising like a magician levitating. "Look," he says a second later, pointing out the window where another plane is passing below us. We're above the clouds, looking down on the world, and when he tells me to take the controls, I laugh and agree.

"Pull back," he says, guiding his own yoke.

"It's like a video game," I say.

"Yeah, except that you can kill yourself and there are no game restarts." He laughs when he says it, though, and so do I.

As much as I hate John, I have to thank him for this.

CHAPTER THIRTY-EIGHT

After a stop to refuel and two more hours of flying, we get to Providence with just enough time to borrow a truck from the airport and grab Subway sandwiches.

As Grant drives toward the campus where John will give his reading, it's my turn to be nervous. I can feel my leg bouncing much like his was earlier. Is it something I learned from him or that he learned from me?

"I've never understood the smart car," he says as he speeds past one, trying to distract me. "It's not even a car. It's like two motorcycles with a bench between them."

The size of most cars in Bali, I think.

We pull up to the campus bookstore, and Grant follows me as I slip inside and find seats in the back. The room is crowded with young, attractive college students holding copies of John's newly released collection. A man whom I assume is my father holds court at the front. I search his face, trying to find something familiar, the curve of my eyes or the flatness of my nose, the shape of my lips. His brown eyes lock with my brown eyes.

"He's looking at me."

Grant follows my gaze. "Don't be paranoid."

"I'm not paranoid. I'm a-nnoyed," I say.

John starts making his rounds at the front of the room,

looking similar to the picture I saw online. Even in his sixties, his hair is still mostly black. He's trim, moving through the room as if he truly has made a deal with the devil to keep himself frozen in time, as my mother suggested. He shakes hands with an older man and an older woman. A few young blonds take turns hugging him. It makes me want to kick him in the balls, like I did once while traveling in India when a man approached me and grabbed my ass. He crumpled to the ground. I want to feel the same satisfying power now.

You don't seduce my mother and get away with it! I think, feeling high and mighty for once.

But did he seduce her? I'm not sure.

All I know is that I can be angry with him—this man whose sperm made me—and that for once, that anger is completely justified. Unassailable.

"I'm going to talk to him. I'm going to demand that he tell me the truth." I rock in my seat like I'm going to get up but then fall back down. "I'm going." I say, really getting up this time.

"Just wait," Grant says, pulling me down by the arm. "Wait until after. You can talk to him more then." He lays his hand on my shoulder, encouraging me to stay in my seat, as if he's afraid I'll run away if he doesn't. The same way he's been hovering since I came to Memphis, the gentle encouragement to stay, stay, stay.

Then John is at the podium. This man, my real (?) father, is clearing his throat in a way that seems so familiar, is adjusting his glasses, is brushing back a loose strand of too-long hair that curls at the end. The gesture reminds me of something from my childhood.

"Thank you," he begins. "I have a habit of thinking each of these collections will be my last, that each of these tours will be the last before I give up and move to some remote cottage where none of you can find me and adopt a few dogs."

The girls erupt in giggles.

"But here I am, and here you are again, and for that, I thank you. For this collection, my editor—she's in the audience there…" A woman stands, waves twice to applause, and sits back down. Is that The Editor, I wonder?

"She asked me to revisit some of the stories that have been trapped in drawers for many, many years. And not even computer files, like some of you may think, but real drawers, stories that were typed on a real typewriter. Do you know what that is, Beth?" He winks at someone in the front row.

"Shall we begin the reading, then?"

There's some clapping and cheering, and then he does.

"This is a story I began writing decades ago, about a girl I once knew, who seduced a neighborhood boy and suffered the consequences."

Ophelia spent her life ready for the final judgment. Each day, she rose by herself in a tiny cabin built by men she didn't know. She studied her mother's Bible, though it didn't do her any good. She made herself breakfast. She read. She watched for the mailman, her only human connection, who brought the cash her father sent at random intervals and without a return address. She walked through the fields in the Texas heat, the tall rows of corn her neighbors grew, disappeared in the maze until she got lost and tired enough to curl up in the sweater she tied around her shoulders and fall asleep.

She was sure she would meet her judgment maker in those stalks. So far, she had met only a cow. The acres spanned for miles in all directions.

She was waiting for either a thumbs-up or thumbs-down from the universe, because even though she was young—either fifteen or sixteen, she could never be sure, since she didn't have a birth certificate—she had a secret.

She had allowed her mother to wander off into these same stalks during tornado season. She hadn't rung the bell when she heard the sirens on the radio. She simply grabbed the supplies she always did, but this time, she walked into the cellar with Gracie the cat and bolted the door behind them. They moved to the back, where they couldn't hear pounding on the cellar door, and listened to the wind dismantling the house's roof.

And when she woke up and came into the light, there was no sign of her mother, and there hadn't been in the six months since.

She was ready for a sign, one way or another, so she could figure out what to do next.

That was when she met Jude.

My breath catches in my chest. He's reading my mother's story!

"That's my mother's!" I whisper to Grant.

"What?"

"She wrote that. He's lying!"

A woman in front of us turns around to shush us.

I've never heard a story written by my mother that wasn't her own, though maybe this, too, is more than fiction, and as much as I would like to listen fully, I can't. I'm too full of rage at John. For stealing my mother's work, for not sending it off to his publishing friends like he said he would, for burning her writing, for burning her soul. For making her think she was just like Ophelia, a lonely girl seducing Jude in a maze, only to kiss him near a lake and awaken the serpents, who drag her underwater and down to hell. Was it this story that first made my mother want to sink like Ophelia, down to a darker unknown, one she thought she deserved?

One I thought she deserved too. Once.

And all this from the man who made me. For the first time, maybe, I feel myself missing Dennis. Even after he torpedoed my credit, even with his lies, I know that despite not loving me as much as he did her, he *did* love her. Something I will never say about the man in front of us.

When Ophelia's soul dies in hell, the story is mercifully over, and the audience applauds.

"And thank you," John says now, with mock humility and no hint of what he's hiding. Jude isn't an angel, like the story says. I agree with my mother: Jude is the true villain. John would never know that, though, and I never want him to.

"Now for a poem," he continues.

"Come on," I say in Grant's ear before I bolt out of the room. I'm shaking, and I dive into the truck, twisting the key, barely waiting for Grant to shut the door behind him before I'm off. I can't listen to another word from John.

CHAPTER THIRTY-NINE

I pull into the parking lot of the first bar I see, head inside, and immediately order two shots of tequila. And no, I do not care what type.

Grant walks in slowly and takes a seat next to me at the bar.

"Two more, please," he says, knowing the two I ordered are for me.

I throw one back.

"Lex, are you sure you don't want to talk to him?"

I take the next shot, and Grant pushes me the first one of his, then on second thought pushes them both toward me.

"You can have it," he says. "Do you want your pilot anxious and hungover?"

He has a point. I swallow another, and he orders a beer.

"No, I don't want to talk to him. And do you know why?"

I can feel the drink snaking through my veins like my mother's serpents, pulling that girl under the water into hell. This liquid dulls what I want to dull, quiets that voice inside my head, banishes the baby's scrunched-up face. Could I see John even in that face? The shape of his eyes, perhaps, plucked from my DNA and combined with Otto's into something new, something fleeting?

I take the fourth shot.

"Because he doesn't deserve it. He's terrible." I point at myself too violently. "He doesn't deserve to know me."

Grant looks at me skeptically. He leans forward to sip the overflowing foam off the top of his beer.

"Do you have burgers here?" he asks the bartender.

"Yeah, sweetie. You want one?"

"Yeah, we're going to need a few."

"I'm not hungry," I say.

We sit together, him watching me drink with amused eyes.

"What would you do if I wasn't here?" he asks.

I know he wants me to say that I wouldn't have been able to come without him. But I can't. I would have come by myself. I would have been fine. I would have come to this same bar and found another guy on a barstool, alone, and figured out what words he used when he came. I can be on my own. Like Ophelia from the story, alone without her mother in that cabin, I know how to take care of myself, to survive.

But it's those times you're alone when the men like Jude seem to enter your life. And isn't it better to fill that spot of your own accord?

I'm not sure I want to be alone anymore. Even if I have all the words in the world. Even if I have my passions. Even alone with fresh languages and unexplored cities and unsuspecting strangers.

"You're looking at it," I say.

He frowns. "I worry about you."

"You don't need to worry about me. I can handle myself."

"That's why I worry." He motions to the bartender for another shot, who is already ready with the bottle. "Why did you come back, really?"

"No fair!" I say, swallowing it. "You can't ask truth questions now!"

I think of all those Truth or Dare sessions on Cami's roof. We never were very interested in dares. Instead, it'd be truth, truth, and truth again, just an excuse to tell someone else the feelings we had never told anyone before, to tell the only person worth telling. Everything is easier if you think someone is making you do it.

Like my mother perfecting that stolen story.

Like Grant flying us here.

Like me coming back to Memphis.

Like telling Grant the truth now.

He orders a water from the bartender. "Drink."

I take a sip and a breath.

"Sidney Henry," I slur back at him, telling myself

truth,

   truth,

      truth.

Grant's brow crinkles.

"Sidney, your grandfather?"

"No." I swallow the urge to cry. I've never said out loud before the name I intended for the baby. Otto or not, I knew from the first test that I was going to name him for my grandfather, the nicest man in my family. The only…legitimate…grandfather, I realize, that I knew.

"There was a baby," I say, and Grant's face immediately softens. His hand goes to my back and starts to rub it. "It… He…died."

"Lex, I'm so sorry."

I start to cry now; I can't help it. I cry all the tears I've put off since Otto left the hospital. I don't tell Grant about Otto, though, because he's nothing.

He doesn't matter.

"I lost him," I say, before realizing how nonsensical that language sounds. Lost him—where? At the mall? Why do people always say that when they mean "died"? It makes me think of Cami, and I start chuckling to myself, imagining *The Dictionary of Word Origins* resting on my bedside table at her house, as it did so many years ago. In some ways, it's as if no time has passed, but it has. Time and people and memories, all victim to some unknown force. Some unknown test Jude has set for all of us.

That bastard.

I smile, remembering my mother's joke.

Hamburgers materialize, along with the bartender, who hovers and looks concerned. "She's fine," Grant assures her, and reaches for the mustard I'll want for my fries.

When I stop crying, I tell him the whole story, starting in Mexico, then to Ecuador, to India, to Bali and more, all the places I've been, telling him the funny parts and telling the sad parts as if they are the funniest, forgetting what I've said and needing to double back.

Eventually, we finish and pay, and he takes us back to some motel he's managed to book using his newfangled phone. As he's shutting the door, I walk over and hug him.

"I love you," I say, falling into his arms, almost falling over. Really meaning it.

"I love you too, Lex." He kisses me on the forehead.

"Let's lie down," he says, leading me over to one of the double beds.

"Wait." I pull him toward me and put my lips on his, kissing him with all the passion I can summon.

He flinches, then stays completely still. I jerk away, realizing what I'm doing.

It's not the first time I've kissed him, and it brings me back to that time. My first kiss. His first kiss. Us together after camp when we had just met. When we hadn't yet figured out we were friends, when I didn't know how to be friends with a boy, or friends with anyone, and maybe he wasn't sure either. I don't remember who did it—probably me—but we both pulled away after the first second.

"Ew!" he said then, and I said it back, and then we laughed and decided to be friends forever.

"Ew!" I say now, laughing to myself, laughing at myself in the memory, and his face looks relieved at my reaction. *Cami, another thing you were wrong about!* I pat him on the chest. "Sorry, sorry."

"It's all right."

If only Jude's test for Ophelia were that easy. If only John's test for my mother were that easy. If only she had listened to Cami. If only, if only, if only.

But then I wouldn't be here.

If only there were no Otto and no Bali and my mother didn't die and we got along, but then there would be no Sidney Henry, however briefly he was on this earth. Then I wouldn't know that I wanted someone all my own. I would be on my own, or I wouldn't exist at all, still lurking in the lake with Jude, waiting for an unsuspecting Ophelia to stumble upon us in her search for damnation.

So where does that leave me?

I fall into bed with my shoes on.

CHAPTER FORTY

The next day, I wake up, head pounding. The last thing I remember is eating a hamburger that Grant demanded contain double bacon. I have a feeling it didn't taste as good on the way back up, but that has been thankfully blocked from my memory.

On the way to the airport today, there are hardly any preflight jitters. Grant goes back and forth with someone about our altitude or something, humming to himself as we fly, but I can't really pay attention. Each jerk of the little plane makes me feel like I'm going to barf, and this is exactly the wrong place to barf up the remainder of the hamburger and an unknown number of tequila shots. More than five, I'm sure. Ugh.

I sleep in Grant's Buick on the way back to Cami's house, thinking, *I have to know. I have to know the truth. About everything.* I sleep in the way you can in cars when you're a kid, half asleep, half listening to Grant singing along to the radio, my mind still turning as much as my stomach.

When I knock tentatively at Cami's door, wondering again if I belong there, she says, "Come in, Lex." Her preparedness makes me wonder if Grant called to warn her.

Paranoid. That I remember from last night. She probably saw his Buick on the street.

Cami sits at the dining table with her coffee, like she did the first morning she told me about my mother's writings. As they were then, the envelopes are spread in front of her, but this time, they're open. A full wineglass and an empty bottle keep vigil next to her, like she's been sitting here all last night, memorizing her friend's words.

"Where were you?" she asks me, not meeting my eye.

"Give me the last envelopes, Cami."

"Lex, honey."

"Seriously, I need them." She looks down at the envelope in front of her that's still sealed. "Give me them!" I say too loudly, and my voice cracks at the end.

Cami hands me another one of my mother's envelopes, and I tear it open and read.

MARGARET

She took the money the American soldier gave her, not bothering to think too hard about whether he thought she was a prostitute or just in need to money. Both true in their own ways.

She sat on her bridge, thinking of motherhood, all the ends it meant for her. She thought of the little almond in her stomach. It was nothing. She could get rid of it, but she didn't have the money. Perhaps if she asked the soldier for it? She wouldn't know how to contact him, though.

Everything went to complete shit the second she began planning her life. Did she regret it? This trip? John? Everything?

~~Yes~~.

~~No~~.

~~Yes~~.

~~No.~~

The only thing she could be sure of was this—writing helped. So she kept doing it.

Her limbo on the bridge could go on forever, like picking the petals off a dandelion when she was a young girl on the playground, before school, before Dennis, before Cami even, when her father had a job and her mother stayed home and her parents were happy.

On the bridge, she admitted with a sinking feeling that she wanted it. The almond was an excuse to start over.

Margaret had already decided it was a she, and that she could be anything. The girl could become everything her mother couldn't. Margaret would help her, guide her, and she'd never make the same mistakes her mother had. This child would live up to her full potential. She'd be grateful for all she had. She'd live with a lightness Margaret never had. The girl would be free.

No—to do that, she would be better off without Margaret. She was no teacher. Was there one thing in her life she could refrain from destroying?

Probably not.

Margaret wished the girl could suck out the little wisdom, her mother's few good traits, and leave the body a crumpled shell to be tossed over the bridge from which she once planned to jump.

If only they weren't linked, so the girl could continue here and Margaret could leave.

Wish, wish, wish.

She headed to Notre Dame to ask for forgiveness. She looked at the stained glass, ~~went~~ shuffled to the front, where Christmas decorations were wedged everywhere. Christmastide in Europe.

Dickens-like. She watched a service. One of the altar boys picked a piece of communion bread off the floor, to stares from the priest, and it made Margaret realize she was hungry.

She thought about calling John—the girl's father, the scoundrel—considered heading back to that house in Italy to see if he was still there. And if he was, if he was still there alone.

But instead, she spent a few more days lolling around, frittering away the money the soldier had given her until she was on her last dime. Drunk on two glasses of wine, a barf-induced empty stomach, and adrenaline, she stumbled to the phone and dialed collect, talked to the operator, waited for the ring, prayed no one else would pick up.

Something she expected to believe more with each hour: You can't know if you're in love or not when you're in the thick of it. Like that imbecilic saying, you can't know how much someone means to you until you lose them. And all of a sudden, she knew.

When she heard a familiar voice at the other end of the phone, she broke down sobbing. "Dennis?" she croaked. "I'm sorry, please forgive me."

"I'll take care of everything. Just come home," he said. He offered no details, and she didn't ask for them.

As she followed his instructions, traveling back to Memphis, she thought about him on the baseball field when she'd left with John, standing there dumbfounded, thought of him drinking coffee and smiling at her over the mug, thought of him watching her carefully at church to see how she would react to what the pastor was saying.

She didn't deserve him.

She saw the wisdom of her mother's words. Who had she been

the last year? It was like she'd been in a movie theater back in
Memphis with Cami, watching the protagonist live her life and
make all her mistakes and choices, and now she was walking out
of the theater into the light, into her real life.

As in *Emma*, she had lived twenty-one (less) years in the world
with very little to distress or vex her. Or so it seemed now, and
here it was all at once.

You know what it was?

All Margaret's mistakes had just gotten saved up. She'd saved
them up her whole childhood, until this year, and then she'd used
them all at once. Like a cat, Margaret had nine lives, and now
she'd used all but one.

And the flight home would be the end of Margaret Green.
Soon she would be someone else entirely. Margaret Henry, hardware princess. Her mother would be proud.

That new Margaret had to thank John—her Jude—for this
test, for what it proved to her. The ashes of her writing bestowed a
rare chance: to rewrite her story, to live twice, as Natalie Goldberg
said in *Writing Down the Bones* (the book Margaret dropped in
the book return slot on the way to the Memphis airport with
John).

Goldberg wrote: "Writers live twice. They go along with their
regular life, are as fast as anyone in the grocery store, crossing
the street, getting dressed for work in the morning. But there's
another part of them that they have been training. The one that
lives everything a second time. That sits down and sees their life
again and goes over it. Looks at texture and details."

Margaret had been good at that first part. Living as fast, if
not faster, than those around her. John had given her a chance to

do the second. And when she did, she saw someone who failed almost every test put in front of her.

Now she would be the perfect wife. Or she would try anyway. In a few weeks, it would be a new decade, and Margaret would be a new person. She would trust Dennis, follow him, her savior, who had whisked her back to Memphis. Her and the almond. She didn't deserve the girl either.

She pictured them together in that house by Overton Park. Maybe the girl wouldn't look like the man she'd think of as her father, but she would be his. She'd have his gentle way.

And Margaret would stay as far away from her as possible. She would save the girl from her mother. She would do nothing. As much nothing as she could do.

CHAPTER FORTY-ONE

LEX

"Give me the rest," I say, my hand already out, mind thundering with all the words about how I wanted my own baby but also the guilt that I felt the same as she did.

Unsure.

Afraid.

Ruinous.

"There aren't any more," Cami says.

"What?"

"That's the last one."

"No, it's not."

"It is." Cami looks at me like she might start crying, both of us on the verge of tears, surrounded by my mother's words, my mother's ghost. Her ability to traumatize us even from the grave seems unparalleled. "There aren't any more."

I sit back down in the chair and stare off into space.

Can I hold my mother's thoughts in the journal against her? That she couldn't dive headfirst into motherhood? That she lied? That she took advantage of someone she loved?

I am my mother's daughter, I think.

"I'm just like her," I say, my head in my hands. And I hated her—that's easier, less complicated to believe than any alternatives. Absolutes are easier. *I hate her and I hate myself,* I think.

But I also loved her.

But I also understand her better than I ever have.

"No, you're not."

"I am, Cami! Why can't you see that? I push everyone away. I say the wrong things. I lie." So many lies, I think, that she doesn't even know about, all the people in all the cities with their too-eager faces as I spouted lies about who I was. "I hurt people, Cami. I take advantage of people. I use people."

She moves to sit next to me but lets me continue, crying: "Look at you. All I've done my whole life is take, take, take from you, be a deadweight, a burden, and now you're sick, and I wouldn't even have been here. I wouldn't even have known."

"You were never a deadweight to me, honey."

I take a breath that sounds like I've come up for air and need oxygen before I plunge down again.

"After my father died, I got myself tested," she says. "I had it too. Lynch syndrome. The gene mutation that led to the painful cancers that whittled away my father. And I knew I would never have kids. I didn't want to make anyone else live through what he lived through, what I'll live through."

I start crying harder.

"You gave me the chance I never thought I would have. To be a mother, in my own way. You and your mother gave me that chance. I was just glad she was willing to share you."

"She wasn't willing to share me," I bawl. "She was trying to get rid of me!"

"She did her best. Both your parents did. She was very sick, sweetie."

"What?"

"Why do you think you came to stay with me that first time in Florida?" Cami says.

"Because my parents didn't want me around in the summer, like sending me to summer camp."

"I know you don't remember this, but you were with me for almost a year."

"No, I wasn't."

"You were. It's funny how memory works." She brushes a hair away from the stickiness of my tears. "Especially when we're young."

"I didn't go to school."

"I homeschooled you."

I remember us playing school and it not being terrible, the summer stretching endlessly, aided by the Florida heat.

"Your mom was in a hospital. That was her first big breakdown that we knew about. That was when they finally got her on some medication. Your father couldn't take care of you and the store and her. And I was happy to borrow you."

"He wasn't my father. John's my father, and we're the reason. We did it. He and I. Father-daughter duo. And even Dennis, at the end. We're all the reason why she was in the garage that day."

"You read the letters. Your mother had been thinking about taking her own life for a long time. As far as I know, since Italy. It wasn't your fault. It wasn't your father's fault."

She doesn't say whether she means Dennis or John. And before I can ask, she continues: "How do you think I found you, the day your mother died?"

Cami knowledge is what I'd always thought.

"She called me, but I wasn't home. It went to my machine. I called the police and ran over there as soon as I heard the message, but for her, it was too late. She was already dead. I've thought so many times about what might have happened if I hadn't gone out for lunch that day. But nothing any of us said could have changed it.

"I know it's hard to admit, Mamacita, but everything isn't about you, and that's good. That's why I gave you these envelopes."

I tell myself to be mad at Cami, even though I'm not, even though I'm leaning toward her with my arms outstretched.

"I know. You're right. Thank you."

I hug her.

"I'm sorry I didn't tell you I was sick," Cami says. "I didn't want to put any more burdens on you."

"It's okay. And if he makes you happy, that's okay too. That's okay with me."

"What?" Cami pulls away. "What are you talking about?"

"You and my… Dennis," I say, since I don't know what else to call him.

"Honey, your father and I aren't together. We're friends. We've been friends for a long time. He's the oldest friend I have, actually."

She laughs as if she's just realizing it now. "When my father died, your mother was still in Europe. I was devastated. But Dennis came. We were suffering the same loss of your mother, and he came and he helped and he cleaned our apartment top to bottom and did all the dishes in the sink and made me eat.

I know he's made mistakes with you—both your parents did. Sometimes he was blinded by how much he loved your mother, but he has that quiet way about him, of helping without you needing to ask, of showing you exactly how he feels. I know how much you like words, Mamacita, but sometimes you have to listen for what people say through their actions."

I stare at her, wanting to ask the question from yesterday, wanting to ask how long Cami has left on this earth. Wanting to ask her so many things I don't have the words for.

"No one's perfect, Lex. Not even me. I've done plenty of things I regret. For one"—she took a breath—"I lied to you about being married. I left him at the altar and didn't tell him about my illness, why I didn't want to have kids, any of it. I guess I wanted to be normal for once. He has four kids now, I'm pretty sure."

I can't think of anything to say, so I only stare at her, my face softening.

"And you don't have to be perfect either," she continues. "We all still love you."

She hugs me again.

"Come on, let's have some brunch," she says. Food always seems to be the solution when you don't know what to say.

She puts bacon in a pan and cracks eggs into a bowl. I cook the scrambled eggs while Cami reads the last letter. After, we're both quiet. The first thing she says, maybe in light of her new religious streak, is a prayer for my mother.

"I forgive you, Margaret," she says to the sky.

She should be saying that to the floor, I think out of habit, then immediately regret it. I think of that naive girl on the base-ball bleachers, watching the man she wasn't sure she wanted to marry, imagining her future. I think of her smoking alone on that bridge in Paris, of her cooking that terrible meal and watching the pages ripped from her notebook. For the first time in my life, I dare to ask the question of my mother—was she doing her best?

"What happened when my mother did come back?" I ask Cami. "Why didn't you ever talk about what happened?"

"I didn't talk to her or to your father for the few years I was traveling. I wanted to see everything. I wanted to see all the places my father couldn't see while I still could. And when I came back to Memphis, she was here with Dennis. Here with you, only a toddler. As soon as we saw each other, it was like not a day had passed. But the past was too painful to relive. We looked forward. You helped bring us together again. I was so honored that they waited for me to come back and made me your godmother. We celebrated it right along with your third birthday."

Cami, Camila—in Roman times, she was a warrior, so fast that blades of grass turned to ash under her feet, so invincible that as a baby, she survived being tied to a spear and hurled over a raging river. It's a myth that holds true for us both.

CHAPTER FORTY-TWO

Once Cami and I talked and cried and drank and talked and cried until she finally had to go take a bath in the bathroom Dennis had put back together while Grant and I were finding John, I nap. Then I sit at the table alone, staring at my mother's envelopes, puzzling over what they mean, reading and rereading her words.

My mind is full of memories of her. Her and the man I thought was my father.

Were they in love?

I asked Cami. She said yes.

I don't know why I care, even sitting here, listening to "Love Me Tender" on repeat. It's a melody I can't avoid, like it's in my blood. The part of my mother's heart that loved Dennis, still there, still inside me, perking up at the tune of this song.

I think of Dennis. Taking on a baby who wasn't his. Accepting my mother back. I think of him shielding me, protecting me in his own way, from my mother's moods, calming her. My mind replays the snubs, but now I wonder, were they snubs, or were they protection? I've always thought I was the one who saw my mother at her worst. But maybe that's not true.

I think of my mother, always an arm's length from me, and I wonder if that wasn't a type of protection too, a misguided type of protection. I know what it's like to be afraid of yourself, to be afraid of what you can do. I think of the Margaret Green on that bridge, tormented by Jude from the story, the last piece of my mother's writing that John eventually stole. Was that boy—that devil she first thought of as an angel—with her that day when she ran after me on the way to Cami's? Was he telling her lies about herself? Was he whispering to her then?

These things, I'll never know.

No one will.

But the image I can't get out of my mind is of my mother in Notre Dame, praying to be a new woman. And after countless readings, I notice something.

"Cami!" I yell. "Cami!"

She rushes out of her bedroom, quickly enough to make me feel guilty, her hair witchlike from her nap, taken when it was still drying out of its braid. "What—what's wrong?"

"Listen to this," I say, reading from my mother's last entry. "In a few weeks, it will be a new decade, and I will be a new me."

"So?"

"A new decade. But that can't be right. I wasn't born until 1991."

Cami comes up behind me to look at the letter, studying it.

"Maybe she was struggling and got confused?" Cami shrugs.

But I can't get it out of my mind.

CHAPTER FORTY-THREE

The doorbell rings.

I go to the door, unsure what to say to whoever it is. I'm not ready to see Dennis, and I don't want to see anyone else in this town.

Before I even open it, I feel Grant's presence on the other side of the door, the porch quaking under his tapping foot. I don't even want to see him.

The memories of last night have come back to taunt me: the thought of standing on my tiptoes to kiss him and his body frozen like a statue fills me with embarrassment.

Not that I even wanted him to kiss me back. I just don't want to have kissed him in the first place. It was like I was back in Ecuador or Bali or India, reaching out for whomever seemed closest to avoid thinking. It's a habit I'd like to stop, and one I'd never like to engage in with Grant.

Surely he remembers the kiss, has remembered the entire time. But he just blurts out, "My mother asked me to come pick you up."

"Why?" My chest seizes with panic over whatever I've done wrong. Does she know about the kiss? Does she know about my many years of corrupting her son? I've been waiting for a call from her my entire life, truthfully. Will she tell me to leave them in peace? That feeling makes me panic even more, because for the first time, I realize....

I don't want to leave.

I don't want to leave Cami. I don't want to leave Grant.

Grant simply shrugs, like this is the most normal request in the world. He's too trusting. It makes me think of all those girls leading him by the hand around school, and my stomach turns with disgust.

I look behind me to where Cami sits at the table, crying to herself.

"Only if Cami can come."

He shrugs again.

No one talks in the car. Grant and I bounce our legs with nervousness, and Cami and I hold hands in the back seat, like we're a young couple being chauffeured.

When we arrive at Grant's parents' house, we go into the living room, where Grant's mother, his father, and my (former) father all sit on the couch together with two armchairs across from them.

Grant looks at me in panic, and I look back at him, stifling the urge to say *I told you you're too trusting!*

"What is this, an intervention?" I say instead.

"Lex, sit down," Dennis says to me.

"Your days of telling me what to do are over," I spit back at him out of habit before immediately feeling bad about it.

"Lex," he says in that singsong way, like I'm being difficult, that way that's so fatherly.

"Don't do that." I start tearing up. "I know you're not my father."

He steps back as if I've cut him.

"Lex, I am your father."

"I read Mom's journal. I know the truth," I tell him, bringing back memories of fighting with my mother in this same calm, controlled voice that has always seemed so unlike my own. Grant stands next to me, too stunned to say anything. Cami lingers behind us, no one surprised at her presence.

"SIT DOWN! NOW!" Grant's mother says, reminding me where we are. Shocked by the outburst, Grant and I sit down, and Cami stands behind me.

I've never seen either of my parents talk to Grant's parents. I didn't even know they knew each other.

"We have something to tell y'all. The both of you," Grant's mother begins.

Dennis and Grant's mother both look at his father, and he clears his throat, like he does before he sings. Their motions are so choreographed, I wonder how long this little intervention took to plan.

Grant's father looks at him as he begins.

"I knew I was in love with your mother the second I saw her picture," he starts.

I immediately roll my eyes, and Cami kicks me lightly on the shin.

"Ouch!" I say.

"Be quiet," Dennis says.

I am quiet.

"I was saying," Grant's father continues, and Dennis looks at his shoes, "I first saw your mother when we were graduate students at Memphis State. She was a transfer student from way out in California, and I remember how they would publish the bios and photos of the new students. I opened up that month's magazine, and I saw your mother's picture, and I knew." He snaps his fingers. "Like that."

His parents grab hands, and Dennis scoots two inches away from them on the couch, obviously uncomfortable to be sitting so close.

"Later that year, I asked her to marry me, and she did me the honor of saying yes."

He looks at his wife, and she speaks: "But we were older. We had both given up on love, or so we thought. And when we got married, when we figured out that a family was a possibility, we wanted it desperately."

"But we had some issues," his father jumps in.

"As you know," his mother says, and as if on cue, all eyes go to the ten-seater dining room table.

I feel a glimmer of the panic Grant must have experienced in that cockpit. The table. That seems like its own kind of incredible pressure. How parents torture their children is so unique, I realize, like the many languages on earth.

"We weren't sure what to do about it," Grant's father says. "But we knew we had to pray. And that's when we joined the church. Dennis's father was the welcome leader then, and he was so helpful to us. He and Dennis and Dennis's mother."

Dennis continues to look at his shoes, refusing to meet anyone's eyes.

"And then, like a miracle, a solution came."

My mind starts turning, putting the pieces together, realizing what's happening, realizing the possibilities of this admission, but Grant only stares at his parents with a naive smile. Too trusting.

Always too trusting. Why have I never said anything about that before? Oh, I have.

"Dennis knew a woman who wanted someone to adopt her baby. A woman he loved. A woman who loved him. We trusted her."

"Your mother," says Grant's mother to me.

The line about my mother starting a new decade with good intentions enters my mind. The missing year.

Grant looks on, still not understanding. Cami's hand goes to her mouth. "*Dios mío*," she whispers.

"She didn't want anyone to know. She was embarrassed was all, and I understood. She wanted to be able to come back home on her own terms and marry Dennis," Grant's mother says. "I got to know her well then. We spent months together in a house on the outskirts of Memphis, since no one knew she was back yet, and we told everyone at church I was having a difficult pregnancy."

"I helped deliver you," she says to Grant. "And you were my baby from the first moment I saw you. You were our son."

"So?" I say, not completely understanding again. "What then?"

"After," Dennis—my father?—jumps in, "your mother came home and told everyone she had just arrived. We dated for as long as we could stand, got married, and she got pregnant with you soon after. And we had you."

"So we're…" I start. "Cousins?"

"Siblings," Grant's mother says now.

"Half," my father corrects.

I look at Grant, searching his face for a reaction, but he won't meet my eyes. In a second, he's up. He's out the door. He's diving into his Buick.

"Grant, wait!" I say, running after him.

But by the time I get out the door, the Buick is squealing down the street, faster than I've ever seen it go, and I stand there, watching. Watching him leave me again.

"Let him cool off," Grant's father says. He's not his biological father, but it's impossible to describe him any other way.

My own father comes up behind us, and all three of us stand with our hands in our pockets, watching the driveway from which Grant has disappeared, as if he might materialize again.

"Let's grab a cup of coffee," my father says.

I nod, still bewildered by this new information, and follow him, kicking stones, down the sidewalk to a coffee shop I've never been to, where he sits down. I expect him to order a coffee, as I read about him doing at the Arcade when my mother worked there, but instead he orders green tea.

In response to my expression, he defends himself, nervously saying, "I mean, I like coffee. I love it. I like the smell, the taste. It just doesn't agree with me anymore." He's still talking and rubbing his stomach when the waitress comes to bring our drinks.

"How's your knee?" I offer, remembering the limp he had last time I saw him.

"Oh, it's okay. I tried physical therapy, but it's just expensive stretching."

I take a sip of my coffee, wishing it had two shots of bourbon. He clears his throat.

"Look, Alexan—Lex. I know I wasn't…the father I should've been." He looks down at his hands in his lap, fiddling with the bitten-down cuticles. "Your mother, she was all I could see. But

I think it's good. It's good that you know more now. That you know what happened."

I study him, unable to say anything else and hoping he won't start crying. I've never seen my father cry, not in all those nights with my mother that led to all those trips to Cami's house for the summer that I now know were because my father had to admit my mother to the hospital. How hard that must have been for the Dennis in the letters to do to the love of his life!

If he were smart, he would have fallen in love with Cami, I think to myself. But he's not. And neither am I.

In many ways, I am my father's daughter, I think, running my finger over the callus on my pointer finger from my reintroduction to home improvement.

"I want to have a relationship with you now, though. And I want to make things right between us."

He removes an envelope from his pocket and slides it toward me.

"I've had enough of the mystery envelopes. Just tell me what it is."

"I sold the store and the land and paid back all the debt. I opened a credit card for you years ago, and I've been spending a bit and paying it each month, trying to help build your credit. It's a check for part of the payment."

I open the envelope. Inside is a credit card and a check for fifty thousand dollars.

It brings me back to that last fight with my mother. What must it have been like for her? To have a son walking around, entering her life unbidden? A son that she'd felt pressure to give up, pressure from this town, surely, and her family, and her own fear. A pressure I never felt in Bali.

"I—Cami and I—really hope you'll stay."

"I'll think about it," I say.

"What, um, what are your favorite words right now?" he says, coached by Cami, no doubt. And I have to smile and respond, because it's the perfect question.

I consider telling him about **family**, the entry in my *Dictionary of Word Origins* that I've flipped to more times than I care to admit. Latin *famulus*, meaning "servant." It felt so fitting to me at the time—*familia*, first used to describe the domestic servants of a household.

But I'm not sure anymore. I'm unsure of the exact meaning of "family" in any language, or maybe we're creating our own— Cami, Grant, my father, Grant's parents.

I don't have a word to describe what they are other than family, so instead, I tell my father the words people say and used to say when they couldn't think of a word:

doo, as in "doodah, doodad, doofer, dooshanks, doings, doohickey, doojigger."

what, as in "what-do-you-call-it" or "whatdicall'um, whatchicalt, whatd'ecalt, whatchacallit, whatchamacallit."

thing, as in "thingy, thingummy, thingamajig, thingamabob, thingummytite."

Until we're both laughing and spewing nonsense words.

That's my new favorite thing about language.

CHAPTER FORTY-FOUR

After saying goodbye to my father, I borrow Cami's car and look for Grant. I go to the flight center, where they haven't seen him. I go to the middle school where we went to camp, where we had that ill-fated kiss. I go to the playgrounds we used to frequent at midnight, though by high school, we were much too old for them. I go to Christian Brothers. I drive by the old Spanish movie theater and the church and my father's old store and Cami's flower shop and the Urban Outfitters where I bought the shirt I'm wearing.

I drive all over Memphis, crossing the city to the Mississippi, going down to Graceland and over to Germantown and back again, snaking through neighborhoods without real direction, looking for a glimpse of his Buick. Second to my bedroom at Cami's, that passenger's seat will always be home to me.

Grant; my brother. It's still difficult to wrap my head around.

Eventually, I give up and go back to Cami's. She's already asleep, and though I go to my room and crawl under Cami's mother's blanket, I can't sleep.

I've never been afraid of Grant deserting me—that was always my job—but now I am. After all, it's in our blood. Leaving, deserting, disappointing. It's in our DNA. It's in the DNA we share.

I sit in bed with my *Dictionary of Word Origins* hugged to my chest, cycling through all the words I know for what I've experienced this week.

father, in English. Or *"padre, tad, athair, vader, ayah, tatti, janke."*

brother, or *"hermano, frate, bruder, bror, brat, veli."*

mother, or *"madre, mami, ammee, me, mama, ibu, more, ma, meme."*

friend, or *"amigo, venn, cara, sóber, amico, vinur."*

What do these words mean anyway? Are they nouns or verbs? Labels or actions?

Because Grant has been my brother for as long as I can remember. Before I knew we shared blood. And there's no universe in which Grant's parents don't belong to him and he to them.

"Mother"—Grant's has been more of one to him than mine was to either of us. And Cami, she's spent more time mothering me than anyone. Even when my own was afraid to, even when she refused to.

But words have meaning. That's something I believe, something I have to believe.

Don't they?

I jump, sending Edgar scrambling and scratching off the bed and leaving a mark on me that feels as if it will bleed, at the sound of a knock at my window, morphing into the camp theme.

I smile.

He's back.

I run over to the window, open the latch, and throw myself into his arms like I did last week.

"I'm so glad you didn't leave." This time it's my turn to say, "I'm so glad you're back."

"Care for a drink?" he says.

When the rum has been poured and I've brought out a blanket from the bed, we sit on the roof and stare at the stars. With what we know, this time is different, maybe, but our actions are the same.

I decide to be brave, to break the comfortable silence. "For what it's worth," I say, "I think you got the better deal here."

He looks at me, narrowing his eyes. I think he might argue, but then he nods.

"So, can I start calling you Sissy?" He laughs.

"Please don't."

"Why not, Sissy?"

"No!" I scream, batting at his drink, which he whisks away with surprising dexterity, any genetic footprint of which must surely be from John, since my mother had no athletic ability. And I certainly ended up with none.

As if reading my mind, he stops.

"Are you going to contact John?" I ask.

"What?" he says, looking at me with mock shock. "That asshole? He doesn't deserve to know me!" Grant points a finger at his own chest, crumpling with the force and laughter, mimicking me from the other day.

"I didn't really sound like that, did I?"

"You sure did, Sissy."

We sit, drinking from our mugs.

"It doesn't change anything," I say, remembering his words from yesterday in the car, since he has always been better at this kind of stuff than I have. "Your parents are still your parents."

Unlike I did then, he smiles at me, like he's pleased and grateful for this fact.

"I know," he says.

CHAPTER FORTY-FIVE

I won't say anything about the next year was easy.

It wasn't.

It was hard. But it wasn't the hardest time of my life.

It was so painful but so funny, arguing with Cami about whether I would bury Edgar with her once he died. No, I wouldn't. She wanted to be buried next to her father.

"They did it in Egypt," she told me, petting Edgar as he purred on her chest. He lingered so much in her room those last few weeks, as if he knew what was coming, as if he was saying goodbye.

It wasn't easy, helping Cami into the new bed, lower to the ground, that we bought for her room, the overeager mattress salesman assuring us it had a lifetime guarantee.

"Her life or mine?" Cami said, laughing so much she had a coughing fit.

It wasn't easy, taking care of her at night. I took to lying down outside her bedroom door some nights when she told me she was fine, to go to sleep, just to listen to her breathing. It reminded me of those nights outside my mother's door, though at least now I knew I could go inside come morning. I could go in and hug Cami and tell her I loved her and hear it in return.

It wasn't easy, sleeping next to her in the hospital bed, tucking the blankets around her that last night, watching her fade away, holding her hand at the end and feeling her body grow still, as she had done with her own father.

That night, though, as hard as it was, part of me had to smile.

Holding Cami's hand, with my father's hand on one of my shoulders and my brother's on the other, for once, I felt something I'd never felt before.

For once, I knew I was right where I belonged.

For anyone who visits the nightspots of Beale Street,
who travels to Faulkner country just to the south,
eats ribs at Rendezvous, or buys voodoo powder at Schwab's,
the sultry mysterious Memphis that gave birth to the Blues,
to Rock 'n' Roll, and to soul will cast its luxuriant, disturbing spell.

—American Heritage (1998)

READING GROUP GUIDE

1. Lex ends up calling Cami because she realizes she has no one else to call. Who would you call if you were suffering halfway across the globe?

2. How did you feel about Lex trading Cami's tasks for her mother's entries? Do you think it would be fair for anyone to withhold information about your family? What would you have done in Lex's place?

3. Many of the changes Lex notices around Memphis are the results of gentrification. How does Lex feel while observing these changes? What is lost when a neighborhood is gentrified?

4. Describe your first impression of Margaret from her letters and journal. How does your first impression compare to the Margaret of the final entry? What do you think is the way she changed the most?

5. How would you describe John in one word? How does that word influence the dynamic between John and Margaret?

6. Which of Cami's assignments was your favorite? What was her strategy?

7. When Lex and Margaret argue about the fraudulent loans keeping the hardware store running, Margaret insists, "You just don't know what love is." What does she mean? Do you agree with this definition of love?

8. Describe Lex and Grant's relationship. Do you have a friend who acts as your platonic soulmate?

9. Lex reluctantly goes with Grant to visit with old high school classmates. Have you ever run into an old classmate? How does your experience compare to Lex's?

10. Throughout the book, Lex often thinks of her mother as hypocritical. Knowing all the secrets Margaret was keeping, do you think she was a hypocrite?

11. Reexamining her childhood, Lex realizes that many of the actions she had thought of as snubs from her parents were actually their attempts to protect her from the realities of Margaret's mental instability. How could that miscommunication have been prevented? How would you talk to a child about mental illness?

12. The book delves deep into the concept of family. Do you think there's a significant difference between the family that raises you and the family you choose? Are there people in the book, or in your life, who straddle the line between chosen family and blood family?

A CONVERSATION
WITH THE AUTHOR

What was your inspiration for this book?

I started with Memphis—I'll talk about that in the next question—and with the idea of writing about a powerful friendship, even love, that wasn't romantic love. I've read many books that dive into the complicated and beautiful world of a sister-like friendship between two girls, but I'm not aware of many books that focus on a friendship between a boy and a girl when both identify as straight that doesn't end in romance.

I started thinking about these two kids from very different lives, each lonely in their own way, who were friends above all else and without explanation, when everyone around them thought they would eventually be more than that. I grew up as "one of the boys," and many of my oldest friendships are with men. Grant is named after one of my best friends. Like Lex and Grant, we decided in middle school not to *like* like each other and have been close friends and support systems for each other since.

Memphis is the vibrant setting for this story. How did you pick Memphis, and how well did you know it before you started writing?

Before I started researching, I knew Memphis only from the stories my grandfather told. My mother's side of the family has a deep history there—my mother was born there, my grandparents both graduated from what is now the University of Memphis, where he "picked her out of a magazine," as Grant's father does with his mother, and I still have some distant family who live in the city. My memories of my grandfather have always been laced with Memphis, through the accent I'd study, different from my Georgia relatives, and through his stories about listening to the police blotter the night MLK was murdered, about BBQ from the Rendezvous, his school days at Christian Brothers High School, fishing at his uncle's pond, where he saw the Peabody Ducks, his paper route for the *Memphis Press-Scimitar*, and the portrait of Elvis his mother displayed proudly, which she got from one of her friends who worked as a maid at Graceland.

I researched both in person at the Memphis libraries and in books while writing. Some of my favorite reads were the Ask Vance columns in *Memphis* magazine by Vance Lauderdale and the writings of G. Wayne Dowdy, especially *Hidden History of Memphis*.

I also visited the city with my mother. I truly fell in love with Memphis while writing this book and while visiting with the people who live there. Unfortunately, COVID-19 interrupted my plan to travel there with my husband and force him to love it too so that I could convince him to move there, but I haven't ruled it out!

As each secret is revealed, Lex gets one step closer to understanding who her real family is. How do you define family?

Family can be about blood, but it doesn't need to be. I'm fortunate to be close to the people I'm related to by blood and also to people who I am not but still consider family. As I wrote in the dedication, I believe the best types of friends are those who feel like family, and the best types of family members are those who feel like friends.

All the characters in the book feel like real people. Do you ever base your characters on people you know? Did you have a favorite character to write about?

The characters I write are all composites—they include some characteristics of real people, both people I know and people I don't. They all include some of me. They include characteristics I've made up, dialogue I've heard on the subway, imagined histories I've concocted while watching someone standing in line at the grocery store. I always take inspiration from real life.

In my first book, *How to Bury Your Brother*, the main character's life circumstances and personality are very different from my own. Lex's personality is much closer to mine.

I loved writing the Margaret sections the most—she cracked me up endlessly. And in another example of finding inspiration in the weirdest places, her character was first sparked by a family story I read on Reddit about a woman who said that getting all of her belongings stolen while backpacking in Paris in the eighties was the best thing that ever happened to her. Margaret might say the same.

Has your writing process changed at all since your first book? If so, how?

My writing process has gotten much faster! *How to Bury Your Brother* took me four years to write, while I wrote the majority of this book in a year. The writing process was much less painful, since I had a better idea of what I was writing before I started. The process also involved a lot more research, since I needed to research Memphis and its history as well as linguistics.

Learning to Speak Southern, **and your first book,** *How to Bury Your Brother,* **both deal with the complicated process of grieving someone while learning about the life they truly led. Do you think we ever really know the people around us? Are there some things that we can't know until our loved ones are gone?**

People vary in terms of how open they are, but I do believe it's impossible to know *if* you know someone fully. You can see the picture someone is presenting to the world, and perhaps that picture is 90 percent of the full canvas, or perhaps it's 30 percent. I'm not sure it's possible to know every single facet of a person— even of yourself. Different situations bring out different qualities in people, and we're always changing and evolving.

I've always been interested in how families reorganize themselves after a death, and I'll likely continue to explore that theme in my writing. Death, especially an unexpected death, often erases a person's privacy. Perhaps it's morbid, but I think about this sometimes with my own writings. I'm a dedicated journal keeper (like Margaret). Even someone's diary, though, is just another picture of them—the one they are writing down. Humans are endlessly complex.

What are you reading these days?

Like many people, I've been making a large effort to read more diverse voices, especially books written by African Americans.

Some books I read recently and recommend: *My Sister, the Serial Killer* by Oyinkan Braithwaite, *How to Be an Antiracist* by Ibram X. Kendi, *Such a Fun Age* by Kiley Reid, *Red at the Bone* by Jacqueline Woodson, and *The Vanishing Half* by Brit Bennett. I've also celebrated the releases of many fellow 2020 debut writers this year and enjoyed reading their books. Some recommendations: *Brontë's Mistress* by Finola Austin, *The Better Liar* by Tanen Jones, *Saving Ruby King* by Catherine Adel West, *No Bad Deed* by Heather Chavez, *Fifty Words for Rain* by Asha Lemmie, and *Age of Consent* by Amanda Brainerd.

ACKNOWLEDGMENTS

Thank you to my agent, Katie Shea Boutillier, for finding me a great home at Sourcebooks and for your valuable feedback and quick responses to my panicked emails. I'm so glad I found you! Thank you to the entire team at Sourcebooks. Shana Drehs makes books shine brighter with every word that crosses her desk. Diane Dannenfeldt and Jessica Thelander have never-ending patience in correcting grammar and style mistakes.

Thank you to the people who interrupted their grieving over the pandemic to provide valuable feedback on early drafts of this book—Anne Beyer, Julia Carpenter, Alex Laughlin, Dana Liebelson, Stephen Mays, Allison Prang, and Jaci Shiendling.

Thank you to the many people who guided my research, including Charo Henríquez, who shared her memories of growing up in Puerto Rico; Rinka Perez Gunn (founder and director of the Social Enterprise, which helps trash-picking children in Indonesia) for sharing her experiences as an expat there; Dr. Naixin Zhang for his medical expertise; Dr. Rebecca Adams of the University of Memphis for sharing her experience as a linguistic educator; and especially Dena Elisabeth Arendall for her help in fact-checking Lex's many rants about linguistics. Any mistakes are my own.

Thank you to the many people I met in Memphis who made

ABOUT THE AUTHOR

Lindsey Rogers Cook is the author of two novels, *How to Bury Your Brother* and *Learning to Speak Southern*. She works at the *New York Times* as a senior editor for digital storytelling and training and graduated from the University of Georgia. She lives in Hoboken, New Jersey, with her husband and a small zoo of rescue animals.

me feel welcome and were happy to share stories with me, especially to Benjamin Bradley for helping me sort out the locations for this book and to Alexis Holt for her recommendations. I love your city. I've tried to capture Memphis's history and locations to the best of my ability, but I've taken artistic license with a few places to serve the plot, like with the church where Grant's parents first meet Dennis and the school that Dennis, Cami, and Margaret attend.

Thank you to Grant for letting me use your name, for your years of friendship, and for many retellings of your childhood fall off your family's porch, which was not necessary for my writing process but was always entertaining. To me, you are family.

My novel-writing career has happily become a family affair, and my books include a piece of all of us. Thank you for trusting me with portions of our story. Thank you to my mother for her many readings and for openly and tenderly sharing her experiences with a late miscarriage. Thank you to my father for a quarantined summer on the porch, during which he finished my first book and answered my questions about flying airplanes. Thank you to my brother, Davis, for taking me on an unforgettable joyride over Atlanta in his Cessna 172. Thank you to my grandparents Dennis Springer and Dr. Jennie Springer for your memories of Memphis and to my grandmother/editor especially for your many readings of this book. Thank you to my mother-in-law, Dr. Sandy Sipe, for helping me figure out the perfect diseases to kill off any character of my choosing and for her readings.

Thank you always to my husband, Kevin Sipe, for your never-ending support. Safety first, then teamwork. Love you.